The Republic of Trees

SAM TAYLOR

faber and faber

First published in 2005
by Faber and Faber Limited
3 Queen Square London WC1N 3AU
This paperback edition published in 2006

Typeset by Faber and Faber Ltd
Printed in England by Mackays of Chatham plc, Chatham, Kent

The right of Sam Taylor to be identified as author
of this work has been asserted in accordance with Section 77 of the
Copyright, Designs and Patents Act 1988

A CIP record for this book
is available from the British Library
ISBN 978-0-571-22294-0
ISBN 0-571-22294-3

2 4 6 8 10 9 7 5 3 1

for my parents

Contents

Nous veillons dormant, et veillant nous dormant.

Montaigne

ONE

1

The Daydreamer

My name is Michael Vignal. Michael, not Michel. My mother was French and my father English. Not that it matters. Countries are countries and, as for my parents . . . well, their role in this story is crucial but brief: they gave life to my brother Louis and myself, and then they died.

My father was the first to go, back when we lived in England. I was still at nursery then, and can remember almost nothing about him. Not his voice, not his face – when I look at the photographs I see a stranger.

I do remember waving to him one morning from the sitting-room window. In the memory, he is in the front garden, though I can't actually see him; only my hand, and my faint reflection in the glass, and, in a blur beyond this, the edge of the porch and some sparkling grass and a low grey sky. I can sense, but not see, my mother standing behind me, encouraging me to keep waving.

It might have been any morning, I suppose – my father was probably on his way to work – but I can't help associating it with his death. He was killed on 1 April, the fool, when he accidentally ran his electric lawnmower over its cable.

I have only one other memory of our life in England. I remember staring at a distant patch of woodland, and the way it made me feel. I had no word for the feeling then, of course, but I suppose you might call it *longing*.

We lived in a suburban housing estate in the Midlands. Ours was a long street: two rows of detached modern houses with neatly trimmed grass verges laid out in front like placemats. Two hundred years earlier, it would have been part of a great forest, but now the only trees were

3

pruned dwarfs, planted at regular intervals next to the road – little slave-trees, kept to remind all those managers and accountants and salespeople of the vast green wilderness crushed beneath their patios.

From our bedroom, though, if you stood on a chair and leaned on the windowsill and put your cheek to the glass and looked as far sideways as you could, the end of Commercial Drive was just visible. There, beyond a barbed-wire fence and a muddy field, was a forest.

My memory is of staring at it one dusk: the sun was setting over the treetops, turning them silver and gold, and I had to keep rubbing my condensed breath from the window-pane so I could see it properly. I felt sad and excited at the same time, and a little afraid, though I don't know why.

A few weeks after my father died, we moved to France – to stay with our mum's elder sister, Aunt Céline.

This experience, too, is pretty much a blank. According to Louis, who was six at the time, we took the boat from Portsmouth and drove down through France, staying with various relatives en route, and reached St Argen in the late afternoon. He said Aunt Céline seemed different then – younger, kinder, less angry. He said the four of us went for a walk up the road to look at the Pyrenees, and then came back and ate dinner together. He said that our mother seemed happy. He said that was the night he and I made our pact always to speak English together when we were alone.

You can believe as much of that as you like. Personally, I give more credence to Aunt Céline's recollections: that she asked me to choose a bunny rabbit from the hutches by the side of the house, and that, when the one I pointed to was picked up by its ears and killed with a single slap to the head, I cried. Our mother comforted me, but Aunt Céline just rolled her eyes and said, 'He'll learn.'

Seven months later our mother died. I have no memory of that, either. According to Louis, we were kept behind at school later than usual while her body was removed from the house. She had cut her wrists in the bath that morning, and our aunt found her when she got back from work. I didn't discover that until much later, though; at the time, Aunt Céline told us she had died of a broken heart.

When I look at the photographs of her, I get flickers: half memories of her face hanging over mine, the softness of her voice and her skin. But I don't know how much of that I truly remember, and how much I have stitched together from other people's remarks. Everyone in St Argen remembers my mother. I have her eyes, they say.

Apparently, I was inconsolable when she died, though the only emotion I remember feeling in later childhood was annoyance. It seemed a careless way to go, breaking something as important as a heart.

Aunt Céline claimed I was a normal, happy, outgoing child until then; only afterwards did I become sullen and withdrawn. I am sure she's right – I did change at that age – but I'm not convinced it was because of our mother's death. I suspect it had more to do with the clocks.

I had seen clocks before, of course, but I probably imagined they were just funny ornaments. It was not until I went to school that I fell under the spell of their ticking – under the universal tyranny of time.

Before you go to school – before you believe the lies that clocks tell – time is liquid and mysterious. Yesterday. Tomorrow. Eleven o'clock. These are only names, their meanings unguessable. I have a vague memory of seeing Yesterday as a man's face, with a moustache and a hat, his features sharp and frowning. Tomorrow was a woman, turned half away, her eyes wide and agleam. Eleven o'clock was a jolly, mischievous little goat-boy in a green suit.

But when you go to school, time starts to freeze, to take

those false shapes you will later know and hate. At school, you learn to obey the numbers; you learn to see the bars of your cage. Of course they may be imaginary bars – the cage may be an illusion – but that does not mean you are not imprisoned by it. It is not what exists that matters, after all. It is what you believe exists.

And so, at some point during that purple-skied autumn when little Michael started school and little Michael's mother slit her wrists, the dead skin of the happy child was shed, and I emerged.

Aunt Céline even gave me a new name to go with my new personality. She called me The Stranger.

It is hard for me to recall The Stranger's first memories. They are all not so much blurred as superimposed, one upon the next, hundreds of days the same: the same actions, the same sights, the same moods repeated *ad nauseam* (literally, on certain occasions). The prevalent mood I suppose you would call melancholy, though that sounds more poetic than it felt at the time. How it felt, in retrospect, was deathlike. Or rather – and this really is a fate worse than death – the feeling of *never having lived*.

Luckily, I had a secret. I had found a way to escape this feeling, to escape between the bars of my cage and leave time behind . . .

I daydreamed pretty much all the time as a child, but if I had to choose a single memory to capture how it felt, it would be of sitting at the kitchen table, staring at the slices of boiled carrot that I had removed from my stew. Of staring at but not seeing the carrot slices. Of hearing but not listening to Aunt Céline's Gothic threats ('If you don't eat your vegetables your skin will turn yellow and you'll die').

Of being in the kitchen, with its brown and beige wall tiles, its dark-stained oak beams, its ever-burning wood stove, its ever-ticking wall-clock, and simultaneously of being in a parallel wonderland. Of the saucepans not squatting drearily on the hob but floating through space.

Of myself not sitting silently at the table, a fork suspended halfway to my mouth, but flying secretly, invisibly, out of my body and through the window, across the yard, over the village, and away into the twilit woodland which I could see silhouetted beyond the reflection of the electric lamp in the glass.

The Chateau

St Argen was not a picturesque place by any standards. Like most farm villages in this part of France, it was basic-looking and long past its peak. The old slate roofs had been replaced by cheap red tiles, and many of the outlying houses and barns were derelict – half-crumbled mudbrick walls, window frames empty, earth floors turned to pasture for cows. In spring the village stank of cow shit, and in summer it stank of the human kind – which was flushed, often unprocessed, into the roadside drainage ditches.

But the land . . . the way it rolled. The thought of it brings tears to my eyes. The valleys were all wheat and corn, meadows and narrow paths, while the hills were forested with oaks, beeches, chestnuts. The air was alive with sparrowhawks and swifts, and deer leapt through fields.

I don't know how much I noticed all this when I was little. Presumably I just thought that's how the world was. Then one day I had an experience which I can only describe as the birth of my conscious self. I opened my eyes and thought: this is me – I have a mind of my own – I can choose what I want to do.

That day I saw, with fresh eyes, how ugly our house was – a grey breezeblock box, two up, two down. Louis and I lived in one bedroom, Aunt Céline in the other; downstairs were the kitchen and the salon. At the back there was a roofless bathroom patched with plastic sheeting. In the yard were a couple of Elf oil barrels and a dusty old cement-mixer. It was surrounded by a low brick wall, and beyond the wall was, to the side, a concrete electricity pole; and in front of us, the main road that ran north–south from Arbeville to Beaufort. Before, all this had just been 'home'; now it looked dead and dismal, in contrast to the beauty of the surrounding land.

Perhaps my mind is merging together separate events here, but I think that was also the day I understood, for the first time, that our aunt did not love us. I suppose I must already have been vaguely aware of this, but now it seemed cruelly obvious. I watched as she vacuumed our room, banging the machine against skirting-boards, shouting over the noise, 'Are you sick or what? What the hell is wrong with you? You're not right in the head!' I heard the anger in her voice and realised it had nothing to do with the toys on the floor. She was angry with us because we had ruined her life.

She used to get drunk and talk to the cat. At night, from our bedroom, we could hear her through the floorboards. We were bleeding her dry, that's what she said. This house – it could have been so beautiful. Slurring her words, she enumerated all the luxury features she had imagined for it. By the time she got to the underfloor heating in the bathroom she was usually choking back sobs.

I can't blame Aunt Céline for the way she felt. She did her best – fed us, clothed us, kept us clean, taught us manners, took us to church. But . . . *love*? We were lucky she didn't batter us to death with the Hoover.

This makes us sound like a tragic pair, doesn't it? Louis and Michael, the brothers triste. Yet that's not how it felt, because we had each other.

At night we stayed up for hours, speaking English. Louis told me about *The Adventures of Huckleberry Finn*, which he'd read three times. He said books were like doors; you opened them and entered and all the old rules disappeared. In books, anything could happen. Sometimes, like Huck, we plotted our escape. Down the river, over the mountains, into the forest, across the sea . . . Anywhere seemed better than here.

And then we heard the news – the most exciting news heard in St Argen for years.

You see, when I said that the village was not picturesque, I was omitting one important detail. At the far south-western edge, on a hill of its own, encircled by a tall iron fence and almost hidden behind overgrown gardens, was the place that the locals called *le château*: a vast, pale building with four towers, set in acres of land. Aunt Céline thought it vulgar, but I had always loved it, imagining myself riding horses in its grounds and shooting arrows at enemy soldiers from the third-floor windows. For years it had been empty. The news was that it had been sold – to an English family with two children.

In preparation for their arrival, a team of gardeners came from Toulouse. We could hear their chainsaws and diggers roar and whine all day. Even after dark, the men worked by torchlight. When Aunt Céline had put us to bed, Louis and I used to open the shutters and watch the lights move mysteriously around the hill. In the morning you could still smell the petrol and crushed vegetation in the air.

The garden was reduced to desert and replanted. The holes in the house were repaired, the roof and shutters replaced, the walls and doors repainted. By April the chateau was born again. It looked like something from a dream.

It was a Saturday, warm and bright, when they moved in. Louis and I cycled up to the hill behind the chateau and watched the arrival of *les étrangers* over a picnic of cold chicken and crisps. It was better than Christmas, that day, watching the big blue trucks arrive and all those huge cardboard boxes unloaded.

To start with, there were only the removal men and Mr Sillitoe, who was large, with angry eyes. He didn't carry anything, just pointed and shouted. The mother and children came later in the afternoon, as our blanket fell into shade. We were on the point of leaving, but when I saw the kids my heart leapt. They were our age, a boy and a girl.

The boy was round-faced and noisy. In his hands was a toy machine-gun, with which he sprayed imaginary bullets at the removal men. The girl was tall and thin. She had long, curly, light brown hair and wore a plain white dress. She stared with wide eyes at her new home, then lay on the grass, stroking it with her palms. I remember thinking how unalike they looked. I couldn't believe they were really brother and sister.

We spent many happy afternoons that spring on the hill behind the chateau, watching the Sillitoes. Even after Alex and Isobel started at our school and became our friends, we still used to go there and watch them, hidden by bushes, as they played in the garden and a firm of workmen dug the swimming pool.

Then, one Sunday in May, we were invited to spend the afternoon there. It was the first truly hot day of the year. The pool was still being finished, and Mrs Sillitoe let us watch the workmen fit the blue liner. I remember thinking how magical it seemed, a swimming pool with no water. Whenever I went to the lido in Arbeville, I always dived to the bottom to feel the smoothness of the tiles and watch the kicking feet and bubbles of air drifting up past long, pink legs. Everything looked different from down there. But the air in my lungs pulled me up to the surface. If only I could hide on the floor of this empty pool, I thought, then maybe when the water crashed over me I would be pinned in place – and see the world always through the strange blue eyes of a dream.

That day was one of the best of my life. We played hide-and-seek in the garden and sprayed one another with water guns. Afterwards, dried and dressed, we ate chocolate cookies and ice-cream under the retractable awning, and I looked down at the concrete stumps and red roof of our aunt's house and wished I never had to go back.

'Where do you live, Michael?' Mrs Sillitoe asked, pleased that her children had found some friends who spoke English and could thus 'ease their passage' into French society. 'Can you see your house from here?'

I pointed out the grey blot on their view.

'Oh, really? That's nice.'

It was a clear day. We admired the Pyrenees, white and sharp against the blue horizon. Mrs Sillitoe asked me if I liked living near mountains.

'I don't mind,' I said.

'Isn't it lovely seeing them every morning when you open the shutters?'

'We can't see them from our house,' I said. 'There's a rise in the land.'

'Oh? Yes, I see. That's a shame. You pay for the view, I suppose.'

'Really? How much do you pay?'

'No, I didn't mean . . . Ah, would you like some more lemonade, Michael?'

I loved the softness of her voice.

It was homemade lemonade; I had never tasted it before. She poured it from a glass jug, not a bottle, and there were ice-cubes and slices of lime and lemon floating on top.

From that day, I began to dream that Mrs Sillitoe was my mother. She took over the role in my imagination from the big-eyed cartoon Englishwoman in the Disney video of *Peter Pan*; the one who says to Wendy and the boys, 'Don't judge your father too harshly, dears. After all, he really does love you *very* much . . .'

Like all adults, though, Mrs Sillitoe was quite weird. I remember when she got the chickens, a few weeks after our first visit to the chateau – five fat hens and a scrawny rooster, whom she named Freddie and cooed at like a baby. She commissioned a local artisan to build a large, elaborate shed for them inside one of the barns, and she would lock the door on them at night, whispering, *'Bonne nuit'* to the six dark chicken shapes.

To start with, she was in raptures about them. It wasn't just the daily miracle of fresh eggs, which Mr Sillitoe ate fried on toast, but the 'calming' effect they had on her. She liked the way they waddled around the estate, pecking methodically for worms. It made her feel, she said, like she and her 'little family' had finally put down 'proper roots' here.

But then something unforeseen happened; unforeseen by Mrs Sillitoe, anyway. The chickens shat everywhere – on the terrace, on the lawn, near the pool, on sun-loungers and in flower beds. Their turds were large and soft; they stank and left black stains. Mrs Sillitoe took it personally.

One time she made the mistake of feeding them leftover pasta, and thereafter they would come begging at the door of the house. Any normal person would just have chased them off, but Mrs Sillitoe was frightened – their scaly toes made her 'skin crawl' – so she ended up barricaded inside her kitchen with the chickens squawking remorselessly outside, until her husband returned from the golf course and swung a five-iron at them. By the end of summer, Mrs Sillitoe hated the chickens so much she paid a farmer from up the road to come and kill them all.

We were there that day, banished to Isobel's room so we would not be able to witness the horror. But when we heard Mrs Sillitoe's car drive away, we sneaked down to the barn where the farmer had set up his roadcone with a hole in the end and his razor-sharp knife and his grey plastic bucket. We helped him catch them; it was great sport, running round the garden in the August heat, feathers sticking to our sweaty skin.

Each time we caught one, the farmer would take it from us, pin its wings back with one hand, and stuff its head through the hole in the roadcone. The chicken would squeal, then the razor would end its terror. The bodies were stuffed in a giant bin-liner; we could see the black plastic twitch for ages afterwards. The bucket caught all the blood. The farmer was, we all agreed, an artist. He soaked up our admiration in cool silence. Alex stared with fascination at the bucket of blood.

We all thought it was fun until Mrs Sillitoe came back. Her voice was trembling as she told the farmer to take the 'mess' away with him. The farmer must have seen the look of disbe-lief on my face, because he dropped off two of the chickens at our aunt's house on his way back. She casseroled them – their flesh was too tough to roast, she said, because the Sillitoes had let them run around. Our aunt was contemptuous of such behaviour. She kept her chickens in little wire-fronted boxes and fed them grain through a drip. They did, I have to admit, taste delicious.

I do have other happy memories. I don't mean to suggest that the only bright moments of my childhood were spent in the Sillitoes' garden. But half those memories might belong to anyone: birthday parties, ski trips, days on the beach, nights at the fair. These are just experiences that you buy, and we had less money than most of our friends.

When I look at the photos the feeling I get is of a vague, guilty disappointment. I knew I was supposed to be having fun – that happiness was paid for – but somehow I kept let-ting everyone down. In the photos I look bewildered, secretly worried, as though happiness were a plastic token that had slipped through a hole in my pocket.

I was older now, but I didn't feel it. I was waiting, but I didn't know what for.

3

The Forest

The year we escaped, I was in my last term at the village school while Isobel and Alex went with Louis to the *lycée* in Beaufort. I didn't see them so much any more.

Two years had passed since their arrival. Isobel had grown taller and prettier: the gap between her front teeth was all that remained of her tomboy days. She wore dresses and lipstick, read novels, kept a diary, went to drama class, stayed in her room while we rolled in the grass below her window. Sometimes, in town, I saw her sitting in cafés and bars, or coming out of shops . . . always with friends, always laughing.

Alex, though closer in age to me, was Louis's friend. I didn't like the way he looked. His hair was too long – he kept having to flick it out of his eyes – and he chewed with his mouth half open. His French wasn't fluent; he talked in the present tense all the time and didn't bother trying to pronounce properly. It sounded weird.

Louis had changed, too. He shaved his head and his face and exercised with dumb-bells every evening in the yard. You would never have guessed he was asthmatic. The girls in my school all thought he was *trop beau* and asked me about him in sickening detail. His voice had broken and when he spoke from the top bunk he sounded like someone else altogether.

And the stories he told me now before I fell asleep . . . In my mind the *lycée* loomed like a dark fairytale castle, brimming with violence and awful, exciting discoveries. I would ask Louis about Isobel, and he would say casually, 'Oh, she's going with X,' and I would ask him what he meant, and he would kind of half laugh, half sigh into his duvet. His talk was full of new, evil-sounding words, casually spoken but all the more ominous for that. Words like *lovebite* and *whore* and *hashish* would evoke bizarre images in my head; always in themselves beautiful and alluring – hashish, for instance, I remember imagining as a sort of hazy gold bar lying on a bed of straw – but crawling on the margins with snakes, insects, blackness.

Louis was growing up in other ways, too. He worked part time on a duck farm and spent all his earnings on books. And he didn't read novels any more. He liked facts and formulas, theories and solutions. He read books with grave words in their titles like *manifesto* and *philosophical* and *society*.

I don't want to make him sound boring. In many ways Louis was my hero: father figure, best friend, teacher. He loved me and thought I was special, and that alone was enough to raise him, in my eyes, way above the rest of humanity.

The point was it seemed like they had all grown up, while I was frozen in time. My school reports were always the same: 'Michael is a bright and well-behaved boy with a remarkable imagination. However, he is somewhat head-in-the-air and often on the moon.'

Souvent dans la lune. Aunt Céline still smacked me across the head whenever she caught me daydreaming, but the *maître* at our school was more laid back – he just called my name in a gently sarcastic sing-song voice or snapped his fingers; then, when my eyes refocused, he would make the rest of the class laugh by saying, 'Welcome back to the land of the living, Michael.'

I never saw what was funny about that. To me, it just seemed he was wrong; that the places I went in my mind were much more *living* than the grey, striplit classroom to which he made me return.

'The moon my arse!' Aunt Céline would snort when she read this phrase in my report (as she did every year). 'What he means is that you waste your time daydreaming instead of concentrating on your work. I always said that man was too soft. Wait till you get to *lycée*, boy. They won't stand for it there. I'm going to make sure . . . Hey! Are you listening to me or what?'

I knew my aunt was right – that my private universe would soon be under attack by the grown-up armies of discipline and focus. I knew I would have to wake up soon.

But school didn't start until September. First I had the summer to dream through.

One night in June, just before the school holidays began, Louis said something from the top bunk. The shutters and windows were open and I was staring through the window frame at the silhouetted hills in the distance, tracing the shapes of the treetops. I had been staring so long that it seemed almost as if the scene outside were inside and I on the outside looking in. When Louis spoke I was entranced in this vision and I didn't hear him clearly.

'Sorry?'

'I said, "You know how we used to talk about escaping to the forest?"'

'Oh . . . yeah,' I sighed. 'It would be great, wouldn't it?'

There was a pause. I could hear canned laughter from the TV downstairs.

'We're going to do it.'

'What?'

'We're escaping to the forest. Me and Alex and Isobel. And you too . . . if you want to come.'

For a moment I was speechless.

'You don't have to,' he added.

'Of course I want to.'

'Good. I don't know how long we'll stay. Maybe all summer.'

'But Louis, I don't understand. When are we going? When did you decide all this?'

'Oh, I've been thinking about it for ages,' he said. 'We go next week.'

We escaped before dawn on bicycles. Alex and Isobel were waiting for us outside their gates. We shook hands with Alex and kissed Isobel on both cheeks.

Once we were out of the village, I relaxed. The only sounds were our own breathing, the mechanical whirr of the bicycle wheels, the distant crying of peacocks. Now and then a dog barked on someone's farm. I could smell the moisture in the air, cool and fresh, and the earth of the surrounding fields. For the first time in my life I felt truly alive.

By the time daylight began to bleed over the fields and houses, turning hay from grey to pale yellow and grass from grey to pale green, we were two valleys clear of St Argen.

Some time later, we crested the hill to yet another empty road. To our left, a rich man's white-walled holiday mansion, the garden surrounded by a tall wire fence. The shutters all closed, no car in the driveway. A painted sign: *CHIEN MÉCHANT*. Louis said something about this, but I do not remember what it was because, at that very moment, I saw it, suddenly there, in front of us, below us and above us, covering two lines of hills and the whole wide valley between: the grand, dark sweep of the forest. It looked like an inky mirage, a black hole, a magic doorway through which we might disappear . . .

'God,' I breathed.

As if orchestrated, the sun emerged between two clouds. We looked behind us: the new corn was shining. From the top of the hill, it looked like lush grass – a sloping sea of green. By the side of the road, a tractor track plunged into the trees.

I leaned back in the saddle. Spiders' webs shining with dew hung from branches and stuck to our clothes and hair as we passed. Black-stemmed climbing nettles grabbed at our ankles and knees. The path, all ruts and rocks, was tricky, but I was too entranced to care. The sheer vastness of the place overwhelmed me. They'll never find us in here, I thought: *never, never, never.*

Briefly, I looked back. A patch of pale sky receding. Dark branches closing their arms around us. And that was it – the moment was over. The known world disappeared. We entered the forest and the forest entered our lives.

I have no sense of time, of how long the descent lasted, but I remember thinking it impossible that the ground could keep plunging so steeply. And then . . . the trees ended, the ground stopped falling. We stood, looking out at a meadow. The grass was short, like a lawn. Across the meadow ran an electric fence, red handkerchiefs tied to the posts, and on one side was a herd of cows.

'Cows,' I said stupidly. The others laughed.

We crossed the meadow and re-entered the trees.

The hours that followed are a blur. Mostly what I remember is the fear. It was my first time in the forest, and each time I turned around to see the same perspective-defying view, each time I looked up at the thin crack of sky bitten into by dark branches, I had to fight back a tide of panic.

As a place it felt both claustrophobic – dark verticals everywhere, as though you were imprisoned at the centre of a giant cage – and cruelly exposed. Here, there were no walls. Everything was alive. I sensed that the forest had eyes, that it was watching me.

There cannot have been another human for miles – when we were silent, so was the forest – and yet everywhere we came across traces of civilisation. A row of beehives, wheel ruts in a path, sawn-off tree stumps. I felt like we were walking in a circle, that at any moment we were bound to end up back in the meadow with the cows.

I don't know how we got there, but it was late afternoon when the path we had been following narrowed and ended, as the ground fell away almost vertically. And then, unwarned, we found ourselves in a magical place: a steep hillside of giant trees and hanging vines, the air swimming with green light.

'It's like being underwater,' said Isobel. 'The bottom of the sea.'

We had to half climb, half slide down the slope, dragging the bikes behind us. At the bottom of the hillside we walked across a patch of dry ground and crossed a river. It was deep in the middle, and the current was surprisingly strong. We rested on the shore and looked into the thick forest that rose, more gently, above us.

I stared up at this place and something caught in my chest. *Déjà vu*. It reminded me of a place I had been to or seen or dreamed or felt, somewhere, some time . . . but I couldn't make the memory fit.

We decided to pitch the tents then and there. Louis and I dug a hole for the campfire, and Alex said he was off to try to shoot something for dinner. I laughed – I thought he was joking. But then he pulled a long, thin canvas pouch from his rucksack and unzipped it. Out came a black shotgun. 'Twelve-bore,' he said, when he saw me staring at it.

'Do you know how to use it?'

He gave me a disgusted look. 'Course I do. I've been hunting with my dad loads of times.' Then he turned to Louis. 'Come with me, if you like. I hunt with Victor normally, so I could do with a spotter.'

Louis said OK and the two of them walked away.

Isobel called out, 'Don't get lost!' then looked at me as if she had forgotten who I was.

'Who's Victor?' I asked.

'Our dad's hunting dog. You've seen it before. Horrid, hairy thing. Drools all the time. Bit like Alex, really.'

I laughed for a long time. It wasn't really that funny, but laughing gave me an excuse not to say anything.

Isobel said, 'Will you help me blow up my air mattress, Michael? You can do the pillow and I'll do the main bit.'

It was faded pink canvas and the nozzle had white bitemarks around it. I held it in my mouth while I blew and watched Isobel do the same at the other end, the fat cylinders growing between us like a raft of flesh.

Afterwards, red-faced, we sat together on the bed of air and listened to the electric silence.

Some time later, Louis and Alex came running back towards us. They were shouting, excited.

Isobel stood. 'What have you caught?'

'It's not what we've caught, it's what we've *found*.'

'What do you mean?'

'Come and look. Come *on* . . .'

We ran after them, up the hill. We came to a ridge, which gave way to a plateau. Here, the trees grew closer together and a new silence reigned.

'Look . . .'

I looked. Darkness and impenetrable vegetation. Louis pulled apart some of the creepers. There was an open space, a rough archway, big enough to walk through if you stooped; and, in the dimness beyond, what looked like a stone wall.

'What is it?'

'See for yourself.'

Isobel went first, and we heard her gasp on the other side. I crawled after and found myself inside the ruins of a house.

It was basically just one room, not much bigger than our bedroom, but with a low wall dividing one corner from the rest. Two holes for windows, one for a door; all empty. The roof was half gone and there was a huge old tree trunk lying across the middle of the room, fused to the walls by a network of creepers. The walls, made of mudbrick and rocks, were crumbling, but three of them were more or less intact. The back wall had been half crushed by the tree and now provided a sort of terrace window, in the shape of a V. This looked out on what must once have been a garden, bordered by thick bushes and small trees.

'We can hide the bikes in there,' said Louis, pointing at the corner room. 'And the four of us can sleep here.' He crouched down and caressed the earth floor.

'Who do you think lived here?' I asked.

There was a blackened fireplace in one wall, and a stone mantelpiece, thick with dust. Louis trailed a hand through a mass of cobwebs. 'Whoever it was, I think they've moved out.'

I walked through the gap in the back wall. It was overgrown – bindweed and nettles everywhere, the grass stems long and featherheaded – yet it was still recognisably a garden. And, oh, the joy of seeing open sky, of hearing birdsong. We were deep, we were hidden, and yet we could breathe. It was perfect.

The rest of the evening passed cheerfully. We dismantled our tents and carried all our things to the shelter; we played cricket in the gloaming with a stick and a stone and three lines carved into a birch; we flattened the long grass with blankets and sat together in the garden, talking and eating as it grew dark; we breathed in the night smells, looked up at the stars and fell quiet; and then we settled down in our sleeping-bags: Alex, Louis, me, Isobel. In the moonlit dark I watched her float slightly above me, and imagined my breaths and hers together, holding her body up from the ground.

4

The Green Days

I opened my eyes in panic but the spell was not broken. I had half expected to wake up at home, in the bottom bunk, but above my face was open sky. It was blue and cloudless. The air was warm. I sat up and found myself alone in the shelter; the other three sleeping-bags lay like abandoned skins. I slithered from mine and hurriedly pulled on a pair of shorts and trainers.

In the garden, Isobel was sipping black coffee from a tin mug. Steam came from her mouth when she said hello. Her hair was mussed and her eyes were half closed.

'Morning,' I said. 'Where are the others?'

'Gone exploring. Louis wants to make a map, apparently.' She raised her eyebrows. 'He told me to say sorry, but he didn't want to disturb you. They'll be back here for lunch. They need your help building a roof or something.'

'Oh,' I said. A roof, a map. It all sounded ominously organised. 'So what are you doing this morning?'

'I'm going to find somewhere to get washed first. And then I'm going to get to grips with this garden. Cut it down to size.' I sat next to her and she passed me the cup of coffee. I drank from the opposite side. 'What about you, Michael?'

'Oh, I don't know. Maybe climb some trees . . .'

I made it sound casual, but I was actually relieved that I had missed Louis and Alex. I did not want to walk around the forest, making a map. I wanted to climb. In my daydreams all week, I had been Tarzan – swinging from vines, leaping between branches.

We talked for a while, Isobel and I. Well, mostly she talked and I listened. I tried to look in her eyes when she spoke, but they gave me vertigo. I spent a long time sipping coffee, staring into its blackness. Isobel ate crispbreads as she talked.

23

'So are you looking forward to going to *lycée* in September?'

'Mmm . . . I suppose so.'

'What's the matter – you're not worried, are you?'

'A bit.'

'Why? You're intelligent.'

'I daydream too much. Aunt Céline says I won't get away with it there.'

'Oh, what does *she* know? They probably still used the whip when she was at school. It's fine, honestly. And I bet the reason you daydream in St Argen is because you're bored. In Beaufort you'll be having too much fun to . . . What is it? What are you looking at?'

I blushed and shrugged. In my mind I was up in the trees.

She laughed and a fine golden dust sprayed from her mouth. Her hand touched my chest. 'Oh no, I'm sorry! Now I've got crumbs all over you.'

I crouched on the branch of the oak tree and looked across: the branches of the beech reached out, hand-like, ready to catch me. Then I looked down: the ground swam. I tightened my grip on the branch and thought: if I fall, I die.

I had always been a natural at tree-climbing; Louis used to say I had monkey blood. It was one of the few things, perhaps the only thing, at which I was better than him. I had never climbed in a forest before, but in my imagination the close-ness of the trees meant I would be able to move easily between them. But, here and now, it seemed impossible.

I closed my eyes and saw the grey yard, the cat asleep in the shadow of the electricity pole. Where would I rather be? I opened my eyes again. Sunlight glinted on the veined beech leaves. Below me the forest floor lay in shadow. One by one I wiped my damp hands on my T-shirt. I took deep breaths and the nausea faded.

I crawled to the end of the branch, as far as I could before the wood started to yield. There I half stood and bent my knees. Breathing through my mouth, thinking: it's not so high. Wavering, waiting, muscles tensed. Finally I sprang forward. A hissing in my chest as I flew.

I made it across the gap easily, but because I was so scared and excited, I jumped too far and ended with my face crashing into the branch above, leaves covering my eyes, sharp twigs gripping my skull. I slipped and fell backwards – and for a moment felt nothingness below me.

I might have died, had my T-shirt not snagged on a branch. Instead I hovered above the void, stupidly, miraculously, wondering what was happening. Then I scrambled back to the trunk.

I was frightened but unhurt. For some time I clung to the trunk, my heart protesting at the danger. As I sat there, though, I began to fantasise that the tree had saved me. It was no mere accident, I told myself; the tree caught me. The trees were my friends.

I edged back to the point on the branch where I had landed. I looked across at the oak. I stood there for what seemed a long time, trying to slow my breathing.

I jumped.

It was a leap of faith.

The oak caught me.

After that, my actions became surer and faster, my body looser. I began to look around as I moved. At ground level I had found the forest stifling, like a huge building of half-lit rooms, the doors closing behind you as you moved. Up in the trees, everything looked bigger, lighter, freer. It was like swimming in a vast ocean.

I stood still on a high branch. The air was hot. My T-shirt was wet, so I took it off and stuffed it in the waistband of my shorts. I started to climb again.

Some time later, I came to a cherry tree. It was shorter than the birch on which I was standing, so I climbed down a little way and hopped across. Below me the ground was covered with a bloody sprinkling of fallen cherries.

I picked and ate some from the branch above me. They were wild cherries: smaller and sharper than the ones you buy. I spat out the stones and watched them fall.

When I'd eaten enough, I climbed down, found a shaded place in the grass and closed my eyes. The colours flickered in my eyelids; a private cinema. I sighed, a contented animal, and fell asleep.

When I woke the sun was much hotter. My tongue was sticky and my throat dry. The pain in my back had stiffened. I felt too groggy to climb, so I walked through the long grass, in search of water, trying to keep to the shade. I could hear the river not too far away. The trees started to thin out, and I could see traces of old footpaths close to the river bank. At random I followed one of these, and it led to a pool made by a bend in the river, like a knee or an elbow. The river was fast and shallow, but the pool seemed still and deep and clear, and it was approached by a flat grass bank which edged into a narrow beach.

I sat down and dangled my feet in the water, expecting icy cold. Instead it was soft and pleasantly lukewarm. I slid down, reaching for the bottom with my toes. Another surprise: it was sand and shingle, not rock. I stood and the water came up to my thighs. I sat down and it lapped around my neck. I rubbed the sweat and cherry juice from my face and scooped two handfuls of water into my mouth.

'Yes,' I said aloud.

The sound shocked me: it seemed ages since I'd heard a human voice. I pulled off my shorts and threw them behind me, and passed the rest of the morning like that: doing nothing, wearing nothing, and feeling happy.

So began our green days; our innocent days. There were three of them, I think, and they were all more or less the same.

Each morning I woke and looked up at the pattern of light coming through the roof. We had made it with branches, the afternoon of that first day. I looked to my right and saw two empty sleeping-bags; then I looked to my left and saw Isobel, breathing imperceptibly through her nose, her arms in a perfect X across her chest.

I got dressed and wandered through to the garden, where Alex and Louis were eating breakfast. We talked a bit, about our plans for the day, then they went off to make their map and I carried the plastic water bottles down to the river. The walk back was slower because I was carrying the full bottles, but I would rush the last part and, each day, time it perfectly to see, with a silent gasp, Isobel standing in her vest and knickers, smiling at me.

I was nervous so I never said much, but she didn't seem to mind. I would lean against a wall, in shadow, drinking water, and she would talk to me while she dressed. I would listen and watch and breathe in her scent. She smelled of vanilla and rosewater, but I didn't know that then; only that it seemed to make me breathe faster.

In the garden I would boil water on the stove and make coffee. 'Thank you, Michael, that's lovely,' Isobel would say, insisting that I share it with her. Sometimes our eyes met and I would become oddly aware of my body, as though it were a too-large glove I had borrowed from a friend.

I would stay there until Isobel started clapping her hands and talking about all the work she had to do: already she had cut the grass and pulled out the nettles, and now she was planting a vegetable garden with Louis's trowel and seed packets stolen from her mother.

One morning she told me what was planted in each row: 'These are melons, these are cucumbers, these are strawberries, these are tomatoes . . . and these are courgettes.' Then a conspiratorial smile. 'Alex hates courgettes.'

'It must have been hard work,' I said, 'with just a trowel.'

'I'm stronger than I look.' She tensed her right bicep and

invited me to feel it. It was thin and long but surprisingly hard. Isobel had a swimmer's body; each morning in the warmer months she would do lengths in her parents' pool.

'Wow,' I said. I couldn't think of anything else to say.

On the third morning I told her about the cherry tree. She was very excited and asked me to show her. We stayed there for a while; me in the branches of the tree, picking cherries, and her underneath, catching them in a sheet. 'Oh my God, you're just like a little monkey,' she said as she watched me dart between the branches. From up there, my vision was filled with a constellation of red stars and a shifting maze of dark, knotted wood. Floating around in the grass way below, I could just about see Isobel's white dress and the white sheet that she held between her outstretched hands. I dropped the cherries and they sped down to her. It didn't take long to fill the sheet.

'Stop! That's all I can carry,' she called.

'Climb up,' I said. 'It's amazing up here.'

'I'm sure it is, but I've got work to do.'

'Come on . . . please!'

'I can't.'

'You're not scared, are you?'

'No, I'm *not* scared, you little monkey. I'm busy.'

'But Isobel . . .'

'I'm going now,' she shouted cheerfully. 'Bye!'

It was hot, but not too hot: the shade of the trees and the wind from the mountains kept the temperature bearable, except for the hours after lunch when a great torpor fell like a net from the sky, trapping us all. It felt a little like death in those hours. So, while Isobel slept in the shelter and the other two went hunting, I would lie in Elbow Pool and daydream of her: the smell of warm suncream on her back as she lay in the garden, or the way her fingers touched mine sometimes when she talked to me.

Other times, I would think of our forest. I would move through it mentally, remembering the trees I had climbed, navigating my way slowly around its borders. To me, it seemed an island of freedom surrounded on all sides by discarded reality: cattle to the north; cornfields to the south; to the east, the stream and the underwater forest; and to the west, a bramble-spiked cliff-face.

It was often much later when we saw one another again. When I got back to the garden, Isobel would be boiling water to cook the dried pasta or rice that Louis had brought from home. He had only brought a few boxes, so we were on strict rations.

Soon after that, Alex and Louis came back together, faces flushed and eyes glittering, and if they had shot something they would walk to the river together to wash away the blood while Isobel and I prepared the meat with Alex's hunting knife.

Isobel was surprisingly good at this. With rabbits, for example, I would hold the warm feet while she pulled off the pelt. As I was squeamish, I watched Isobel's face. Her lips went thin and pale with concentration.

I had to dispose of the unwanted parts while Isobel sliced the meat for cooking. Unthinkingly, I dropped them by the side of the shelter, on the grass. Before long, this became home to a colony of flies – the heads and hearts covered by a writhing dark blanket. Every time I saw this, or heard its moan, I felt anxious and ashamed. Thankfully, it was around the corner of the shelter, so that didn't happen very often.

What did we talk about, those first evenings, as the fire smouldered in its hole? Louis told us about the books he was reading – *The History of the French Revolution* and a book by a Swiss philosopher, Jean Jacques Rousseau, called *The Social Contract*. It was, Louis said, about how to create the perfect society. Isobel talked about nuclear weapons, and the hole in the atmosphere, and the Third World, and how complacent her parents were about it all. She said their generation had ruined the planet, and we would have to clean up the mess.

Alex didn't say much and neither did I. It was in the evenings that I most felt my shyness. I could have told them about the trees, I suppose, about my climbing, but I was scared that they would laugh at me. Mostly I was content to listen, and watch the changing expressions on Isobel's face. I loved the way her eyes widened when she became excited.

Sometimes, too, we talked about ourselves: this fantastic thing we had done, the people we had left behind. None of us could quite believe it, I think, even as we sat in the garden in those humid dusks, seeing the clouds turn pink and the trees blue, hearing the crickets grow louder.

One evening Louis and I tried to say in English how we felt about being here. It was 'marvellous', said Louis. Isobel wrinkled her nose with distaste. 'Fantastic,' I said. 'Wonderful,' said Louis. 'Terrific.' 'Fabulous.' We knew what these words meant – what they truly meant – but Isobel said they were never used like that now. 'They're the kind of words my mum uses to describe cleaning products,' she explained. 'So how would *you* describe how it feels?' we asked. 'Unreal,' she said. 'Like a dream.'

Yes, that was how it felt. Unreal. Like a dream. Too good to be true.

Though we never talked about being caught, I could sense our fear in the silences between the words. In the evenings nothing looked the same – the forest became ghostly, insubstantial – and when I closed my eyes at night I worried that it wouldn't be here the next morning.

Time moved differently, too, in the forest. Freed of clocks, it seemed to bend and shift, so that I might dwell for ages in the space between two breaths, or whole hours could be swallowed up and disappear. And the days, which ought to have been shortening, seemed to stretch and deepen the longer we stayed there.

Yet if it felt like a dream, it also felt more real, more *living*, than the world we had left behind. The colours were brighter, the sounds sharper. And the higher I climbed, the more heightened this feeling became. The further away the ground receded, the brighter the leaves around me seemed to shine.

The treetops were my favourite place. What I missed most of all, living in the forest, was the vision of it I had seen from a distance – the magical surface of green light and green shadow; that veneer of perfect mystery. From the tops of the tall trees I could catch a glimpse of this. Above the flies, above the trapped heat, I could see the forest slide away, a haze of green, reaching out to the horizon.

It looked so lovely that I wanted to run my lips over it, to taste it, swim in its glory. Though utterly grateful for its beauty, somehow I felt cheated – empty with longing at the thought that I could only *see* all this, could never enter it and become it as I dreamed.

And then I found something else to dream about.

5

The Bathers

Isobel was sitting in the sun, drinking coffee. She smiled when she saw me. I sat down next to her and she passed me the cup. I blew on the surface of the liquid and watched light ripple in the black. As usual in her presence, I could think of nothing to say.

She closed her eyes for a moment and let the sunlight rest on her face, then she opened them again and asked me what I wanted to do when I grew up. She wanted to be a nurse, she said, or possibly an actress. In my dreams I was always a cowboy or a spaceman, but I knew she would think that childish, so I said the first thing that came into my head.

'A doctor? That's interesting.'

'Mmm.'

A long silence, while she looked at me and I tried to think of an appropriate response. Finally she looked away. 'Michael, you never ask me anything about myself, you know.'

'Sorry,' I said, taken aback. It had never occurred to me.

Another silence.

'Well . . . go on, then.'

My mind was a blank. Finally I blurted out: 'Have you got a boyfriend?'

'Oh God, of all the questions you could have asked . . .'

'Sorry.'

I was about to ask another, blander question, when she went ahead and answered it anyway.

'Have I got a boyfriend? Well . . . not really. I did have a boyfriend . . .' She giggled. 'God, how do you *know* about this stuff anyway? Ah, it's having an older brother, I suppose. Anyway. Yes, I did have a boyfriend, but . . . I can't believe I'm telling you this! He . . . wanted something that I didn't want to give him.' Her eyes flashed at me. 'Does that make sense?'

'Yeah.'

'Does it?' There was a thrilled smile on her face. 'Do you actually know what I'm talking about?'

'I think so.'

She gave me an evaluating look and touched the top of my hand. 'God, you're a quiet one. Mind you, they say it's the quiet ones you have to watch!' She leaned back on her elbows, face flushed, still smiling in a disbelieving sort of way. 'OK, ask me another one. A bit less personal this time, if you *don't* mind . . .'

She was wearing a little gingham dress which buttoned up the front, and when she leaned back the hem of the dress edged up her brown thighs, revealing a line of white skin near the top. That, I guessed, was where her blue shorts – the shorts she wore for sunbathing – came down to.

I tried to think of something more positive, less personal to ask her. 'Do you like being rich?'

She laughed so much, and in such a surprised sort of way, that she began to choke. When her coughing had died down, she looked at me, shaking her head. 'What *are* you like?'

'I was trying to be nice.'

She laughed again. 'Oh God, I'm going to wet myself. You were trying to be nice. That is *so* funny.'

'Sorry.' I was blushing and annoyed.

'Oh, it's OK,' she said, seeing my face. 'Do you really think we're rich, though?'

I thought of the chateau and the swimming pool. 'Yes.'

'Well . . .' Her eyes cooled. 'Maybe we are.' She looked away for a few seconds and a curl of hair fell over her right eye. She brushed it back. 'It never felt like we were rich before, though . . . in England. We were just like everyone else I knew then. Just normal. You know?'

'You mean all your friends had swimming pools, too?'

That clear, high laugh again. 'Oh, Michael! No, we didn't have a swimming pool then. There wouldn't have been much point in England . . . although a couple of my friends *did* have them, actually.' She frowned slightly, remembering. 'I don't know . . . now I think about it . . . maybe we were *poorer* than some of our friends.'

We both contemplated this for a while.

'So what happened?'

'What do you mean?'

'Where did the money come from?'

'Oh no.' She smiled. 'What I mean is . . . things are cheaper here, aren't they?'

'Are they?'

'Oh yes. Much cheaper. I mean, your aunt could probably afford to have a pool if . . .'

The unspoken words hovered between us.

'Sorry,' said Isobel, her eyes lowered. 'I wasn't thinking. Does it . . . does it make you feel sad?'

'What?'

'Your mum and dad, being . . .'

'No.'

'You mean . . . ?'

'No, it doesn't make me feel sad.'

'You're angry, you mean.'

'No.'

'You sound angry.'

'No,' I said, softening my voice, 'I'm not angry.'

'You don't want to talk about it?'

I shrugged.

'I understand,' she said, and reached forward to touch my hand. I looked at her long fingers and had a sudden urge to stick them in my mouth and suck them, bite them, bend them backwards.

I swallowed. My heart was pounding. 'Isobel . . .'

'Uh-huh?'

'Come with me this morning. I want to show you something.'

It was hot when we got to Elbow Pool, and there were streams of sweat on Isobel's pink face. 'Oh God, it's fantastic,' she said when she saw it.

'The water's warm, too,' I said, my shyness lifting for the first time that morning. 'Well, not warm . . . but not cold like the river. Put your fingers in.'

I watched as she touched the water and the ripples spread towards the centre of the pool. 'Amazing.' Her eyes were wide. For the first time I noticed their colour, a soft grey. We looked in each other's eyes for a long time.

'Let's go for a swim,' she said. 'Skinny dipping.'

'OK.' My voice sounded tinny and far away.

We undressed, facing away from each other, and dropped our clothes behind the big oak tree. She ran in first and dived underwater. I followed, seconds later.

I don't know how long we swam and played in the water, but I never forgot the way it made me feel. If I closed my eyes afterwards, I could still see the sunlight glinting on the surface of the pool, could feel her fingers tickling me, too hard, my stomach muscles tensing . . . could hear the strained, excited, high-pitched breaths she took when I swam up, a shark, between her thighs . . . could see her gappy teeth, half bared between tight-pulled lips . . . the glistening drops of water on her face . . .

People think of innocence being neutral, unsensual, but it can be charged too, sometimes overpoweringly so. Not having a name for the way you feel, not understanding its meaning, not knowing that this is something everyone experiences . . . Innocence is like blindness – all your other senses are heightened in compensation.

So we played our little games, diving down and resurfacing, blowing bubbles, splashing each other. A few times the tip of my erection touched her back or hip. She must have known about it. She was older; she'd had a boyfriend. And yet . . .

Isobel stood up, dripping and magnificent. My eyes chastely followed hers as she rose.

'Stand next to me,' she commanded. 'I want to see how tall you are.'

I did as I was told. Our eyes stayed locked together, face to face, body to body. I had to lift my head a little. Neither of us looked down.

'Put your head flat,' she said.

I obeyed and stared at her lips, her chin, the tendons in her neck, the shaded hollow between. She put her hand flat on my head and moved it across to her face; it reached the tip of her nose. I looked up and all I could see was her pale, wrinkled palm, the blue of her veins and three pink lines that I could not read: love line, money line, life line. I don't remember if they were long or short, smooth or jagged.

'Half a head taller. Funny to think you'll be bigger than me one day . . .'

I couldn't speak. Time was moving so slowly I could see the shadow beneath a fly's beating wings. I could hear leaves tremble in the trees above.

So there we stood, both of us naked, the water up to our thighs. Isobel looked away for a second. I glanced down. Her skin was tanned, except for a pale band over her breasts and another band, achingly white, that ran from the top of her hips to the top of her thighs. Her nipples were hard and long and she had thick, dark hair growing between her legs. I felt the same fear I had felt on the branch of the oak, contemplating that first jump. If I fall

I fall

I fall.

My erection pulsed. Against my will, I swayed and it brushed her thigh. Isobel looked down, surprised. I looked down too.

'Oh, I didn't think . . .' she began, and put her hands to her mouth. Then she started to make a strange sound. I looked at her face, expecting to see fear or embarrassment or anger. After a heartbeat I realised she was giggling.

To hide my humiliation, I dived underwater and crouched on the shingle. I held my breath and closed my eyes.

When, some time later, I opened my eyes, I saw stars in the water, flashing lights. I could hear a distant sound, shrill and hysterical but a long way off. I felt sleepy but, at the same time, I knew I ought to put my head above the water soon, or I was going to be in some kind of trouble.

I wasn't prepared for the effect my little escape act would have, either on Isobel or on my own body. For my part, I was spitting water, gasping, flopping around like a landed fish. I could see myself doing this, as if from above, and was embarrassed at my lack of dignity. But Isobel was even worse. Her face was red, her eyes were full of tears, and the veins in her pretty, slender neck bulged blue as she screamed.

A little later we had recovered, more or less, and were lying, side by side, on the grass bank. She was squeezing my right hand. We were both breathing heavily.

'Promise me you'll never do anything like that again.'

'Like what?'

'Going underwater. Disappearing . . .' She struggled to find the right words. 'My God, I thought you were *dead*!'

'Dead?' This hadn't even occurred to me. So that's why she was screaming. I felt pleased, in a guilty sort of way.

'Yes, you idiot! You must have been down there for . . . two minutes or something!'

'No, if I'd been down there two minutes, I really would be . . .'

'Well, *whatever*,' she snapped. 'It was a long time. Just *please* . . . please don't scare me like that again.'

'OK,' I said, mildly.

'Jesus! What were you *doing* down there anyway?'

'I don't know.'

'You don't know?'

'No . . .' I looked up at the branches of the oak, tangled against the blue sky. 'I was just . . .'

She was sitting up now, looking down at me. Her face was still unnaturally pink, and there were tear stains glistening on her cheeks. But then, perhaps because she misread the look in my eyes, her expression turned tender; she bit her bottom lip. 'Michael, when I laughed . . . I didn't mean to upset you.'

I was still in a state of shock, so I said, without thinking, 'OK.'

'It's a nice one, you know.'

'Sorry?'

'Your . . . thing. It's nice. A nice shape, I mean.'

'Oh . . . is it?'

'Yes. Honestly.'

I had no idea how to respond to this. There was a long, long silence.

'Well, anyway . . .' said Isobel, letting go of my hand. 'It's been a funny old morning, hasn't it?'

'Mmm.'

Another long silence. Her face flushed. 'Maybe we should get dressed?'

'OK.'

I stood up quickly and walked around the tree. To my relief, the clothes were still there. I put my shorts on and, feeling more relaxed, circled back to Isobel, holding her clothes out to her.

'God, you're a strange one!' she said, and turned round to get dressed.

6

The Knife

The rest of that morning passed so slowly I wondered at times if I were dead. I felt too weak to climb trees so I walked instead, listlessly, aimlessly, around the borders of our forest. I sat looking across at maize fields, seeing nothing. I lay alone in Elbow Pool.

I sighed and moaned and felt like crying, but could make no tears. I was angry, anxious and resigned. I rolled between moods like the ball in a roulette wheel, resting at random on this or that, wondering at its significance, then spinning off again. I was not 'me' any more; I had no solid idea of who 'I' was.

Is-oh-belle. I said her name, aloud and in my head, so many times that it became a kind of song – beautiful and then maddening; impossible to forget.

Am I 'falling in love', I wondered. Is this what it feels like?

When I saw her at lunchtime I was paralysed by fear. I couldn't look at her. I couldn't speak. I couldn't eat. No one seemed to notice any difference in me.

After lunch the other three went for a nap in the shelter, and I dozed alone in the garden. In my half dream it was grey and I was underwater. I could see a girl's legs and silverish bubbles floating upwards to the light, and I was falling

falling
falling.

Louis shook me awake. I was in shade and the air was cooler. 'You're coming with us this afternoon,' he said. 'It's time you helped out.'

'OK.' I blinked. I was a paper bag; the wind could blow me wherever it liked.

I looked at Isobel's calm, sleeping face as I walked through the shelter. She seemed colourless and distant, like a ghost. My sadness, I noted, was at bay. The gentle twisting in my stomach was due to a simpler desire: I was hungry. I told Louis this and he shook his head wearily. 'We'll eat in a couple of hours – I know a place where there are loads of blackberries. But first we need to get on with this map. I want to get it finished. The map is the first stage.'

'The first stage of what?'

Louis just said, 'Come on.'

Alex was waiting for us, sentry-like, in the entrance to the shelter. He was wearing his favourite black T-shirt: **KILL**, it said, in letters seemingly scrawled in blood. The shotgun leaned against his shoulder.

'What do you need that for?' I asked. 'I thought we were mapmaking.'

'Just in case. And Louis says if we get enough mapwork done, we can go hunting afterwards.' He gave me a cool look. 'You don't need to come.'

The sun was in our eyes when we reached the western border. Louis and Alex were poring over their map. I yawned and looked down at my feet. Mapmaking was dull work. Their voices mumbled on and I stifled a second yawn. I was staring intently at my trainers. The day before, I had noticed a hole in the left one; if I wiggled my toes I could see it now, a black eyelid opening and closing with a flutter of pink flesh underneath.

Bored, I kicked a stone down the cliff at our feet and started thinking about Isobel. I remembered again the pattern of minute lines on her water-wrinkled palms, the shadow they cast over her lips, her chin, her neck . . .

'Michael!'

I looked up.

Louis was smiling at me, a little grimly. 'Daydreaming again?

I shrugged.

'We're going to get the blackberries now. After that, I want to go back to the shelter and get this stuff down on paper. I thought you and Alex could go hunting together. It'd be nice to have some meat tonight.'

I had never been hunting before, though of course I had seen the men of the village parade off on the *chasse* in their orange vests. I had heard their crude jokes and the damp, clinking bells that the dogs wore on their collars. I had seen the boyish self-importance in their eyes as they patrolled the cornfields or the forests. It had always seemed like a big game to me.

The way Alex hunted was different. He moved with a quietness and grace I would never have expected of him. He seemed more animal than boy.

I was his spotter; his 'second pair of eyes'. The most important thing, he told me, is patience. He was proved right. For ages we saw nothing. Birds fluttered in trees, but Alex said they were too small to bother with: 'The smaller they are, the harder they are to hit.'

'And the less meat they have.'

'Exactly.'

'What about if I went up into the trees?'

'What for?'

'I might see something from up there that you can't see from down here.'

'You'll make too much noise – you'll scare them off.'

'I can be very quiet,' I said. 'Watch . . .'

Up in the trees, I felt instantly lighter. Hopping from branch to branch, scanning the ground for flickers of movement, I had no time to worry about Isobel and our strange morning.

After a while, I spotted a twitch of brown among trees to my left. I counted one, two, three deer, standing in a perfectly spaced line, noses aloft. I looked down to where Alex was creeping, gun at the ready, behind me.

'Alex!' I whispered.

He looked up, but didn't see me. I called again and waved,

warily. I looked back at the deer; they had heard me, but had not moved.

Alex saw me, and his mouth opened into an O. I put my finger to my lips, then pointed towards the deer. His eyes followed my finger. He blinked in acknowledgement. With infinite slowness, he lifted the gun to his shoulder and moved his eye to the viewfinder.

A dusting of hooves, and they were gone. I looked back at Alex. He pulled a resigned face. Then, making a circle with his thumb and index finger, he hissed: 'Good spot.'

I smiled, embarrassed, and we began moving again in hunters' tandem. It was like a dance, with its own ever-changing steps, the two of us far apart but held together in a kind of magnetised radius.

When we eventually killed a rabbit, it was anticlimactic; the creature was so slow and unconcerned that its death required barely any skill at all. I saw it hopping below me and gestured towards it. Alex walked up and blasted a hole in its throat.

He was leaning over the corpse by the time I came down from the tree. 'Nice fat one,' he said. 'Come on, let's go to the river.'

I could have taken him to Elbow Pool but that was a secret I wanted to keep, so we undressed by a wide straight in the river and plunged into the cold. We splashed and soaped our-selves, giggling through clenched teeth, and Alex talked loudly about all the different animals he had killed before. What he really wanted to hunt, he said, was a wild boar. He had seen them killed, but had never done it himself. 'That would be the ultimate. I tell you, they are fucking *beasts*.'

Afterwards we towelled down on the bank and he said sincerely, 'You were great, Michael. I've never seen anyone climb trees like that. It was a good idea, too. It really helped.'

I was overcome. 'Thanks, Alex. You're a good shot.'

I looked in his eyes and noticed, for the first time, that the irises were the same soft grey as Isobel's. His face was in the sun and his pupils were huge. We stood for a moment, naked but for our towels. Alex stared over my left shoulder with his mouth half open, as though he were about to say something. His right hand rose from his side, his towel dropped, and I thought for a heartbeat he was going to touch my waist – I thought: he actually wants to *dance* with me – but then his hand fell back again and he cleared his throat. 'We ought to get back.'

'Yes,' I said.

We could smell the woodsmoke from inside the shelter. Alex started to tell the story of the hunt, but I could tell from the look on Louis's face that he wasn't listening. He looked tense, expectant. 'I've got some good news,' he said, when Alex had finished. Isobel was by his side, smiling with secret pleasure.

'What is it?'

'I've finished the map.'

'Oh. Is that all?'

'You won't say that when you see it,' said Isobel. 'It's a wonderful map. Really inspiring.'

The map was pinned to the wall over the fireplace. It had been drawn on the back of an OS map, so it was impressively large. It was also beautifully detailed. Above it in neat, large, black letters were the words: *The Republic of Trees*.

'What does that mean?'

'It's ours,' said Louis. 'Everything inside those borders belongs to us. This is our declaration of independence.'

I found, to my surprise, that I couldn't stop looking at the map. 'You're right,' I said to Isobel, my voice rising uncontrollably. 'It is inspiring.'

'You see?'

'Thanks.' Louis smiled. 'The difficult bit was getting the proportions of the borders right. I'm not saying it's *exactly* right, but that is basically the shape of our forest.'

'It's funny . . . I would never have guessed it looked like that.'

'It makes you proud, doesn't it?'

'Yeah,' said Alex, 'like the shape of Great Britain makes you proud.'

'Or France.'

'Yeah.'

'But this is better than either of them,' said Louis. 'This is ours. It belongs to *us*.'

I looked more closely at the map. Louis had got the shape of Elbow Pool, but he had not named it or given it any prominence. I guessed he had never touched the water. The trees were marked as identical faint lines, like a covering of grey fur. There was only one word written on the map, apart from the imperious title Louis had given it. Just above the little square representing our shelter, it said 'Home'.

'And this is just the beginning,' said Louis. 'Now we can really start.'

'Start what?'

'The revolution.'

'Huh?'

'That's why we came, isn't it?' he said. 'To create a better place.'

In the corner of my eye I could see Alex and Isobel talking over the skewered rabbit, could see the smoke rising into the high blue sky.

'But this *is* a better place. It's perfect.'

'Not yet,' said Louis. 'But it will be.'

When it's perfect, I thought, will Isobel fall in love with me?

He pinched my arm. 'You might have to stop daydreaming soon, Michael. This is going to be better than anything you can imagine.'

'I don't know about that,' I said. 'I can imagine quite a lot.'

The next morning, I opened my eyes and heard Alex say, 'It'd be better with three, you know. They're bastards to kill, and he's great in the trees. Have you seen him?'

'Yeah, but he's tired. Let him sleep.' It was Louis's voice.

'But he just moved. I'm sure . . .'

I felt their eyes on me. I gave a sleepy sigh and turned on to my side.

'Leave him. We'll be fine.'

I heard them go soon after that. Some time later, I heard Isobel rise, yawning, beside me and walk the other way – into the garden. The air outside the sleeping-bag felt warm now, and I was fully awake, but I lay there a while longer, eyes closed, rehearsing the lines in my head.

I had come to an important decision: I would talk to Isobel about what had happened between us. I would declare my feelings. In my imagination, she reacted to this revelation in various ways: broke down in tears, or slapped my face, or kissed my lips, or laughed until I ran away in anguish.

Finally I stopped torturing myself with all these potential branchings of the future. I knew there was only one way to find out what would happen. I unzipped my sleeping-bag, stood up and walked outside.

Isobel was sunbathing, and for a second I thought she was naked. I blinked. She was wearing her blue shorts, but their satin surface reflected the light; from a certain angle they were visible as nothing but a too-bright gleam. She sat up when she heard me coming. I saw her back, golden brown, and the quick descent of her white T-shirt, like a curtain going down on stage.

'Isobel . . .'

'Good morning.' She smiled, but it was only a thin smile of politeness.

'I need to talk to you.'

She got to her feet and moved towards the shelter. 'Oh. I was about to go and wash, actually . . .'

'It's important.'

She stood still, hands on hips, her eyes blankly resting on mine. Her irises were pools of smoke.

'What is it?'

I sat on the grass, hoping she would sit next to me, but she stayed standing so I had to crane my neck. Her face eclipsed the sun; a halo burned around the edges of her hair. Her arms were folded, the T-shirt pushed up under her breasts, exposing a small patch of taut, curved, brown stomach. Her bare legs rose before me like the pillars of heaven.

'Well?'

I stared up at her adoringly. I could have stayed like that for ever, her beauty towering over me, her eyes focused only on me, her body tensed, waiting for what I would say.

'I don't know what to say.'

'Oh, for God's sake!'

I looked at the ground: Alex's eight-inch hunting knife glinted from the grass. I picked it up and stared at my warped reflection in the blade. All the rehearsed lines flashed through my head, uselessly. What I eventually came out with was: 'You hate me, don't you?' – probably because it was the only question I could think of to which I didn't fear the answer.

'Of course I don't hate you,' she said. Her voice was cold.

'Don't you?' I asked, pathetically.

'Of course not. Don't be silly.' I waited for her to add, 'I love you,' but she didn't.

'Did I do something wrong?' I asked, trying not to stammer. I could feel the tiny muscles in my upper lip go into spasm. 'Yesterday morning . . . in the pool?'

She frowned and looked away. 'What do you mean?'

My words sounded hollow. 'Did I upset you or something?'

'No.'

'It's just you seem . . . different . . . since then . . . to me.'

'I don't know what you're talking about.'

My tongue lay dry in my mouth. 'Do you regret it?'

A pause, while I stroked the side of the knife blade with my fingertips. Isobel sighed heavily and sat down, her knees pulled protectively to her chest. 'Do I regret what?'

'What we did.'

'We didn't do anything, Michael.' She wasn't looking at me. I looked down at her hands. She was pulling chunks of grass and weeds from the garden.

'But being . . .' – I heard a drum roll in my head – '. . . naked.'

The ghost of a laugh. 'What about it?'

'Do you regret it?'

'I suppose so, if I ever thought about it. But it's really not important.' Her knuckles were white.

'It was important to me.'

'Well, it shouldn't be,' she said crossly. 'It didn't mean *anything*. If you're going to make such a big deal of it, I'd rather you just forgot it happened.'

I stared at the shelter. I was trying not to cry.

'Please?' she said. Then, more firmly: 'Look, I *do* like you.'

I gripped the cool pearl handle of the knife; admired the smooth curve, the fine workmanship; prodded with the blade at the ground.

'Can't we just be friends?'

'I don't want to forget it,' I said quietly.

'Oh, for God's sake . . . stop acting like such a *child*.'

She stood up and walked to the shelter. Her body disappeared into darkness. I wiped the tears from my eyes and carved a circle in the earth. I felt like the world was ending.

A few moments later Isobel came out of the shelter again, smiling as though nothing had been said. 'I'm going down to the river to get washed. See you later?'

I shrugged, said nothing.

'Ohh-*kay*,' she drawled, as though bemused by my silence. 'Well, I'm off now. Have a nice morning.'

When she was gone, I stood up and, with all my strength, hurled the knife at the spot where she had stood. To my astonishment, it flew with a circular whoosh and landed deep in the earth. The anger drained from my body instantly. Sickened and excited, I stared at the hilt of the knife and imagined how it would have looked embedded in Isobel's stomach. She was so thin, it would have stuck out the other side.

7

The Kiss

The morning hunt had not been a success, so it was a dull, meatless lunch. Isobel and I pretended nothing had happened. She seemed to find this easier than I did. I stared at the grey rice in my bowl and listened to the others talking about how bored they were. The afternoons were growing longer, hotter, emptier.

After lunch Isobel went to sleep in the shelter and Alex made a sport of killing flies. Louis sat in the mouth of the shelter and read *The History of the French Revolution*. There was a painting of a guillotine on the cover.

I asked Alex if he wanted to go hunting but he said it was too hot, so I went to Elbow Pool and lay there in the water, thinking sullenly, obsessively, of Isobel. I tossed mental coins into the air: love, hate, love, hate, love . . . The circumference of the coin was indifference. I prayed the coin would land on its side, but it just kept spinning.

Later, it clouded over and Alex took me hunting. We searched for the boar run – he was sure there had to be one – but found nothing, and in the end he shot a wood pigeon, near the Republic's western border. I had to scramble down the cliff-face to retrieve its light, warm corpse. It was risky, going out into the open like that, but there was something reassuring about hearing the gunshot fade and the silence of the evening rise again. I scanned the horizon: not a soul.

In the garden Isobel had changed into cut-off jeans and a pink T-shirt emblazoned with the word **KISS** in large, powder-blue letters. Her hair was damp from the river; her forearms were brown and pricked with tiny golden hairs. She smiled at me when I gave her the dead bird.

Evening brought a gentle breeze, and the smell of burning

flesh seemed to relax us all. As we sat in a circle round the fire, nibbling bones, Louis stood up and said, 'I've had an idea – something to do in the afternoons.'

We all looked up expectantly. 'What's your idea?'

'History games' he called them, and we groaned.

'Not *history*,' pleaded Alex.

'It's just dead people,' said Isobel. 'Who cares about dead people?'

'What sort of games?' I asked.

'Make-believe,' said Louis. 'Like we used to do at your house, Isobel. Remember when we did *Romeo and Juliet*?'

'Oh yes, I was *such* a good Juliet.' Isobel smiled. 'I still think it should have had a happy ending, though. Which play do you want to do?'

'Not a play,' said Louis, 'something real. The French Revolution.'

Alex made a face.

'There's lots of blood,' said Louis, holding up the book with the picture of the guillotine. 'And it has the perfect role for you, Isobel.'

Isobel looked at him blankly. 'What?'

'Marie Antoinette.'

'Oh God, of course! Louis, you're a genius.' Isobel stood up and drawled, nose pointing to the sky, 'Let them eat brioche.' She giggled.

Louis smiled. 'She never actually said that, you know.'

'Hang on,' said Alex slowly, 'this is the head-chopping thing, isn't it?'

'That's right,' said Louis, scenting acquiescence, 'but I think we'd better start at the beginning.'

Isobel looked beautiful that evening. Her eyes were wide and she kept touching us. Once she gripped my hand so warmly I couldn't breathe. And then, the next moment, she was leaning close to Louis, her wrist on his shoulder, whispering into his ear. My hand felt cold where she had held it and then let go. I watched her stomach as the hem of her T-shirt edged upwards – she was leaning across him now – and imagined the pearl handle of the knife protruding from it. I could still see her shocked face, her choking words, her jammy wound, as she turned to me and smiled and laid her fingers on my hand. 'So who do *you* want to be, Michael?'

We drew our roles by chance. Louis wrote four names on little squares of paper, folded them up and dropped them in the empty saucepan. Two of us would be victims – De Launay, the governor of the Bastille, who was the Revolution's first decapitation; and Béquard, an unfortunate soldier. Two of us would be revolutionaries – Hulin, who led the siege; and Desnot, a pastry chef who was part of the mob.

What happened, Louis told us, was this: the people were hungry, and primed for rebellion. On the morning of 14 July, a mob laid siege to the hated Bastille Prison; they were after the government's stock of gunpowder. De Launay wrote a letter threatening to explode the gunpowder, killing everyone, unless he and the guards were allowed to leave unharmed. The letter was posted through a gap in the gate. Hulin walked across a plank and read it aloud. There was a roar of refusal. Hulin prepared to fire a cannon at the gate, then De Launay ordered the drawbridge to be lowered.

The mob rushed in, liberating the prisoners and taking revenge on guards and soldiers. Béquard, who opened one of the gates of the fort, had his hand chopped off. The hand was paraded through the streets, still holding a key. Later, he was mistaken for one of the cannoneers and hanged from a lamppost in the Place de Grève.

De Launay, meanwhile, was dragged through the streets while people spat and yelled abuse at him. Finally he shouted, 'Let me die!' and kicked out; by chance, his boot hit Desnot in the testicles. The mob stabbed him to death and shot him. Someone gave Desnot a sword so he could chop off De Launay's head but he said he preferred to do it with his pocket knife. Meticulously he sawed through De Launay's neck, and his head was stuck on a spike and carried through the streets in triumph.

Isobel shivered. 'That's horrible. I'd forgotten how barbaric it all was.'

But, even as she said this, she was grinning. Alex giggled and that set me off, too.

'De Launay was an enemy of the people,' said Louis. 'He deserved to die.'

'But why carry his head around on a stick?'

'As a deterrent for other traitors.' Louis's face was straight. Alex coughed into his hand; his eyes were moist with the effort of not laughing. 'And because it was fun, I suppose . . .'

Our laughter rose in shrill staccato waves.

Isobel drew first; she was Hulin. 'Oh, the hero, how boring,' she groaned. 'Can't I be Marie Antoinette, and just sit on a branch and watch?'

Alex drew next, and was thrilled to be Desnot.

'That horrid thug,' said Isobel. 'Well, at least you won't need to do much acting.'

'I hope it's your head,' whispered Alex.

Then me – I was poor Béquard. 'Show me your hand,' said Isobel. I lifted my right hand and held it by the side of my face, palm towards her. 'Shame – it's a nice hand.'

I shivered as they howled.

'So I'm De Launay,' said Louis. 'Well, it's been nice knowing you all . . .'

'You're not really going to kick me in the balls, are you?' asked Alex, as we stood up.

'No, Alex. As long as you promise not to really cut my head off.'

Louis and Alex woke me early and the three of us rushed breakfast. We were going on a hunt, in search of the elusive boar. As we were leaving, Isobel emerged through the archway in her pink T-shirt and knickers. It was a cool morning and her nipples made sharp indentations in the **K** and the second **S**. Sleepy-eyed, her hand on his forearm, she asked Louis if she could borrow his book on the French Revolution. She wanted to start 'getting into character'. I watched impotently as her eyes and my brother's met in a deep stare.

'Come on, Louis, it's getting late,' whined Alex.

'Why don't you two go ahead,' said Louis. 'I think I'll stay behind with Isobel. I need to do a bit of reading myself.'

Louis went back inside, and Alex and I trudged away. I heard him mutter something.

'What did you say?'

He looked up, and seemed suddenly to see me. 'Nothing,' he sighed. 'Let's bag a bird or something.'

I climbed, and scanned the forest. When I spotted a movement in a patch of bushes to my left, I gave Alex the sign. He looked, but shook his head.

'I've got to be sure,' he explained later, as we walked back to the shelter empty-handed. 'I can't afford to waste shells.'

'Why, are you running short?'

He nodded. 'I've got enough for another few days . . . a week at the most.'

'And then what do we do?'

A gloomy shrug. 'The pasta's going fast too, so it's not like we can live without meat. Louis tells me not to worry, but . . .'

'Maybe he's got a plan.'

Alex squinted suspiciously. 'Has he said anything to you?'

'No,' I admitted.

'Me neither.' He looked grimly ahead of him, jaw set. 'Come on, we should get back. I've got to cut off his head this afternoon.'

The book lay in the garden, its transparent plastic cover turning soft and bubbly in the sun. Louis sat in shade. In the moment before he heard us, I caught sight of him staring at the ground, his face tight with what might have been anxiety or irritation or frustration. It was not an expression I had seen often on his face. Something, I guessed, was not within his control. I thought of what Alex had said: the lack of ammunition, the dwindling pasta.

Alex coughed, and Louis looked up. 'Hi, did you catch anything?'

Alex walked over to talk to him. I looked across at Isobel. She was standing apart from Louis, arms folded, in full sunlight. Her eyes were closed, as though she had fallen asleep on her feet. Then she smiled and opened them, like an actress about to deliver her favourite lines. 'Hello! You were gone for ages. We were getting worried about you.'

'We did . . . didn't –' I stuttered.

'Have we got any fruit?' asked Louis, to no one in particular.

'Didn't catch –'

Isobel came towards me and touched my arm. I looked at her face and then down at her hand, its long, gripping fingers. I tried to speak but the words stuck in my throat.

'We'll go and pick some blackberries, won't we, Michael?'

I looked over at Louis. He was talking in a low voice to Alex, the pair of them grimacing.

Isobel guided me with gentle pressure on my elbow through the shelter and out into the forest. I expected her to burst into tears as soon as we were outside, so strange was her performance, but instead she slid her arm through mine. The skin under her forearm felt like satin. 'Come on, I know a place over here where they're already ripe,' she said. 'And sweet, too, not those hard, sharp ones.'

She leaned on me as we walked, staring at the ground. The silence between us was tense, but not unpleasant. Thinking of Marie Antoinette, I said: 'Have you been getting into character?'

She laughed quietly, without looking up.

After a few moments she said, 'We haven't got a bag, you know.'

'A bag?'

'To carry the blackberries.'

'Oh! Shall I run back and . . . ?'

'No, don't be silly. You can use your T-shirt.' She glanced at me, a glitter of mischief in her eyes. 'If you don't mind the stains.'

I could tell something was about to happen, but I had no idea what it could be. 'No, I don't mind,' I said, and made an effort to relax.

She started to walk more slowly, by degrees, until she had stopped moving. She pulled at my arm and put her free hand on my chest. She turned her face to mine; her eyes were half closed and she was smiling with her lips together. Because she was leaning on me, I had the momentary illusion that I was taller than her. I don't know if it was the light or the angle of her face, but she looked different somehow; almost like another girl altogether.

She moved her face closer to mine. I could feel her breath warm on my chin. She was leaning heavily on my shoulder, and I was worried that she might fall, so I put my hand to her side; I could feel her warmth and her ribcage through the T-shirt and the throb of her heart under the bones.

'Close your eyes,' she said.

'What are you doing?'

'Please.'

I closed my eyes and felt a foreign wetness on my lips. Startled, I pulled away.

Her face was tilted and she was smiling strangely.

'Who are you?' I heard myself say.

'Close your eyes and open your mouth.'

My first kiss. I was shocked by how thrilling it was. I came up gasping.

'You have to breathe,' she said, amused. 'And move your head that way a bit.'

I did as I was told.

Again the dark currents of electricity inside me. I experimented with breathing through my nose; I could feel the little jets of warm air mingle where our mouths met. I tried to remember that I was kissing Isobel. It seemed easy to forget.

'It's nice, isn't it?' she murmured. I nodded mutely. 'In England they call it a French kiss, you know.'

'I don't know what they call it in France.'

'Open your eyes for a second.'

I obeyed. Her face had a businesslike look which took me aback.

'That stone behind you, can you stand on that?'

It was a roundish boulder. 'I can't get my balance.'

'Oh, well . . . come with me.' She pulled me by the hand further through the forest. 'This'll do,' she said, pointing to a shaded patch of long grass between two large, gnarled tree roots. 'Can you put your T-shirt down?'

I took it off and she trailed the backs of her fingers down my chest.

'Isobel, I . . .'

She put her finger to my lips. 'Don't talk. Come on, lie down next to me.'

We lay there and kissed for . . . I don't know how long. An hour sounds excessive, yet it felt like whole sun-drenched afternoons passed between breaths, like fruit ripened and corn grew and the moon waxed and waned and the forest became detached from the earth and floated away to sea. I remember feeling oddly cheated, that no one had told me about this before. Had everyone done it, I wondered? All those dry, busy adults in the village, all the schoolteachers and bus-drivers and builders; had they all felt this secret lapping of human souls? How did they go on with their dusty, clockwork lives, as if nothing had happened?

Finally she pulled away from me and I lay there dazed, unable to open my eyes.

'I love kissing,' she said. 'Don't you?'

I smiled like an idiot.

A cool wind stirred. I opened my eyes. Isobel was standing now, brushing the soil from her T-shirt, looking back along the path we had walked. I gazed at her and wondered if my time was over.

I sat up and tried to think a little more clearly. 'Isobel . . .'

She turned her face round slowly, and looked at the tree trunk above my head. '*Oui, mon amour?*'

'Thank you.'

Her eyes flicked down to my face, as if just remembering I was there. '*De rien.*' She smiled. 'Come on, we'd better go and pick those blackberries.'

That afternoon, we stormed the Bastille for the first time. It took ages because Louis kept picking faults with our performances. 'I thought this was supposed to be fun,' said Alex, after Louis complained that the drawbridge they had made was descending too quickly.

'I just want to get it *right*,' said Louis.

The sky had clouded over, but the air was damp and hot, and each movement released a little torrent of sweat. Louis, Alex and I were all topless; Isobel had changed into a white cotton bra-top and her blue sunbathing shorts. When I looked at her my throat turned dry.

'I'm going to the river to get some water,' I said, holding the empty bottle up for the others to see.

'I'll come with you,' said Isobel.

Louis sighed. 'OK, let's all take a break.'

As soon as we were out of sight, she grabbed my arm and pushed me against a tree. She kissed me. I felt the sweat slide between our touching shoulders, the dry cotton rubbing against my chest. When she pulled away, a drop of sweat fell from her upper lip onto my tongue. I tasted the salt. Her lips were stained purple from the blackberries we had eaten. She smiled, as if at a private joke, and turned away.

'Does it feel like this with everyone?' I asked as we walked, a body's width apart, towards the river. It was too hot to hold hands, Isobel said.

'No-oh,' she said, in a light, wavering voice. 'It depends on the person. But . . . it's usually very nice. Do you like it?'

'Can't you tell?'

She laughed, and gave a little skip. 'It's fun, isn't it? Oh, I could do it all day . . .'

We reached the edge of the river and filled our bottles. Staring into the water, I found that something was bothering me. 'Isobel, what you said before, when I . . .'

She flashed me a coy smile. 'I changed my mind, that's all. Girl's prerogative.'

I watched as Isobel poured the bottle of water over her hair and face, her neck stretched backwards.

'How many boys have you kissed?' I asked.

When the bottle was empty, she wiped the water from her eyes and looked at me critically. 'Why do you want to know that?'

'I don't know. I'm just curious.'

'How many boys have I kissed?' She looked blank. 'I have no idea. Is it important?'

I regretted the question, yet at the same time her evasiveness made me more determined to find out the truth. 'You must have *some* idea. Roughly how many? One? Two? Five?' She kept looking at me blankly. '*Ten?*'

'Maybe.'

'Maybe *ten*?'

'Or more . . . I really don't know. It doesn't bother you, does it?'

'No, but . . . more than ten! Fifteen? *Twenty?*'

'Calm down, Michael, it's no big deal. I like kissing.' She filled her bottle again, and took a drink. 'Still, I think twenty is highly unlikely. I only started three years ago.'

I lay awake in my sleeping-bag that night, looking at Isobel's profile in the moonlight. It unnerved me now, the way she slept in the same motionless, changeless pose, like a vampire inside its coffin.

I imagined her kissing twenty other boys. Feeling the same easy ecstasy with each of them. I struggled to think of twenty boys' faces. I pictured her with movie actors and rugby players, with huge black men and old stubbly men and small boys.

Three years. So she had been kissing before she even moved to France. I thought back to the thin, faraway girl I had seen from the hilltop above the Sillitoes' chateau. I should have seen it in her face, I thought. She had been kissing. How could I not have seen it?

8

The Pool of Blood

I woke up and looked to my left. There she lay, asleep, afloat.
I savoured the shape of her mouth. That belongs to me, I
thought. Those beautiful, pouting lips are mine. I was so
happy I could not quite believe it. Life seemed too good to be
true. And that worried me.

I had always found it odd how people took this moment for
granted – the moment of waking, when your mind quickly
reassembles all the feelings, ideas, memories, hopes and fears
of the day before, pulling them from an alien world of dreams
that you can never quite remember. Sleepily, I wondered:
What if there were two souls in each of us, leading parallel
lives, working shifts inside the same head and body? The
dayself and the nightself. The sleepself and the wakeself. The
dreamself and the realself. And what if each of these souls did
not believe in the existence of the other, but regarded the life
that happened when it was off duty as a kind of imaginary
netherworld? What if I were, to my dreamself, only a series of
fragmentary images, dismissed on waking as the mind's
waste matter? I tried to remember my dream, thinking it
might give me a clue to the activities of my soulmate, but it
was already fading.

I got up and went outside, where I stretched again and
yawned loudly. There was no sign of Alex and Louis; I
guessed they must have gone hunting. I stood in the garden
for a few seconds, letting my eyes adjust to the light, watching the grass blades shine. Then I went back into the shelter
and knelt next to Isobel.

I was hoping she would open her eyes so we could kiss; I
wanted to wake her like that, but didn't dare. What if her
nightself were still on duty, I thought, and to this soul I was

merely a stranger, a threatening shape? What if Isobel woke and did not remember what had happened between us? That regathering of memory seemed such a fragile process. It had happened only once, after all. What if it were to slip her mind? Or what if she had a change of mind? I imagined her doing it: taking the grey sphere from her head and replacing it with another one. I had dissected a sheep's brain once at school. The teacher said it was the same size as a human child's. I remembered staring at it and wondering how love could exist in something so doughy and sliceable.

These thoughts weren't new to me – I always asked myself unanswerable questions like this in the mornings (or at least I thought I did) – but the uncertainty seemed doubled now that my happiness so depended on the threads of memory inside another human mind. What were the chances that we would both wake up and feel the same way towards each other? One in two? One in four? One in a thousand?

I leaned closer: her hair smelled of woodsmoke, her throat of vanilla. I watched her lips, slightly parted, and the pulsing hollow in the skin above her nostrils. For three or four heartbeats I breathed her freshly expired air; it felt dangerous somehow, unnaturally pleasurable, as though, if we kept breathing each other's air like this, we would soon suffocate and die.

Still she didn't wake so I sat back, legs crossed, and looked at the sunbeams where they came through the holes in the roof and the scattered golden coins of daylight they made on the wall behind her. I rubbed the outside of my arms – they felt cold in the shelter after being out in the sunlight.

I closed my eyes and listened to Isobel breathe. There seemed an extraordinarily long pause between exhalation and inhalation. I imagined her breaths as mountains, the pause as the valley between. That valley was where I longed to live. In that valley, time would stand still. There, our dayselves would hold hands and kiss. Nothing would change, ever.

I went to the river to wash and fetch water. In Elbow Pool I plunged my head under for a moment and when I opened my eyes I saw rainbows through the water drops on my lashes. I breathed deep, then crouched underwater again. Plunge and breathe, plunge and breathe: this was my morning routine, but it felt charged with something extra that day. I could feel my heart contract and spurt, contract and spurt. Everything seemed sharper.

I stood up, watching the water cling in circles to my skin, then dived into the river itself. The coldness was a shock, but I soon turned numb and half swam, half floated downstream. I lay on my back and watched the sky. A wavy blue line bordered by trees. It was easy to imagine that the sky was a river and the river was the sky.

When I'd had enough of floating I grabbed hold of a tree root and looked around, unsure where I was. Ahead, in the distance, I could see light where the forest ended. I tried to swim back upstream and felt a flutter of panic when I realised the current was too strong. In a flash I saw the shelter empty – Isobel gone. It was crazy but I felt frightened. What if I never saw her again?

I scrambled up on to the bank, slippery mud sticking to my knees and toes, and ran through the sharp reeds. My feet were caked brown when I got to Elbow Pool. I towelled myself, dressed, filled the water bottles, and ran to the shelter. In my panic I got lost. The path kept forking and I found myself staring into two dark entrances, hesitating endlessly. Which way now? Which path should I take?

By the time I finally got back I was in a terrible state. I paused in the entrance of the shelter, trying to slow my breathing. I stared through the gloom, at the place where the air mattress lay.

'Isobel?'

She wasn't there.

Desolate, I dropped the water bottles on the ground and walked through the shelter to check the garden.

Then I sighed and, for the first time in my life, felt perfect happiness. Isobel was lying on my purple-stained T-shirt in the middle of the grass, her back bare in the sun. She looked like she was still asleep.

I walked softly towards her. She did not stir.

'Good morning,' I said.

'Oh . . . hello,' she breathed, turning her face to smile at me, her eyes still sleepy. 'Can you rub this in, please?'

She pushed a greasy old tube of suncream over the grass, towards me. I knelt down and kissed her on the back of the neck. Her skin was hot. She made a little murmur of satisfaction. I sat over her back and squirted a long white line down her spine.

'Ooh, it's cold.' She shivered.

I started to rub it into her shoulders. The muscles were tense and rubbery.

'Oh my God . . . that feels *nice.*'

'My aunt used to make me do this to her when I was younger.'

'She used to *make* you?'

'She said I had angel's hands.'

Isobel gave an amused snort and strained her neck up to look at me. 'What else did she make you do?'

'No, nothing like that. She loved sunbathing. And she didn't have a husband or . . .'

'Well, exactly!'

'No, it was never . . . It wasn't like that.'

I wished I hadn't told Isobel about Aunt Céline. The massages were among my few warm memories of her, but now, spoken aloud, they sounded sordid and embarrassing.

'You *are* good, you know,' said Isobel, after a while. 'You could do this professionally.'

'I'm not sure I'd want to.'

'Oh, come *on*, all those older women – they'd be putty in your hands.' She turned her shoulders and looked me full in the face, with a sly smile. 'You little early starter, you.'

'I think you're done,' I said, wiping my fingers on her lower back.

'No,' she said. 'I'm not.'

And she leaned up to kiss me.

So began our purple days.

While Louis and Alex prepared lunch, Isobel would push me through the shelter towards the blackberry brambles and we would kiss. She seemed to love it as much as I did.

'I've been looking forward to this all morning,' she said.

'You're getting good at this,' she said.

'What are you doing for the rest of the summer?' she said.

Sometimes we would experiment – putting soft blackberries on our tongues and crushing them – but the one time in those first two days I dared to touch her breast, she gently picked up my hand between her fingers and put it on her waist. 'Just kissing,' she said, in that crisp, English voice. '*Ça suffit.*'

One time, she gave me a lovebite on my neck.

'I wish I had a mirror,' I said. 'I've never seen one before.'

'They're funny, they're a bit like gobstoppers. You know – the way they change colour.'

'What colour is mine?'

'Red at the moment. But it'll go purple, then black, then sort of greenish-yellow, and then it'll fade away.'

'What shape is it?'

'The shape of my mouth.'

I shivered: the shape of her mouth. Proudly I felt it burn on my skin, like a tattoo of possession.

She would hold hands with me all the way back to the shelter, then let go as we crossed the threshold, and rush in before me, all chatter. Stumbling behind her with the blackberries in my T-shirt, I would listen to the happy, detached trill of her voice, the way she could talk about nothing. I admired her coolness; for a long time after our blackberrying, I was barely able to speak at all.

63

Sometimes she winked at me and I would blush. I suffered with constant erections, like old people suffer with trapped wind. They cramped me up, bent me double. There was no relief.

At lunch we would sit in a circle and Louis would tell us about the Bastille; how Paris had arrived at this boiling point, what it all meant. He taught us the words to the 'Marseillaise' and told us about the King's hunting journal – the only record he kept of the tumultuous times through which he lived, reserved for major events and lists of the animals he had shot. On 14 July 1789, the entry in the King's diary was: *'Rien.'* 'Just because the idiot didn't catch anything,' said Louis. 'That's why there was a revolution.'

In the afternoons, we rehearsed the play. And, under Louis's remorseless direction, we slowly improved. Isobel learned to sometimes dim her electric brightness. I learned to project my voice, not to look at the ground when I spoke. Alex learned to move and talk at the same time. The day of our grand performance was set. Despite the lack of an audience, we became dedicated to giving the best show we could.

The morning of the performance, Louis and Alex woke me early. Alex had found traces of what he thought was a boar run the day before, and the plan was to kill one for lunch, then use its collected blood as a theatrical prop in the afternoon.

The boar run was not in the Republic, but past the Underwater Forest, in a plantation of holly trees and brambles. We let Isobel sleep and walked there in silence. I wanted to talk to Louis, but he had a distant, forbidding look on his face, as though his mind were elsewhere.

As we entered the holly, Alex warned us we would have to be patient. He told us about the boar hunts he had seen; the hours of silent waiting followed by the fast kill. But this time he was wrong: we did not have to wait long at all to see our first boar. When we got to the place where Alex had seen the markings on the ground, we crouched down to inspect them – and a large, dark shape bolted past us into the bushes. I felt its heavy body brush my back.

We followed the creature's tracks: the path wound through holly trees, and we had to crawl. It was cool and dry, but dusty. Eventually we came to a clearing and agreed to wait there, hidden in the bushes at either side. The idea was that Alex would shoot it in the leg and I would try to stab its neck. Louis held a large rock, which he planned to bring down on the boar's head.

We waited, and we waited. None of us spoke. I felt thirsty. I daydreamed of the river and of Isobel's lips and tongue. The boar came just when I had begun to think it never would.

For some reason, I remember the kill as a sequence of still, soundless images: the look of fury on the beast's face; the wide, black body rushing over me; the anguish in Louis's eyes as he slowly smashed its skull; the patch of drying blood on the animal's fur, moving up and down in time with its final breaths.

Some time later, Alex said, 'Fucking hell. I thought it would never die.'

I could do nothing but nod, even when Alex and Louis relaxed and started making fun of my backwards dive through the bushes. I was covered in scratches and bruises, but all I could think of was the violence in those small, dark eyes. All I could think was: it wanted to kill me. I had never known anything so strong, so alive, so terrifically eager to keep living as that boar. Even when its muscles had finished twitching, I was afraid to touch it.

And the corpse weighed a ton.

Our first history play was a great success. Louis made a fraught yet ultimately dignified victim. 'The way you died was important then,' he told us. 'It was your last message to the world. It said a lot about you.'

Isobel was supremely restrained. A little too much theatrical yelling over the fuse of the cannon, perhaps, but there were plenty of classy touches: little movements and gestures which signalled a true acting talent.

Alex's pastry chef was brutally convincing. He gave an excellent grimace when Louis pretended to kick him in the balls, and a savage smile thereafter.

I was pretty good, too. I actually went purple when I was hanged, Isobel told me later. And the scream of horror I gave when I lost my hand . . .

But it was, inevitably, the blood that stole the show. We had to mix it with water to keep it from congealing, and even then there were thick, dark clots like lumps in soup, but the effect was not lessened at all.

Alex splashed a little on to my wrist as the sword descended, but the rest he saved for the neck-sawing episode. Grotesquely, hilariously, it went on for ages: arteries and veins exploding in foul little surges, one after another, like the fountains of Versailles.

At dusk the four of us stood or lay in the garden, eating cold boar, aching with laughter, and taking turns drinking from a bottle of wine that Louis had brought from home. He had been saving it for a special occasion, he said.

I lay on the grass and watched the purple sky spin above me. What a day it had been. My hair and skin were sticky with thick, rich-smelling blood. Isobel sat down next to me and I lifted myself to whisper: 'Shall we take them to . . . ?'

'To where?' Her eyes were huge and unfocused.

I mouthed the words 'Elbow Pool'.

She flinched. 'If you want.'

'Don't you think I should?'

'It's up to you, Michael. You found it.'

It was an impulsive gesture. I felt close to them all. I felt happy. The forest was warm and beautiful and ours. 'Listen, everybody!' I clapped my hands. 'I've got something I want to show you.'

Alex yelled something obscene. Louis gave me a curious look. Isobel turned away.

'Come with me,' I said. 'And bring your map, Louis, you may want to write this down.'

I took them there, and they made all the right noises. They gasped, they splashed, they rubbed my hair. The water turned purple.

I thought of how the people in that Paris mob must have felt, as the giant prison fell at their hands. The yells of *'Liberté!'* The wine-flavoured kisses afterwards, in the sunset. The hangovers next morning, and all those headless bodies, like drained bottles on the carpet after a party. All that clearing-up to do . . .

We trooped back, cold and exhausted in the half dark, hands held in a human chain. And we sang the 'Marseillaise', though none of us could remember the words.

9

The Hot Hand

I was living in a new land. Around me I saw the same views – the mudbrick shelter, the sun-painted trees, the dry grass below, the blue sky above. And yet, I sensed, something had changed.

My senses, stroked by love, had become heightened to an almost unendurable degree. It was like suffering from a thick cold all winter and then, one warm May dawn, suddenly recovering. It was like a dam bursting.

The world was so fresh that for long periods of time I did not daydream at all. There was no music in my head. I did not scratch my hair or grind my teeth or rub the grime from my face.

I did not daydream, yet she was always on my mind. I saw her in river, trees, sky. Her skin rubbed against my insides as I walked. It was as if I had swallowed her whole.

Am I 'in love'? I wondered. Is this what it feels like? What surprised me was how different it felt from what I had supposed was 'falling in love'. Then, I had noticed nothing; the world had revolved mutely in a dark blur. I had felt like an invalid. Finding the lips and skin of the one you wanted was, it seemed to me, like being ejected from the womb into a crazy, alien, overwhelmingly vivid place. It did not feel like something that could possibly last. The seconds were too heavy, as if whole hours had been compressed into each of them.

When I tried to tell Isobel how I felt, she gave a sad, knowing smile. 'Just enjoy it,' she said.

She loved my fingers. After the massages, she used to lift my hands to her face and stare at each finger in turn. She turned the hands round and traced the lines and tiny hairs in silence. Occasionally she blinked. She kissed them respectfully and sucked the ends. 'How did you grow such wonderful fingers?' she asked.

I told her that her fingers were the first things I had noticed about her. She pulled a sour face. 'I hate my fingers. They're too thin and long and the knuckles are too thick. My rings are loose when I wear them, but I need soap to take them off.'

'Your hands are always warm,' I said, holding one of them.

'It's summer, Michael. Anyway, warm hands, cold heart; that's what my mum says.'

'Your mum says you've got a cold heart?'

'When I was little I had cold hands. She told me cold hands, warm heart. But if that's true, the opposite must be true as well.'

'Are my hands cold or warm?' I asked.

'They're neither,' she said. 'They're perfect.'

She was particularly attached to my right hand. 'Will you give it to me, please?' she asked one day, pouting exaggeratedly. I pointed out that I used it for almost everything.

'If you died,' she said, 'would you leave it to me in your will?'

'I don't have a will.'

'Make one.'

'What would you do with my hand if I was dead?'

'I'd hold it,' she said earnestly.

'Nothing else?'

'I'm not telling.'

I raised my voice in mock-protest. 'But it's *my* hand!'

'You're dead,' she said. 'What do you care?'

She asked me to stop hunting.

'Why?' I asked.

'I want you to stay and rub my back.'

And so I did. Louis and Alex walked off without me each morning, and when I got up, Isobel was waiting for me in the

69

garden, lying topless on my ruined T-shirt. I watched her from the mouth of the shelter, framing the beauty of her shape in my mind so I would never forget it. She lay like an adorable doll on the grass and I saw dark insects crawl between the blanched stalks. I admired the supple arch of her back and the shadowy buds of her breasts, the curve of her tight blue hips, and those long, brown legs, calves waving in a little-girl rhythm that betrayed her excitement at what was to come.

'Oh, hello!' she said, when I eased myself on top of her. 'Fancy seeing you here . . .'

She did most of the talking. The massages made her giddy and flirtatious; the more excited she got, the more she chattered away. She was relentlessly light-hearted, which annoyed me at times, though I tried to suppress the feeling. Sometimes, in the end, I had to kiss her to shut her up.

'If I get rich . . .' she started.

'Nurses don't get rich,' I said, in a low voice.

'No, silly, but actresses do.'

'Some of them.'

'The best ones do, so *obviously* I will! So, as I was saying before you so rudely interrupted me, *when* I get rich . . .'

'When you get rich . . .'

'I'm going to keep you as a slave and make you do this every day. Twice a day if I feel like it. I will keep you in a glass cage at the foot of my bed, and feed you on barbecued boar and macaroni and blackberries.'

I laughed, despite myself. 'Can't I sleep with you, then?'

'Oh no, my husband wouldn't like that!'

'Your husband?' I lifted my hands from her back.

'*Don't stop,*' she pleaded. 'OK, you can be my husband if you insist, but I still want to keep you in a glass cage. And I'll have golden statues made of your hands and put them on my mantelpiece. And . . . oh yes, there . . . that's nice.'

I was quiet, a craftsman concentrating on his work. She dared me to improve on the previous day's labours, to squeeze new sensations from her body, and I applied myself seriously. It was a highly intimate form of slavery.

I always started at the top. She pinned her hair up with butterfly grips so I could touch the back of her neck, which I loved. There was a little triangle of blond fur there, and the last, large bobble of her spine. From there, I moved across to her shoulder muscles, kneading them with thumbs and rows of knuckles, then stroking gently . . . down her spine, up from the coccyx in a light spreading of fingers, fanning out over her shoulder blades. I used the back of my hand to glide over her pleading pores, offering the gentlest of touches. Then, a kiss on her neck; a little shudder in response. More solid work on the back – a kind of soft pummelling, awakening the skin, warming the muscles.

I would slide off her then, and crawl around to her feet. I didn't touch those – the only time I did, she went into a paroxysm of horrified laughter – but softly caressed her calves, which were surprisingly defined. I loved the rubbery tautness of her muscles. I liked to kiss and lick her calves. She said she didn't know how I could, with all those hairs and bramble scars, but I enjoyed the light pricking sensation on my lips and face. The hollows of her knees were beautiful, but oversensitive; I just traced the thin blue veins until she snapped her leg shut on my hand. And then up her thighs. The skin was so soft there, like sieved flour. I had to push her legs apart to make room for myself. Around this point, I would sit up and take a rest, trailing my fingers lightly over her thighs while I admired the view: the luminous blue of those silken shorts, the golden-brown glow of her back, the pink and blue plastic butterflies shining from her glossy hair.

'My God,' she would whisper, 'where did you *learn* all this?'

'*Marie Claire.*'

'I hope you didn't do *this* to Aunt Céline,' she would breathe, as I finally slipped my fingers inside her shorts and stormed the Bastille.

And I would laugh, with the joy of her sudden silence.

Sometimes I wished Louis and Alex would come back early one of those mornings and catch us at the crucial moment, just so another person could admire the tortuous architecture of our body shapes, the look of surprised seriousness on Isobel's face.

Just so someone could witness the balance of power tip, for one of those heavy seconds.

All through lunch I would savour the smell of her on my fingers, mingling with the odours of boiling pasta and smoking meat. The smell relaxed me. It meant I could watch Isobel's taunting, flirting coolness, hear her empty, ironic words, and think: oh, you . . . but I know the truth.

Isobel was having a grand time: the mornings devoted entirely to her sensual pleasure; the afternoons to her dramatic talents. And what a role – Marie Antoinette!

'Why did they call her a whore?' asked Isobel at lunch.

'The rumours were that she was sleeping with almost everyone in the Court,' said Louis. 'Paris was full of dirty cartoons of her. They thought she was the wickedest woman in the world.'

'Was she really that bad?'

He shrugged. 'Probably not. But the truth wasn't really important. It was what people believed that mattered.'

After lunch, Louis told us about the progress of the Revolution: the fishwives' march, the flight to Varennes, the massacre in the Champs de Mars, the declaration of war, and the Queen's real treachery – sending French military secrets to her family in Austria.

Alex wanted to build a guillotine. 'Then we could chop off the Queen's head.'

Isobel stuck her tongue out at him.

Louis laughed. 'And how are you planning to build a guillotine?'

'We can use the blade from your wood axe,' said Alex. 'And for rope . . .'

'An axe blade wouldn't work,' said Louis. 'It's too light and it's the wrong shape. You'd need a steel sheet or something. Not to mention a saw, a hammer, lots of nails, some kind of pulley, a counterweight, probably a drill . . .'

'But . . .'

'A pulley?'

'Listen,' said Louis, his face suddenly focused again. 'I know a way we can do it, but it's too soon now. You have to trust me. If I promise to sort out the guillotine for later, will you listen to the rest of the history?'

Alex leaned forward excitedly. 'OK, but what's your idea? How do we build the guillotine?'

'Later,' said Louis, and then he laughed.

'What's funny?'

'I was just thinking of the nicknames they had for it. After 1792, you see, there was the Terror, and the guillotine became a way of killing lots and lots of people. No one thought about it as death any more, apart from the ones getting their heads cut off. It was just like being ticked off a list or something.'

Alex stirred. 'What were the nicknames, then?'

'The national razor. Looking through the republican window. Spitting in the bag.'

'Ugh,' said Isobel.

'Shaking the hot hand . . . I really like that one.'

'I don't get it,' I said. 'What's the hot hand?'

'The devil's, I suppose,' said Louis. 'You shook his hand as you entered hell.'

That evening, before dinner, Louis offered to help me gather blackberries. Isobel looked at us strangely as we left.

'Are you having fun now?' asked Louis, when we got to the place where the brambles grew. The light was slanting through the trees, and the whole familiar scene was heart-rendingly beautiful.

'Absolutely,' I said, starting to pick the ripe fruit. 'I'm having a wonderful time.'

'I thought so. You seem happier. You're glad we came?'

'Of course.' It seemed an absurd question. 'Aren't you?'

I looked at Louis as he thought about his answer. People always said that we looked alike, and I knew what they meant, but the same individual features in each of our faces produced very different effects. His face was all angles, his lips were thin, his cheekbones wide, his forehead high. His green eyes were clearer, brighter, less muddied than mine. He had the kind of face that people trust.

'I am glad,' he said. 'But you have to realise that things won't stay like this. I told Alex the same thing this morning.'

'Told him what?'

'It's going to get harder . . . soon. Harder but better. More exciting. I feel like we're waiting, at the moment. Killing time.'

'I don't feel like that at all.'

'I know. But you've got . . . distractions.'

He meant Isobel, I guessed. I looked at the tree in whose roots she had lain down my T-shirt for our first kiss. I wondered for the first time how much Louis knew; what he thought about it. I could never work out how close he was to Isobel.

'I just think we all need to be prepared,' he said.

'For what?'

'For change.'

There was something ominous in his voice, or perhaps it was just the thought of change – any change – that struck me as ominous then.

'What's going to happen?'

'I don't know yet. But something has to. We're running out of . . . well, everything. Food. Bullets. Patience.'

'Patience?'

'Not ours. I mean the adults in the village. It's been a long time.' He looked away, in what I assumed to be the direction

74

of St Argen, though all I could see were trees and patches of pink sky.

I had completely forgotten about the outside world. It seemed unimportant. 'What do you think they're doing?'

He shrugged. 'Looking for us, I suppose.'

'You don't think they'll find us, do you?'

Louis said nothing. He started to pick the berries again.

'Have you got a plan?' I asked.

'Of course.' He smiled smoothly, pouring a handful of berries into the stained, waiting folds of my T-shirt.

'Can you tell me?'

'Not yet.'

'When?'

'Soon.'

'How soon?'

A hand on my shoulder. 'I honestly don't know, Michael. But don't worry.' And then he gave me what was beginning to sound like familiar advice: 'Just enjoy it.' A curl of thin lips. 'While it lasts.'

The four of us ate dinner together and Louis told us more stories of the Revolution. When it got dark we lit a fire. Isobel and Alex went to bed. The stars came out. Louis and I sat together and he showed me the books he was reading. I recognised their covers: the thick one with the guillotine and the thin one with the shining eye.

'This', he said, holding up the first, 'is about the most important events in the history of Europe, and this' – he held up the second – 'is just a few ideas written by a Swiss philosopher. And yet all this' – the first again – 'would not have happened without this' – the second.

'Why?' I asked dutifully.

Louis smiled – his teeth shone in the firelight – and he began to recount the life of Jean Jacques Rousseau (1712–78), composer, novelist and philosopher. As he described his early life, I reclined on my elbows and closed my eyes, and imagined I was back in our room, listening from the bottom bunk.

'Europe was full of philosophers at that time,' said Louis, 'all giving their theories of life and the world. But Rousseau was different. He cut through all the crap and asked, "Why are people unhappy?" And the answer was because they had lost touch with their innocence. Animals are not unhappy, he said. Primitive man – the noble savage – was not unhappy. Unhappiness came with civilisation. It came with progress, cities, money. What Rousseau said was that if you take away those things, and return to nature, you can find happiness again.'

'Like us,' I said.

'Exactly. We understand him, but in those days people laughed and said his ideas were pie in the sky. So he wrote a book about how to put these ideas into practice.' Louis held up the book with the shining eye. 'In 1762 he published *The Social Contract*. The government realised how dangerous it could be, and sent orders for his arrest. Rousseau was forced to flee to England. He returned to France five years later, but his ideas were never accepted in his lifetime.'

I could feel myself falling asleep, so I sat up and hugged my knees and stared at the fire.

'But after Rousseau died, things began to change. People realised he had been right after all. Soon everyone was visiting his grave, which was on an island in Ermenonville, surrounded by beautiful woods. Even Marie Antoinette went there, and was so inspired that she had a little grove built at Versailles where she could feed lambs and be natural. By the time of the Revolution, Rousseau was a hero and his ideas were everywhere. Robespierre carried a copy of *The Social Contract* around in his jacket pocket. It became the bible of the Revolution.'

'So what went wrong?' I asked.

'What do you mean?'

'Well, the Revolution happened ages ago. So why isn't France the perfect society now?'

Louis grinned. 'Historical gravity.'

I yawned. 'Historical' and 'gravity' were, to my mind, two of the most boring words in the English language. 'I don't understand,' I said.

'Everything that rises must fall. Revolutions . . . empires . . . our lives. They all have the same pattern. They rise until they reach a zenith, the highest point possible, and then they begin to decline. As far as the French Revolution is concerned, it's hard to pinpoint where it went wrong. Maybe it was when the Jacobins conspired against Robespierre and had him executed. Or maybe it was before that, when Robespierre signed Danton's death warrant. Or maybe it was the death of the King, or the invention of the guillotine, or the war . . . but this is all hindsight. That's the thing about zeniths. They're invisible. You never know them for what they are at the time they happen.'

'But then what's the point?' I asked. 'If everything that rises must fall, what's the point of having a revolution in the first place?'

'Because maybe it won't fall, this time.'

'Do you really believe that?'

'We have to, Michael. We *must* believe.' He gripped my hand, stared into my eyes. 'Because if you believe, there's a chance you might succeed. If you don't believe, there's no chance at all.'

'Hmm,' I said.

It wasn't that I didn't believe him, just that I was too sleepy to care.

I woke late the next morning and found myself alone in the shelter. I walked to the edge of the garden. It was empty. I stood with my eyes closed, breathing the warm air, feeling the sun on my face, and then I heard soft movements in the shelter. I did not open my eyes.

A moment later, Isobel was hugging me from behind. '*Bonjour*,' she sighed, kissing me on top of my head. I pulled her hands apart and turned around.

77

I looked up at her, suspiciously.

'Have you been growing in the night?' She rubbed the sleep from her eyes, and yawned.

I looked inside her mouth: black nothingness and a long, pink tongue; the little nodule at the back of her throat hanging in the darkness like a pale teardrop.

'Oh, pardon me,' she said, and squinted at me. 'What's the matter?'

'Nothing. I was just looking in your mouth.'

She wrinkled her nose. 'Mmm . . . I would kiss you, but I think I need to brush my teeth first. Shall we go to the river?'

At the river, as I splashed my face and hair, Isobel sat with her toes in the water, brushing her teeth and looking at me. She mumbled something, but the toothbrush made it impossible to understand.

'Sorry?'

'I said: "I had a nice dream last night. You were in it."'

'What was the dream?'

'Not telling.'

'So why mention it?'

'Because I know what it means.'

'What does it mean?'

'That it's time I gave you something.'

'What sort of something?'

'Your reward. For being a good boy.' A knowing smile, aimed at the white sky. 'Phew . . . it's hot, isn't it? Let's go to your pool. I fancy a dip.'

It was the first time we had been there together since the fall of the Bastille. 'Look,' she said, 'the water's dark.'

'It's the blood,' I said. 'You were right. I shouldn't have brought them here.'

'Bathing in blood, what a thought!'

She laughed as she threw her dress and knickers behind the tree, then slid into the stained water. I followed her in and we played together.

'Isobel, do you remember that first time, when you called me a strange one?'

'You *are* a strange one.' She grinned. 'And yes, of course I remember. It was only last week, you know.'

'Was it? Seems longer . . .'

She swam back a little way, and looked at me. I felt a trickle of sweat on my forehead. 'Come here,' she said.

I swam over to her, my knees dragging on the smooth stones. She rose above me, and I stared into her forest of dark hair. Then she pulled me up by the hands. A long kiss. Our faces separated for a moment. She bit her bottom lip, as if making a difficult decision, and looked down. I felt her fingers tighten around my erection.

'What are you . . . ?'

My breaths turned heavy. I thought about that phrase as she started to drag my foreskin up and down. Heavy breathing. How many times had I heard those words, and never thought of the reality? The air that came from my mouth felt almost solid. My legs were weakening beneath the weight of all those heavy breaths. I had to hold Isobel's shoulders for support. The brown freckled flesh turned white beneath my fingers.

I watched her face. It was tightened in a grimace of concentration. She looked like someone about to receive an injection. I heard myself moan, and felt a wave of warm air flow over the skin of my thighs.

She stopped for a moment. 'You're hurting my shoulders.'

'Sorry,' I gasped.

She knelt down in the water, her face reddening. With one hand she held on to the back of my thigh, while the other hand kept pumping away.

Watching her like that, from above, I thought of the little girl she must once have been, polishing a table leg under her mother's anxious gaze. She looked so serious, I felt like laughing.

'*Come on*,' she said through gritted teeth. 'My wrist is killing me!'

'What am I supposed to do?' I cried.

And then it happened.

I closed my eyes, grabbed a handful of her hair, pressed her face to my stomach as I felt the wave crash over me.

'Ah . . . bingo!' she said gleefully, from below.

'Oh God,' I said. 'Is that what it feels like?'

I was lying on the grass, staring at the sky.

'Didn't you like it?'

'I thought I was going to die.'

'You were so quiet, I wasn't sure I was doing it right.'

'I think you must have been.'

'Yes, I think so, although there wasn't much of it. My friend said it was like watching fireworks.'

'What was?'

'The stuff coming out.'

She showed me two of her fingers, which were sticky with some kind of clear glue.

'Oh . . . is that it?'

'Yes. But normally it's white.'

'Oh.'

She put some on her tongue. 'Not very salty at all. It doesn't really taste of anything.' She sounded disappointed.

I didn't know what to say, so I lay back on the grass. The sky was unbearably bright. I closed my eyes. There was a cold, hollow feeling inside my chest.

'So are you happy now?'

'I was happy before.'

She murmured something.

'What did you say?'

'Nothing.'

There was a parched silence.

After a while she said, 'Have you really never done that before?' She sounded as if she were miles away, on a distant shore, the wind carrying her voice over the water.

'No.'

'You don't do it to yourself?'

'I didn't know you could.'

'Well, there you go. You're one of the lads now.'

Something in her tone of voice made me uneasy. There was a pause and then she sniggered.

'What?' I sat up, feeling paranoid.

'I was just thinking about Louis and Alex. It's funny to think they've probably just done the same thing.' Her eyes were narrowed, coolly mocking.

'What do you mean?'

'Why did you think Alex was so keen on hunting with Louis?' There was a slight tremor in her voice as she said this.

'You mean . . . ?'

She gave me a sardonic look.

I couldn't quite imagine what Isobel was suggesting. '*Together?*'

She snorted derisively.

'How do you know?'

'Oh, I saw them once. Anyway, they're so obvious about it. Didn't you guess? Why did you think they always looked so pleased with themselves when they came back from "map-making"?'

'I thought they were pleased with the map.'

She turned her face away. 'Alex is so disgusting. It's all he thinks about.'

'What about hunting?'

'Same thing. To him.'

I remembered the movement he'd made with his hand, in the river, after we shot the rabbit. I had thought he wanted to dance.

Isobel stood up and got dressed. There were no words in my head. She stood above me, staring at the water, and her shadow lay over me. 'Maybe I'd better go,' she said.

I nodded, too tired to speak, though I didn't really want her to leave.

She rubbed my hair, one of those sad little gestures meant

to signify more than they do. I looked up and she had gone.

I crept close to the water and stared at my reflection. My face stained red; black holes for eyes. 'So this is what it's like . . .'

A bird of prey hovered high above me in the dazzling heavens.

10

The Guillotine

I opened my eyes in panic and turned to the left. Blood was banging in my ears and for several fearful moments I couldn't see her. Was she there? I rubbed my eyes and stared through the dimness. In my dream she had gone. I had followed her but she had vanished. Now, stretching from the hole in my sleeping-bag, I had to touch her to be sure. Her cheek was cool. She murmured and I sighed.

I got up and walked to the edge of the garden. The air was warm but the sky was grey. I looked up at it and got an ominous feeling in my chest. Every day since my first kiss with Isobel, the sky had been a perfect blue. Yesterday it had turned white. Now it was grey. I told myself it was only weather, not a symbol, but the ominous shape in my chest did not disappear.

Deep down, I had been waiting for a change like this. I had never really trusted blue skies since I learned in school that they were an illusion. Now when I looked at the blueness, I thought always of the darkness that lay behind – or rather, the darkness that was there, ever present, but which I could not see. I suppose I thought of Isobel's love in the same way.

I walked back into the shelter and watched her sleep for a moment. Feeling sad, I gathered the empty bottles and took them to the river.

When I got back, she was waiting for me in the garden, lying topless on my T-shirt.

Even while we were doing it, I was worrying. I didn't know how the sadness had slipped in, but I could feel it here now, between us. The sadness and the fear. It was as though I had been happily climbing in the treetops and had only now looked down. I had been climbing with ease, but now I looked down and saw the depth of the drop and it seemed impossible to continue. My equilibrium had gone.

Below me Isobel was still writhing in ecstasy, but already I was panicking about the silence that would follow. They were lengthening, our silences. I feared she was getting bored of me. In the dream she had been bored of me. I tried to think of something to say.

'Do you think your parents do this?' I asked her, as I wiped my fingers on the T-shirt.

'No way,' she said. 'My father is such a brute. Not like you at all. Besides, they sleep in separate beds now.'

'Really?'

'My mother says he flails his arms around in his sleep.' Isobel pulled a face. 'He's got a hairy back, you know.'

'Why did she marry him?'

'Oh, she told me once. I forget now.' She closed her eyes and smiled. 'I can still feel the tingles. How do you do it? You're going to have to teach me, so I can do it myself. Just in case.'

'In case of what?'

'I don't know . . . This can't last for ever, can it?'

It seemed casual, the way she said it, but then she looked into my eyes, as if searching for something. I shrank away, frightened of what she might find in there – the emptiness, or worse, that I knew lurked inside.

'Dunno,' I mumbled. For some reason, the second syllable came out louder than the first.

Her eyes looked sad for a moment, then she turned on to her front and resumed her light, ironical tone. 'Anyway, tell me . . . how's my tan coming along?'

'You'll be black soon,' I said. 'Your parents won't recognise you.'

We walked in silence towards the river. Our hands were joined, but the silence hissed between us. For the first time she had talked about the end, and now I began to dread it. There it loomed on the horizon: a hole in the sky, a growing blackness. I glanced at Isobel; her eyes drifted wearily over the sunless trees. Twenty boys. 'Isobel, I . . .'

She let go of my hand and looked at me, surprised. 'Yes?'

I heard them. 'Nothing,' I sighed.

I heard them before I saw them; their excited voices carried through the dividing trees. I had time to wonder, anxiously, if Isobel had heard them before me, if that was why she had let go of my hand, and then they were next to us, our paths converging. Alex carried a dead buzzard; Louis had the shotgun. Their faces were red and sweaty. Alex held the bird by its feet so its noble head drooped grotesquely. 'Not bad, eh?' he said to me, lifting it up to eye level.

'Well done,' I said.

To my consternation, I found myself walking with Alex while Louis and Isobel followed behind. Alex talked loudly about the hunt, so I couldn't hear what the other two were saying, though their voices rose with laughter several times. I wondered if they were laughing at me.

Close to the river, Isobel said, 'Why don't you give me the buzzard, Alex? You and Michael can go to the river and get cleaned up. We'll get lunch ready.'

'All right.' Alex yawned. 'Come on, Mike.'

I looked at Isobel, but she did not meet my eye.

As I stood by the bubbling river and listened to Alex's stupid voice, I got the ominous feeling in my chest again. It felt like a large, jagged shape. All the way back it seemed to rub brutally against my heart, my lungs, my gut.

'Are you OK?' asked Alex, when one of his jokes failed to receive a laugh.

'Feel a bit sick,' I said.

When we got back we found them sitting close to each other in the garden. Isobel's hand was on Louis's forearm.

Louis noticed the look on my face and came over to me. 'Michael, are you all right?'

'Need to lie down,' I said, and walked into the shelter. I did not look back, but I heard her laugh.

I lay there for some time, looking up at the grey sky through the holes in the ceiling. I could hear their happy voices from the garden and I could smell the roasting bird. I thought Isobel would come to see me, but she didn't. The grey shapes blurred and enlarged as fluid formed in my eyes. I didn't wipe it away, only blinked, and let the heavy tears roll sideways down my face so that they crept inside my ears and muffled the voices. The large, jagged shape touched the base of my throat. I closed my eyes.

When I woke, Isobel was kneeling next to me, her hand stroking my cheek, her face set in an expression of tender concern. But for a moment I did not see her like this, as she was, but as I had just seen her, in my dream: coldly smiling, kissing someone else, a queue of boys snaking through the shelter and out into the forest, all of them laughing, making lewd remarks.

'How are you feeling?' she asked.

'OK,' I mumbled.

'Poor darling. Are you hungry? We saved you some meat. It wasn't too bad, actually. The legs were a bit tough, but I made them leave you a breast. Alex wanted it, the greedy sod, but I insisted. I know you like breasts, even if mine are a bit on the small side . . .'

Still I wasn't happy. I felt she was humouring me. I was suspicious of the kindness in her voice, which lacked her usual irony and sounded like an adult telling lies to a child.

She took off her top and lay on the grass while I ate the cold greasy meat. I wiped my hands on my T-shirt and then touched the soft skin of her back.

'Mmm,' she said, after a while. 'I love bodies, don't you?'

'Bodies?'

'All those nice feelings they give you.'

There was a pause while I wondered how to phrase my

next question. Finally, I said, 'Don't you think it matters *whose* body it is?'

'Oh yes, some bodies are much nicer than others.'

'And minds? And hearts?' I was struggling to keep the emotion out of my voice.

'I prefer bodies, though. You know where you are with a good body.'

'Is that why you keep touching Louis's?'

I didn't mean to say it. The words came out on their own.

There was another pause and then Isobel turned round and said, 'Pardon?'

I had spoken in a mumble but I could tell by the shocked anger on her face that she had heard me, and understood.

She sat up and put on her T-shirt. 'What's that supposed to mean?'

'Nothing.'

'Spit it out.'

I could not meet her eye. 'You seemed very . . . close. This morning.'

'You mean I want to seduce your brother. Is that what you think of me?'

I felt nauseous; I knew I had taken a wrong turning, but could not go back now. 'You tell me.'

She shook her head slowly. Her eyes were wide. 'How dare you.'

'Come on, you were all over him . . .' I wanted to say more, but my lips were trembling.

But so, I noticed, were hers. She blinked away tears. 'Oh, not this.'

I had not expected this reaction at all. It was as though *I* had done something wrong, not her. I was confused now, and worried, but my anger was all played out. 'Look, let's start again. I'm sorry if I –'

But she was up already, speeding from the garden. 'Leave me alone, I don't want to see you . . .'

*

I spent the next hour in the limbs of trees, tearing at my skin. I looked up at the darkening sky, and blamed myself for it. In a fury I ran to Elbow Pool. I threw myself in, fully clothed. The water was still dark. Eyes open, I sank beneath the surface and stared through the blue-red liquid at my hands. The guilty hands, I thought. You'll never touch her again. I crouched in mourning until I felt the gathering explosion in my chest, then I bulleted upwards, vision spinning, heart pounding, and lay on the grass, shivering, but not with cold.

And then, to my surprise, I felt utterly calm. Memories of her actions, her words, her glances came back to me, each of them freeze-framed. She *had* been all over him. I had a *right* to be jealous. I sat up and looked at my dripping clothes, and thought: now why did I do that?

I got her alone that evening, having spent the afternoon on my knees, kissing and rekissing her outstretched hand. Louis had persuaded us to act out the fishwives' march. I was Lafayette; Isobel was the Queen. Alex was a vicious fishwife, threatening to fricassee her liver. Louis was the King.

'I forgive you,' she said, before I could open my mouth to apologise.

'I'm *really* sorry,' I said, aware that I was still acting. 'I honestly didn't mean it.'

'Yes, you did.' Her eyes, behind a veil of curls, looked cold. 'But you're right – I *am* a bitch.'

'I never said that.'

'I flirt with everything that moves, it's true. It's not the first time I've been told that, you know.'

'Isobel . . . I never meant that . . . I love what we . . . I don't mind if you . . .' My voice was rising higher with each unfinished declaration; I was running out of octaves.

'It's all right, I understand,' she said quietly. 'You aren't happy with us doing nice things together. You want more, like all the others. At least I know how things are. I can make a decision now.'

'But you *don't* understand. I don't want to change *anything*. I'm happy the way it is now.'

She nodded sadly. 'So was I.'

As we sat around the fire, Louis told us about the King's execution. The sky was black and starless. Louis sat to my left; Alex to my right, eating my rice (I had no appetite still). Isobel sat across from me, staring into the flames.

In most respects, said Louis, it had been a normal execution. The King was not a king – just another enemy of the revolution – and he was treated the same way as all the others. His hair was cut on the scaffold, his hands tied. He started to make a speech, but was interrupted by a drum roll. Nobody mourned or protested.

Afterwards, the executioner held up his severed head for the crowd to see, and later sold packets of his hair and pieces of clothing as souvenirs. Again, this was pretty standard: there were more buyers than for a common criminal, but that was all.

The only unusual aspect of the King's death, said Louis, was the silence beforehand, and the length of his journey. It was a foggy morning in January, and he was woken at six. He got dressed, had breakfast. At eight he was taken by carriage from his prison cell, and had to endure two hours while the driver picked a way through the crowded streets. Two silent hours, thinking of nothing but your own death. Imagine that, said Louis.

While he spoke, I watched Isobel. I couldn't tell if she was listening. Her eyes were blank. Louis started to talk about the King's funeral. Isobel closed her eyes and lowered her head on to Louis's shoulder. I saw him press his cheek lightly to her hair.

That night, in my sleeping-bag, I imagined myself in the slow-moving carriage, listening to the clop-clop of the horses' hooves on the streets, the eerie silence beyond. This was the beginning of the end, I knew. Sooner or later I would be strapped to the plank, my head would be pushed through the hole. The guillotine of love. Lying in the dark, I could sense the blade suspended somewhere above my neck. Silently I listened for what I knew would be the final sound: the hiss of its descent.

In the dream we were kissing, but I was watching us from above, as though I were outside my own body. We kissed for ages. She seemed to love it even more than usual, and so did my body, though I felt nothing, watching them, only a kind of puzzlement. And then we parted, a smile on each of our faces. And I looked again.

A smile on each of their faces.

I made a noise. They turned to look at me and said, 'Hello, Michael.'

I was crouching on a branch above them. 'You,' I said. '*You.*'

They told me to calm down. I became angry, upset. And then I was falling

            falling

                  falling.

I woke, with a whispered scream, and opened my eyes in panic. But there were the shining bright blue shapes above me and the criss-crossed wood, and there was the golden light-shadow on the wall, and there was Isobel, asleep, beside me.

I sat up, remembering the events of the night before. After the King's funeral, Louis had told us about the revolution. Our revolution. He kept talking about laws, equality, ideals, but that was not how I imagined it at all. In my mind the revolution was a girl – bare-breasted, treading on corpses, waving a huge flag. The image came from Delacroix's painting of Liberty, which I had seen in Louis's book. In my imagination, Liberty looked like Isobel. She clung to my side. I fired a pistol into the night air. The past exploded into dust.

Laws . . . Isobel must kiss only me. That was the only law I needed.

I stared at her head for a moment, and then got dressed and walked down to the river. All the way there I remembered my dream, unwillingly. Why did it scare me? Because it seemed so real, so believable. Isobel and Louis. Louis and Isobel. Now the thought had entered my mind, it had a sort of unstoppable power. I could think of no reason why she *would* prefer me to him. I knew myself well – there was nothing to love.

As I brushed my teeth I saw her standing in the river. Not her, but the permanent vision of her that my mind projected. She was wearing her gingham dress and her hands were clasped behind her back. She smiled at me; it was the smile of a sweet, innocent girl. As her lips widened to reveal the gap between her front teeth, I said to myself: She is an angel, she is purer than Our Lady, she is purer than Wendy in *Peter Pan* . . . and then I found myself sinking beneath the water.

Strangely, as I did this, my eyes stayed open and I continued to breathe. My head was underwater now, but I found I could see as if through air, and that the element I had left, the element suspended above me, was the liquid mass. Here I crouched at the bottom of the river with the water held miraculously over my head. It had stopped flowing and was almost still; I could see clouds in the sky through its faint ripples and viscosity. I turned towards Isobel to share this strange vision with her, but I looked at where her pretty, smiling face had been, and now it was in the water above. All I could see of Isobel was her bottom half.

I watched, in horror, as hands crept unopposed down to the hem of her dress and started to pull at it. Up it went, revealing white skin, dark hair . . .

I looked around and noticed that something odd was happening. Pebbles jumped up from the river bed and silently vanished. Large fish swam clockwise through the air, faster and faster, in narrowing circles, and disappeared between

Isobel's legs. It was as though the plug had been removed from a bath.

I felt myself being pulled unwillingly towards her – towards *it*. Trembling, I resisted. It pulled and pulled. I cried out and the water crashed down. The vision dissolved. I opened my eyes.

I spat toothpaste into the river and watched the white circle float away. Then I rinsed my mouth, filled the water bottles, and began the walk back to the shelter.

On the way I became angry with myself. Isobel was innocent, I told myself. And she loved me. All of this was in my mind. She had done nothing wrong. Nothing had changed except my mood. The solution, I decided, was to be positive: to show her love, to stroke her back, to smile trustingly whenever she touched Louis. I would be a good boy. I would win my reward.

I looked up at the sky: it was a perfect, unbelievable blue.

To clear my head, I went tree-climbing. I spent half the morning up there, swinging rhythmically from branch to branch, listening to the forest's silences, thinking nothing and feeling gradually better. At one point I looked round with surprise and realised that I had not been thinking about Isobel. I had, for a short time, been out of my mind. It was a blissful moment.

Finally, I climbed down and, as my feet touched the ground, gravity did its work. I was consumed again by the present . . . with all its pasts and futures. The dream. My fears. Her head on his shoulder. Her hole underwater. My head in the hole. The blade above. The large, jagged shape in my chest.

Gravity and memory. They felt like the same force. Pulling you down, sucking you back. I thought about what Louis had said – a revolution. King Gravity and Queen Memory. If we could execute those two – and Prince Time, too, perhaps – oh, what a world this could be! The blade, suspended above me, might never fall. The sky might stay blue for ever. But I knew that wasn't what Louis had in mind. He saw things differently to me.

I looked up at the treetops one more time, and down at the shadowed land. I sighed. I ought to be getting back, I told myself. She'll be wondering where I am.

Isobel was waiting for me in the garden. She had just woken up and wandered out to find me, she said. She was wearing the gingham dress. She said she wanted to talk to me. Her voice was serious.

'Of course,' I said, forcing myself to stay positive. 'Shall we go to Elbow Pool?'

There was a pause. 'If you like.'

As we walked, I noticed that Isobel kept reaching with one arm behind her neck, as though she were trying to scratch her back. The hem of her dress lifted when she did this, revealing the pale tops of her thighs. I adjusted my erection. She looked like she was in pain.

'What is it?'

'I don't know, I think I pulled a muscle. My back hurts.'

I lifted my hands. 'Allow me . . .'

'Oh.' She looked embarrassed. 'Are you sure you don't mind?'

'My pleasure.'

We arrived at the beach and stood there, the two of us, looking out at our pool. The sunlight glinted on its calm surface.

'Well, here we are again,' I said.

She sat away from me, facing the water, and started to undo the buttons on the front of her dress. She shrugged it down and I saw her brown shoulders. 'Maybe this isn't such a good idea,' she said.

'Lie down. It can't do any harm.'

'Can't it?' she asked, but she lay down anyway, with her calves resting on the sand, her toes dipped into the water. I knelt over her. She sighed as my fingers kneaded her trapezius. 'That does feel better . . .'

There was a silence. What did she want to talk to me about?

'Isobel . . . I'm sorry about what I –'

'Oh. It's OK. No hard feelings.'

'Well . . . one hard feeling,' I joked.

She didn't laugh.

After a while I felt her shoulders relax, and soon after that she started to talk. I was concentrating on her back, only half listening. I yawned, feeling suddenly exhausted. It must be the relief, I thought, the escaped tension. I hadn't slept well either. I had taken ages to fall asleep, and then the dream had woken me.

'You don't know what you'd be getting into with me,' Isobel was saying. 'I'd be a nightmare to go out with. I'm so *demanding*. Look at you – you're knackered already and it's only been a few days.'

'That's not you,' I said.

'No? What is it, then?'

I told her about my disturbed night, my bad dream.

'Oh!' She sat up suddenly and turned round. She was holding my hand now, staring into my eyes with that disorientating enthusiasm of hers. 'Oh, tell me what you dreamed about! Did you write it down?'

I was staring at her breasts.

'Why would I write it down?'

'So you don't forget it, of course. So you can interpret it.'

I rested my hand on her thigh. 'Interpret it?'

She sighed and lay back. 'Find out what it means.'

'Why should it mean anything?' My hand caressed her thigh.

'Dreams are symbols.'

'Of what?' My fingers brushed her knickers.

'Desires and fears.' Her voice was thick.

'Tell me.'

Her knickers were warm and damp.

94

'About your dream.'

I lifted the elastic and felt heat.

'Well . . .'

I wanted to tell her and was afraid to tell her.

'Please . . .'

I wanted to, but was afraid.

'It was in the forest and we . . . you were kissing –'

My finger slid inside.

'Oh . . . no!'

In a sudden movement she pulled away from me and began rearranging her dress. She was blushing furiously.

'What's the matter? I haven't even –'

'I get the idea.'

'What do you mean?'

She gave a bitter little laugh. 'One of *those* dreams.'

I moved towards her. 'Isobel . . .' Gently I turned her face towards me and saw, with shock, that she was crying. 'Isobel . . . what is it?'

She gave a long sigh. 'I know what you want. *I* want it too, or part of me does. Oh, sometimes I wish you'd just take me and then it would be . . .' She moaned, a mixture of ecstasy and agony, and then turned away. 'Sorry, I shouldn't have said that.'

'I don't understand,' I said. 'What are you –'

'It's not easy, you know, being good all the time.'

I wiped a tear from her cheek. She held my hand to her face, which was unnaturally warm, and closed her eyes. Her wet lashes tickled my palm. We stayed like that for a while, her breathing slowing, her skin cooling. With my other hand, I stroked her hair.

As we sat, I thought about what she had said. *I know what you want.* She must mean sex, I thought.

For all my innocence, I wasn't ignorant. Quite the opposite, in fact. Thanks to frequent readings of Aunt Céline's magazines, I had an almost medical knowledge of what was required. But that was the trouble: it sounded so complicated and exhausting, so easy to get wrong. I feared coming too quickly, not making her come, *not even touching the sides*.

But seeing her cry now, feeling her tremble in my arms, I felt myself falling in love again. This surprised me. I had not realised there was any further to fall.

Just as I was developing cramp in one shoulder and thinking about changing position, Isobel opened her eyes and looked deep into mine. There were tiny wells of water on the lower lids of her eyes. She wiped them away with the back of her forearm, then sniffed and said, 'You're sweet. I'm sorry . . .'

I kissed her forehead. I felt confused; as if I were acting in a play and had forgotten all my lines. Or as if the script had been changed without my knowledge. Now I had to improvise. As I thought about this, words came to my mouth but I did not get to say them, because, in a sudden movement, Isobel flung her arms around my neck and kissed me.

Finally she pulled away and said, 'Michael, listen, I've made a decision. That was –'

Decision? I thought. But the words were in my mouth. The words were on my tongue. It was too late to stop them coming. 'I love you,' I said.

And she sighed.

TWO

11

The Long Sleep

In the dream I was running down a path in dark woods. Ahead I kept catching sight of her dress, its white and blue squares lit by random stabs of sunlight. I could hear her footfalls too, and the sound of her breaths, unnaturally loud, as if she were panting or laughing or sobbing.

I was running and running down this path and then the path forked. I stood still, listening, staring down each path in turn. They were dark, these two paths, and I could not see or hear any sign of her. With every heartbeat I knew she was getting away. I knew I had to choose. Which way had she gone? Which path should I take?

When I awoke, I was sure I had forgotten something. I had a feeling that it was something large and important, but I had no idea what it might be.

I opened my eyes. It was totally dark and I was lying on my back. The thought occurred that I might be anywhere: in my old bedroom, or in the shelter, or somewhere else – and how many million somewhere elses were there in the world? I tried to imagine them all, and soon gave up. Better to fall back asleep.

In the dream I stood mesmerised by the split in the path. And it seemed to me as I swayed there, hesitating, trying to decide, that I had been there too long for it to matter any more. I sensed that she had already gone; that whichever path I chose, I would never find her again. Or perhaps that it was not even her, the physical girl, but a ghost of her, a mirage. Or perhaps that she lay waiting down both paths; but that in one of these places she was subtly different; or I was . . .

And as I thought all this, I began to relax. The choice, I saw, was no choice at all. I took a step forward and the two paths became one. As soon as I moved, the decision was made. I entered the path, entered the darkness, and there she was, in a miraculous shaft of sunlight, waiting for me, smiling.

I opened my eyes and I knew where I was. The air was still dark but I could discern now the black lines of the branches against the dark blue of the sky beyond. I looked to my left and then to my right and saw familiar shapes in the darkness.

I listened and I could hear them breathing: Louis, Isobel, Alex. And someone else . . . but who? And then I realised – myself, of course. My wakeself, sleeping. I closed my eyes and tried to remember what had happened. The large, important thing.

The last image in my mind was of the two of us down by the pool. Isobel wearing the gingham dress. I remembered tear stains on her face, my fingers in her hair. I remembered her kissing me.

I closed my eyes.

In the dream the air was grey. I could see the ceiling high above me and the walls close around. They seemed to move slightly, the walls, as though they were breathing. And then they disappeared and the air brightened, and a face appeared above mine. It was a new face – the face of a young woman.

She smiled and asked me how I was feeling. She wore a white dress, with a collar. She wasn't pretty – her eyebrows were thick, like caterpillars, and I could see pockmarks and spots beneath the powdered skin of her face – but she had kind eyes. She asked me how I was feeling and I said I was having a strange dream. She nodded sympathetically.

'You should get some more sleep,' she said.

I closed my eyes.

*

I opened my eyes and saw patches of pale blue through the gaps in the ceiling. I was thirsty so I tried to lift myself up: I normally kept a water bottle next to my sleeping-bag. But for some reason my sleeping-bag felt too heavy to lift. I tried to speak, thinking perhaps I could wake one of the others, but found that all I could do was frown and gurgle.

Then the kind face appeared above mine again. 'How are you feeling?' she asked.

I noticed she had an accent – American, I guessed. '*Pourquoi parlez-vous Anglais?*'

'Because this is the Republic of Trees,' she said. 'We all speak English here.'

'Another dream.'

'If you say so, Michael. Are you feeling better?'

'Better than what?'

She laughed gently. 'I think you're still tired. Perhaps you should go back to sleep.'

'Perhaps,' I said. I closed my eyes and then, remembering, opened them again. 'Who are you?' I called.

But she had gone.

I lay back and closed my eyes.

I opened my eyes. It was daylight in the shelter now, and warm. There was a dull pain in my forehead, but otherwise I felt fine. I got up and walked to the edge of the garden. Everything was as it had been before, except that Isobel's green bubble tent now stood between the vegetable garden and the shelter. I wondered why it was there, but it did not spark any memories, so after a slow tour of the empty garden I walked out into the forest.

It was another hot, bright day – late morning, I guessed, from the position of the sun. As I picked my way down the familiar winding path, gazing with love at the tree roots and shadows and half-buried stones, I tried briefly to make sense of my dreams, the feeling of time lost. But my head hurt when

I did this, so I stopped. And as soon as I gave up thinking, my pleasure in the moment increased.

I did some climbing, and after a while found myself near the southern border. I jumped down from the lowest branch of the last beech and looked out at the world we had left behind. I saw a small meadow – sheep nibbling obliviously in little groups – sloping down towards an electric fence, the dried mud line of a tractor track, and beyond it a vast stretch of cornfields. At the other side of the corn rose the forested foothills of the Pyrenees, and behind those the mountains themselves, half-hidden by white mist.

I stood there feeling shocked – not by the sight of mountains, but by the corn. It was so tall. When we had arrived in the forest it had barely reached my knees. Now it came up to my chest. I looked at my fingernails, grimy and long; I ran them through my hair, lank and floppy. All that lost time. What a long sleep I must have had. And then I wondered, Where *are* they? All that time and still no one had found us. Perhaps they weren't even looking.

Staring out at the maize, at the wide, empty landscape, I was reminded of that hot May day long ago, playing hide-and-seek with Louis, Isobel and Alex in the Sillitoes' garden. I remembered crouching inside a rose bush, sweat trickling over my nose, so perfectly hidden that the others got bored and gave up. I found them later drinking lemonade by the pool, guilty smiles crossing their faces as they watched me arrive.

A dry wind blew from the mountains. It really was pleasant to feel the treeless breeze and breathe treeless air and see treeless sky. I sat down and watched the sheep for a while, then lay back with my head in the long grass. I stared up at the sky. A bird of prey sailed above, a black mark on the perfect blue, like a little scratch, a tiny tear in the surface of the day. What lay behind? What manner of darkness?

My mind was pregnant with memory now. I stood up and began to walk back the way I had come, slightly faster this time. There was something else . . .

I found the river and followed its edge, staring down into its foaming waters as though the secret I searched for lay down there, somewhere. When I reached Elbow Pool, the memory returned. It returned in a single moment – and whole, not in fragments. I sat down on the grass and took off my trainers so I could feel the sand with my toes. This was where I had been sitting.

'I love you,' I said.
And she sighed.
'What is it?' I asked.
'Oh . . . I've been dreaming that you'd say that.'
I waited for her to say that she loved me too, but she didn't.
'Are you glad?'
'Yes.' She smiled. 'I'm very glad.'
There was a pause and then she said, 'That was my decision. I was
going to tell you that I was in love with you, and that I couldn't
continue like this unless you felt the same. You've been acting
so strangely recently . . . I was afraid you might break my heart,
Michael.'
'I would never do that,' I said.
'Promise?'
'Yes.'
And she sighed.
And she smiled.
And she kissed me.

I opened my eyes. So that was it; that was the memory. It had to be. I crawled forwards and stared into the pool. It was clear: the blood had gone. It must have rained, I thought. I took off my clothes, feeling happy, and entered the water.

Afterwards I felt more relaxed. I let the water dry on my skin, then got dressed and walked back to the shelter. I found Isobel in the garden, lighting a fire. 'There you are,' she said when she saw me. 'I was getting worried. How are you feeling?'

'Strange,' I said.

'Now there's a surprise.'

'But good.'

'I'm glad,' she said. 'You look much better.'

'Was I ill?'

'You had a bang on the head. Don't you remember?'

'A bang on the head?'

'We think you must have fallen from a tree. You were out cold for a while.' She blew on the flame.

'How long?'

'Oh, I don't know. You know what it's like here, with time. It seemed ages, but maybe that's just because I was missing you. There . . .' The wood took and Isobel stood up. 'Now come here, you.'

I moved towards her and she put her arms around me. I felt her mouth wet on my neck and then a sharp sucking pain.

'Gotcha,' she said. 'You'll have a massive one tomorrow.'

'A lovebite?'

'Mmm.'

We kissed.

'I love you,' I said.

And she sighed, 'Oh, I love you too.'

It was as if those words were a kind of incantation. I spoke them and a door opened and all the old rules disappeared. Then the door closed behind me and it too disappeared.

Around me I saw the same views, the same appearances – the mudbrick shelter, the sun-painted trees, the dry grass below, the blue sky above. And yet I sensed these were only thin coverings, that behind them lay the Truth . . . and that the Truth was more fantastical, more unbelievable, than I could possibly imagine.

All my daydreams, I understood them now for what they were: not imaginary escapes, but visions of the future. The feeling of *déjà vu* I had experienced when I saw our patch of forest for the first time . . . it must have been a premonition. I knew there were still pieces missing, that the picture was incomplete, but it didn't worry me. My life, having for so long seemed pointless and dull, now vibrated with significance – the central thread in a spider's web of symbols and events.

As Isobel cooked rice, I lay in the sun and tried to think back to the old times . . . the grey times. If I closed my eyes, I could see it faintly: a two-dimensional, monochrome vision. Aunt Céline sweeping the kitchen floor, the shadow of the electricity pole stretching across the concrete yard . . .

'Still with us?'

I looked up. Isobel was smiling at me.

'What do you mean?'

'You looked like you were in a world of your own.'

'Just daydreaming.'

'One of *those* dreams?'

I laughed. 'Not this time.'

She kissed me on the forehead and walked over to the saucepan. She stirred the rice with the wooden spoon. 'It's ready,' she called. 'Shall we eat now? I'm not sure what time the others will be back.'

'OK,' I said.

'I can tell you all the news. And after we've eaten, you can take me to your pool. I fancy a dip . . .'

Isobel passed me the plate of rice and I began to eat. Suddenly I felt extremely hungry.

'So what's the news?'

'Oh, there's so much . . . I don't know where to begin.'

She began to talk, but I soon realised I wasn't listening. Instead I was watching a dark figure inside the shelter. A human figure, moving around silently. A couple of times the figure moved through a sunbeam and I caught sight of an eye, a pair of lips. It was not Alex and it was not Louis.

'What's the matter?' Isobel was looking at me, concerned.

'I can see someone in the shelter.'

'Oh yes, that's right! You haven't met Joy, have you?'

'Joy?'

And then the figure emerged into the brightness. She wore a white dress. She had short, dark hair, thick eyebrows, several spots, and kind blue eyes.

'You,' I said.

'Hello, Michael. Are you feeling better?'

12

Day Zero

I awoke after more strange dreams and walked to the edge of the garden. The tent had gone, and there was a rectangle of flattened yellow grass where it had stood. Isobel and Joy were crouching next to the vegetable garden. Isobel was pointing at the plants and speaking, and Joy was nodding alertly in her usual manner.

'Good morning,' I said, moving a little way into the garden.

'*Bonjour, mon amour*,' said Isobel.

'Hi, Michael,' said Joy.

They both smiled and stood up, and I thought how funny they looked, together like that, so sister-like and yet so different: the hippopotamus and the giraffe.

Isobel came towards me and kissed me on the mouth. Then she turned to face Joy with one hand dangling on my right buttock, as though she had forgotten it was there.

I looked at Joy, and noticed the book in her hand. A giant eye stared from its cover. It was *The Social Contract* by Jean Jacques Rousseau.

'So . . . today's the day.'

'That's right . . . Day Zero.' She grinned nervously and her brace glinted. 'I ought to get started actually.'

'Oh, you've got plenty of time,' said Isobel.

'Not really. And I want to get it right. I would hate to think I was letting you guys down in any way . . . after you've been so good to me.'

'Don't be silly,' said Isobel. 'You'll be brilliant. Won't she, Michael?'

'Yeah, I'm sure. Are you nervous?'

'God, yes! Excited too, though. Just think, tonight we'll be –'

'Yes,' I said, not wanting to hear all this again.

Joy looked at me curiously. I spent the next few moments of silence staring at a mosquito bite on my arm.

'Oh, Joy!' said Isobel suddenly, removing her hand from my buttock and placing it on Joy's forearm. 'I nearly forgot to ask. Will you help me do my hair tonight?'

Joy cringed. 'I'd love to, Isobel, but . . . I feel like the task Louis gave me is more important.'

'Oh.'

'I'm *really* sorry. I'm sure you'll look beautiful anyway. You always do.'

'Hmm.' Isobel turned and looked me over, critically. 'I suppose you'll have to do then.'

'Thanks very much,' I said, in a mock-injured tone.

We all laughed.

As I walked to the river, I thought about Joy. It had been confusing, meeting her for the first time. There had been some embarrassment when I accused her of being a figment of my imagination. Isobel and Joy must have thought I was still concussed. Eventually, though, the story was cleared up. I told them about the two dreams in which Joy had appeared – the first, with the moving walls; and the second, in the shelter – and Isobel explained that Joy had looked after me in the shelter. 'Your dreams must have been recycling fragments of real memory,' she said. 'You must have woken up for a bit, and seen her, then fallen back asleep and dreamed about her. Fascinating, isn't it?'

Isobel even had a theory for my dream of her running away from me, and the fork in the path. 'That was your anxiety about telling me you loved me, and then forgetting my answer. Then when you took a step forward and the path became one, that was a symbol of your memory returning.'

I nodded. 'It all fits.'

'Of course it does,' said Isobel. 'I told you dreams were important.'

The first feeling I had for Joy was a mean one. Here at last,

I thought, is someone even less charismatic than me. As a fellow social inadequate, I recognised the nervous energy being used up by the formation of her smile and friendly words. I quickly registered the plain teenager's face – painful-looking pimples, wide metal brace – and the shiny newness of her clothes and shoes. And then, as we sat there talking, I began to see myself through her eyes: the sun-darkened skin, the unwashed hair, the thin girlfriend draped between my legs. For the first time in my life I felt glamorous.

I reached the river and splashed water on to my face. When I closed my eyes, I saw the two of them smiling at me, their faces together. Joy and Isobel. Isobel and Joy. It was funny to think that my two best friends were girls. Even funnier that I had known one of them for only three days. But the days were so long here, it seemed like years. In some ways I felt closer to Joy than to Isobel. Isobel was my girlfriend, my lover, but Joy was . . . almost part of me, it seemed. It was hard to understand, our closeness. There was something peculiar about it. I did not desire her at all, physically, yet I yearned for her company when she wasn't there. Sometimes I even wished she could watch me with Isobel, the things we did.

I squatted on the usual patch of sand and began a conversation with Joy inside my head. I asked her again how she had found us, what she had been doing in the forest. As usual she answered vaguely and turned the subject round with flattering references to the four of us, our way of life, Jean Jacques Rousseau and the Revolution. I asked her about her home life in Montreal (she was Canadian, it turned out, not American), and she responded thoroughly enough, but as always her tone suggested that her life in the city was unutterably dull next to ours here in the forest. Her parents were 'straights', she said. 'Kind of shallow people, you know?' The only aspect of home she enthused about was the school's philosophy club, of which she was the president. 'I just think that is the most important question of all, you know? What is the best way to live your life? But the adults I know don't even ask it. They earn money, spend money, dream about money. That's why it was such a thrill for me to . . .' And then we were back to the Republic of Trees.

It was a wonder to me, how quickly and fully Joy had been absorbed into the daily pattern of the Republic. She reminded me of one of those leaf-shaped grasshoppers that you notice only when your hand trails too close to them and they leap away. She was so quiet and agreeable that, half the time, you forgot she was even there. That, I thought, was why I felt able to tell her everything. That was why there were no awkward silences. She seemed such a nonentity that talking to her felt like talking to myself – inconsequential. With Isobel, I always weighed my words more carefully, wary of starting a fight or revealing something which might, one day, be used against me.

Without ever being intrusive, Joy enquired constantly about the tiny details of my life. Already she knew all about Aunt Céline (her love of sunbathing, her hatred of 'coloured' people), the precise layout and décor of our house and the Sillitoes' chateau, the physical and human geography of St Argen, the words used in my school reports. She never asked about my parents, but when I told her she managed to be sympathetic without pitying; something Isobel had never mastered.

We felt the same way about so many things. More than any of the others, for instance, Joy loved nature: the feel of tree bark, the songs of birds, the beauty of those forest evenings. It was this aspect of Rousseau – Jean Jacques, as she always called him – that had first attracted her, she explained. He was the only philosopher she had read who seemed to love the innocent, animal world and to believe that human beings were capable of such innocence themselves. 'Like, I can't imagine Locke or Engels rhapsodising over the smell of wild-flowers. Jean Jacques would *so* have approved of what you guys are doing here . . .'

It wasn't only me. She was in awe of us all. To me, she talked in complimentary terms of Isobel's beauty, Alex's shooting skills, and Louis's commanding genius. To Louis, she talked, naturally enough, about Rousseau – and Plato, and Voltaire, and all the rest. Louis, far from being put out, was thrilled to have a superior knowledge from which he could draw. The two of them spent hours together, huddled over his copy of *The Social Contract*, underlining key phrases and discussing how to create the perfect society. Alex treated her like a small boy: he taught her to chop wood and shoot rabbits. And, though she had no great aptitude for either of these activities (any more than she had for tree-climbing, as I discovered one afternoon that ended with her scratched and bruised and dusty-haired), he announced to us all proudly that she was 'plucky' and 'a game girl'.

To Isobel, I know, Joy talked about me: my gentleness, kind nature, and much more besides that I blush to remember. Isobel said teasingly that she thought little Joy had a crush on me. I affected distaste, irritation, disbelief, but secretly I enjoyed the idea, not least because it seemed to make Isobel more attentive towards me. Which is not to say that she felt remotely troubled by Joy's interest in me. Indeed, I think part of the reason Isobel liked her so much was that she was shy and spotty and small. She never thought for a second that I – or any boy – might prefer Joy to her.

But Isobel was also truly delighted to have another girl to talk to. The two of them spent so much time together: walking, cleaning the shelter, watering the vegetables, brushing each other's hair, chatting constantly. The results were that Isobel and I saw rather less of each other than before, but that the intensity of our feelings was, if anything, increased.

'What do you two find to talk about for so long?' I asked Isobel once.

'Oh, you know, lots of girly things. Boys, skincare, parents . . . It feels like we have so much in common. She agrees with everything I say.'

'Boys?' I asked.

'Ooh, jealous? No, sadly, it's mostly you three we talk about. Well, not so much Alex, but you and Louis. She seems fascinated by you. Thinks you're wonderful. As I said, we agree about everything, me and Joy . . .'

I wiped myself with a dock leaf and jumped into the river. The cold sent my muscles into spasm, but I started to breast-stroke against the current – swimming without moving – and soon warmed up. As I swam, I tried to remember what life had been like before Joy's arrival; but it was difficult, hazy. Now, when I recalled treetop climbs or my first kiss with Isobel, I seemed to see Joy's face watching from the bushes, or from some recess inside my mind.

Tired of swimming, I waded upstream until I reached Elbow Pool. There I floated, with my eyes closed and the sun warm on my face, and remembered the blissful routines of the last three days. Each morning had been like this one: myself alone, or with Joy, or with Isobel, thinking, talking, bathing, walking. Then lunch, the five of us together, Alex and Louis telling us about the hunt. Each afternoon, two of us would go on a patrol of the Republic's borders. It was invari-ably quiet. Each evening we talked about our escape from what Joy called 'straight life', and our hopes for the Republic. And each night, as it turned dark, Louis read to us from *The Social Contract*. It occurred to me on the last night that what this new ritual reminded me of was Sunday mass: the dron-ing, relentless voice; the dry, abstract words; the seemingly attentive faces; the drifting thoughts. As Louis talked of the common good, the general will, the sovereign authority, I dreamed of my own revolution.

Liberty, the girl with the flag, joined me in Elbow Pool. She slid into the water, naked but for her red bonnet, and started to pull at my erection as Isobel had done. I held the pistol in my hand. From the bushes I noticed Joy's face, watching us approvingly. I smiled at her and she smiled back. A huge gust of wind billowed the girl's flag and I pulled the trigger. *Bang*. The past exploded into dust. The stuff coming out was like fireworks. It was white. It turned to rubber worms in the water and I lay back, face in the sun, watching the bright, amorphous patterns change and fade inside my closed eyes.

As the four of us ate pasta in the garden, I kept looking at the entrance to the shelter. Somewhere in that darkness, I knew, Joy was working. Reading the book and thinking. Writing the laws of the Republic. Because Joy was no longer simply Joy; she was the Lawgiver. Louis had made the announcement the night before, after he had finished his reading of Rousseau. 'Tomorrow', he had said, 'will be our last day of anarchy. Tomorrow will be Day Zero.'

And now tomorrow was today.

I tried to enjoy the lunch, but there was another taste in my mouth beside the pasta. It was fear.

In my mind what lay ahead was a dark and endless tunnel. I feared this evening as I had always feared dental appointments and maths tests. And, true to my normal behaviour patterns, I reacted not by talking about or even thinking about my fear, but by ignoring it; by concentrating so fully upon something else, something lighter and more present, that all I felt was a lingering, nagging, seemingly sourceless anxiety. I didn't even know what I was afraid of, exactly. The sound of the word 'law'. The prohibition of tree-climbing. The unknown.

Finally, when lunch was over, I decided it would be a good idea to read our new bible. I found the Lawgiver alone in the cool gloom of the shelter, lying on Isobel's air mattress. Her eyes were closed. I could see a patina of grease on her nose and a faint, dark moustache above her top lip. Her pale, plump hands held a solitary sheet of paper to her chest, blank face up.

I knelt close to her and whispered, 'Joy . . .'

She opened her eyes. She looked startled. 'Oh, hi.'

'I didn't wake you, did I?'

'No, I was thinking.'

'I thought you were praying, actually, with your hands like that.'

She laughed. 'Maybe I should.'

'How's it going?'

'Oh . . . it's all right, I think. I mean, I've written it. There's just one part that I'm not sure about. It worries me.'

'Can I help?'

'Oh, that's so nice of you, Michael. But you can't, really. The only person who could help has been dead for the past two centuries. Short of a miracle, I have to work this out on my own.' There was a pause. 'Did you want to talk to me about something?'

'I was wondering if I could borrow *The Social Contract*.'

'Of course,' she said brightly. 'I didn't really need it, to be honest. I know it pretty much by heart. I'm glad you're taking an interest, Michael. It's important, you know.'

We looked at each other for a moment. The intensity in those small, blue eyes made me uneasy. It was the only time I ever felt uncomfortable with her; when she stared at me like this, unblinkingly, as though she were trying to see me through fog.

She passed me the book. I thanked her and stood up to leave. Then, something occurred to me. 'Joy, are you short-sighted?'

She smiled. 'You found me out.'

'But why don't you wear glasses?'

'Oh God, I think I'm ugly enough already, don't you? Besides, I thought contact lenses would be more practical for living in the great outdoors. And they were fine, actually, until I lost them.'

'Oh.' What I felt, above all, was relief that the bulge in her eyes was just myopia. But I couldn't tell Joy that. 'Are you OK, though? Can you see?'

'Just about,' she murmured. 'Talk about being led by the blind, huh?'

I wished her luck and turned to go, then changed my mind. 'Joy,' I said. She looked up. 'I don't think you're ugly at all.'

She smiled and blushed, and I felt myself blush, too.

'You should read the book,' she said.

I did try. Actually, it began quite well. 'Man was born free, and he is everywhere in chains.' That was catchy, and I got the impression Rousseau was not in favour of the chains, which made me feel positive towards him. But then he started talking about all these people I'd never heard of – Philo, Grotius, Hobbes – who sounded like a bunch of circus dwarfs, and I was disturbed by a persistent fly that kept landing on my nose, and the sun was warm, and I felt tired, and then Isobel came in the garden and saw me reading and started talking about how exciting it was, having a revolution, and then she went off to wash her hair and her dress, because she wanted to look nice for the dawn of the new society, and I started imagining her in Elbow Pool, undressing in golden light, and then . . . oh, you know . . .

Smoke rose into the evening air. Isobel opened a bottle of red wine – our supply seemed mysteriously to have been replenished – and we passed it round. 'Let's drink to the Republic,' said Louis, who had lost his sombre air and was buzzing around, slapping backs and rubbing hair. The wine made my chest warm. I knelt on the grass, turning the boar on a spit.

Isobel gleamed freshly. Framed by shining leaves, her curls all damp and golden, I thought she looked like an angel. We smiled at each other across the garden. Louis was whistling the 'Marseillaise'.

'Where's the Lawgiver, then?' asked Alex.

'Inside,' said Isobel. 'She's preparing herself.'

Louis came and crouched next to me. 'Excited?'

'Yeah. A bit nervous, maybe.'

He frowned. 'Nervous? Why?'

'I'm just worried that I'm not going to be as free as I was.'

'Michael, how many times do I have to tell you? You're going to be *more* free! Come on, this is so exciting. What would Aunt Céline say if she could see us now? Drinking wine, cooking wild boar, passing laws . . . Think about how far we've come.'

I nodded, and tried to remember our aunt's face. To my surprise, it was a blur. The whole of our past life, indeed, seemed to be fading. I felt amnesia creeping over me, erasing the faces of schoolmates, the view from our bedroom window, the sound of our aunt's voice. Sensing that I would soon forget this moment too, I closed my eyes and saw again the grey world we had left behind. It was still there, but becoming bleached, like a Polaroid in the sun.

I opened my eyes: the mudbrick shelter, the sun-painted trees, the dry grass below, the darkening sky above. Everything present and touchable.

'Look!' cried Louis. 'Here comes the Lawgiver . . .'

Joy walked into the garden. In her hand was a piece of paper.

Oh, the relief I felt as Joy read out those seven little laws in her friendly, reasonable voice, a shy smile edging across her face as each proclamation was met with a burst of applause.

These were the laws:

1 All citizens are equal and free.
2 Money is forbidden.
3 The prince may govern only with the support of the general will.
4 Any citizen who breaks the law is no longer a citizen, but a traitor.
5 Treachery is punishable by death.
6 Our god is Jean Jacques Rousseau and our bible *The Social Contract*.
7 You must believe.

We gathered around her, congratulations on our lips, and it was then that I noticed her eyes. They were shining – with a certainty I had never seen in them before.

'You look pleased with yourself,' I said.

'Not with myself, Michael.'

'What do you mean?'

But before Joy had a chance to answer, Isobel started to ask her something. 'Do we really need the death penalty? It seems so barbaric . . .'

'Course we do!' shouted Alex. 'I'll knock up a guillotine in no time.'

'Alex!'

'Actually,' said Joy, 'it's interesting you mention that, Isobel. Because that was my great worry, too. In the book, there's no argument. He seems so definite about it. But still, it was written a long time ago and I thought maybe it wouldn't apply any more . . .'

'So?'

'So I asked him.'

'Asked who?'

'Jean Jacques.'

'*Rousseau?*'

'Uh-huh.' Joy was smiling beatifically. 'It was just after you left, actually, Michael. You know you said I looked like I was praying? Well, I thought, why not give it a try? He's our god, after all. So I asked him and . . . he talked to me. He came into the shelter and read the laws and told me they were perfect. In French, of course. I said I was concerned about the fifth law and he said, "It is in order to avoid becoming the victim of a traitor that one consents to die if one becomes a traitor oneself." Then he gave his blessing to the Republic of Trees, warned me that the laws must be enforced vigilantly, and disappeared.'

There was a silence.

I looked at Alex and he raised an eyebrow. Isobel started to laugh, and I was about to say, 'Oh, come on,' when Louis spoke.

'So the laws have been divinely sanctioned,' he said. 'This is the word of God.'

'Yes,' said Joy.

Louis lifted the wine bottle to the sky and said, 'Thank you, Jean Jacques.'

The five of us sat in a circle and ate slivers of cold boar. We voted in favour of the new laws. Then we voted Louis our prince. Both votes were unanimous. Afterwards we lay looking up at the stars and talked of the changes we would make.

Much later, when all the others were in bed and the fire was nearly out, Louis sat down and put his arm round me. 'So how are you feeling now?'

'Fine,' I said. 'A bit drunk.'

'You don't feel less free?'

'No. The laws were all good.'

'I told you.'

I nodded. 'Don't you think it's a bit weird, though?'

'What?'

'That stuff about Rousseau. Talking to Joy.'

Louis narrowed his eyes. 'Are you saying you don't believe?'

'Oh, come on . . .'

'Because if that was the case, we'd have to chop off your head. And I would hate that to happen.'

'Pardon?'

'You must believe. It's the law, Michael.'

I smiled. 'Yeah, but –'

'But what?'

I looked in my brother's green eyes and saw only my drunken face reflected back at me. 'Nothing,' I said. 'Is there any more wine?'

13

Revolution!

The next morning, everything seemed more vivid. The leaves on the trees throbbed and span. There was a strange tingle in my stomach. I thought: this must be how revolution feels. But I was wrong. It was a hangover.

My vomit was purple; particles of dark meat stuck to the grass. Isobel rubbed my back and said, 'There, there,' but she didn't feel much better herself.

We went back to sleep, Isobel and I, dream-heavy and uncomfortable in the heat. I woke, covered with sweat, and suggested a swim. Everyone came. Louis, Alex, Isobel and I went skinny-dipping in the cold river. Joy sat on the river's edge in shorts and a T-shirt, dangling her feet in the water. Every time I turned towards her, she was looking at me. I might have been embarrassed about her seeing me naked, had I not known that she was half blind. Afterwards, the four of us lay wrapped in towels on the grass, laughing and gasping in the sun. I could see my heart move under my skin.

After lunch, in a shady corner of the garden, we sat in a circle and looked expectantly at Louis.

'So, Your Majesty . . .' began Isobel.

'Oh, stop it.'

'But *Prince Louis* . . .'

'No, really. Stop it,' said Louis, looking her in the eye.

The first act we passed stated that each of us must address all the others as 'Citizen'. In 1792, women were called 'Citizenesses', but this was deemed sexist and too difficult to say. The second piece of business, raised by me, concerned the flag.

'Do you think we need one?' asked Louis.

'Of course we do. You can't have a republic without a flag.'

'OK then, why don't you design it, Citizen Michael?'

'All right. But what colour should it be?'

Various colours were suggested: Alex wanted black and red; Isobel yellow and blue. Louis said, 'The original colour of the French Revolution was green. They changed to red, white and blue because green was also the colour of the Count of Artois, but . . . well, that hardly seems relevant now.'

'Green's good,' I said. 'The colour of the forest.'

'What about brown?' said Isobel. 'Trees are brown.'

'Green and brown, then.'

'Art was my favourite subject at school,' said Joy. I remember noticing that she used the past tense: nobody mentioned *la rentrée* any more. 'I could help you, Citizen Michael, if you like . . .'

'Sure,' I said, 'I'll tell you what to do and you can do it.'

Next we changed the calendar. Louis suggested that the four of us take three months each and rename them.

'What about Joy?' asked Isobel.

'Uh . . . she could rename the seasons,' said Louis.

'Really?' Joy grinned. 'But wait, that's not fair –'cos I'd have four and you'd have only three each. Equality is important.'

'Then let's just have three seasons,' said Louis.

'But there are four,' said Alex.

'Only because that's how people divided them. Unchain your mind, Citizen Alex! We can change whatever we want.'

I felt a shiver of power run through me. 'Anything?'

'The days of the week, the names of the planets, the hours of the day . . . I mean, why should everything be divided by sixty?'

'Oh, don't,' said Isobel. 'My head's spinning already.'

'All right, let's leave it at that for the moment. Anyway, now for the important business: naming my ministers.'

I watched Louis's face for clues, and noticed a flicker of a smile. I was hoping for something fun; something to do with trees. He took a piece of paper from the pocket of his shorts and unfolded it.

'Citizen Alex, you're the War Minister.'

'War?' said Isobel, alarmed.

'Well, I was going to call it "Defence", but then I thought it may involve attacks, too. Raids and so on. War seemed to cover both.'

Alex punched the air repeatedly, whispering, 'Yes! Yes! Yes!'

'Citizen Isobel, I'd like you to be Food Minister. I want you to organise mealtimes . . .'

Isobel groaned. 'Chained to the kitchen!'

' . . . and keep an eye on supplies, gather fruit, look after the vegetables, that sort of thing. Without food, the whole thing will fall apart. An army marches on its stomach. And I don't think we can rely on Alex hunting so much now, because he'll be busy with the war. We need a long-term solution.'

Isobel's expression had changed. 'Oh, OK . . .'

Louis turned to me. 'Citizen Michael, I want you to be in charge of propaganda.'

The word was new to me. 'Proper *what*?'

Louis laughed. 'Good start. It means . . . Well, take the flag. The flag is a symbol of what we are. It's a way of telling the world about our revolution. The calendar, too: you can oversee that. Concentrate on those two for the moment. I'll talk to you later about what else you can do.'

'I've got it!' yelled Isobel, triumphantly. 'Chickens!'

'Chickens?'

'We'll steal some from a farm, and then we can eat the eggs.' She stared around, with a madly excited look on her face. 'Eggs are good for you,' she added.

'I like it,' said Louis. 'It's brilliant. Citizen Alex, can you organise a raid on a farm? We can do it tomorrow night.'

'Why not tonight?'

'I've got plans for tonight.'

I gave my brother a probing look, but all he did was smile. 'That'll do for today . . .'

'Um.' A little voice to my left. 'What about me?'

'Oh, Citizen Joy . . .' Louis looked embarrassed. 'Well, you were the Lawgiver, so . . .'

'Right. I can just help everyone else, I guess.'

'Hang on.' Louis put a finger to his lips and lowered his brows in thought. 'Coordination! That's what you can do. Talk to everyone about their plans and ideas, and . . . bring them all together. You can liaise with me.'

Joy smiled. 'Thank you, Citizen Louis.'

Louis caught up with me later that morning. I was on the path outside the shelter, and had just put my right hand on the lowest branch of an oak, ready to climb. That was where I did all my best thinking now: up in the trees. The rhythmic movement seemed to free my mind. And I needed inspiration for the flag.

'Citizen Michael! Wait a minute . . .'

'Are we really going to call each other that all the time?'

Louis laughed. 'I don't know. We'll either get bored of it or get used to it, I suppose.'

'What is it?'

'I wanted to talk to you about your ministry. Are we happy with it?'

'I suppose so. I don't really know what I'm meant to do, apart from design a flag.'

'Well, that's the first thing. You were right – it *is* important. It's part of an overall message, and that message is what I want you to control.' He paused, his face thoughtful. 'You're good at writing, aren't you?'

'I'm OK. Not as good as you.' I was not as good as Louis at anything, apart from climbing trees.

'That's not true,' he said. 'I'm good at facts, essays. You've always had a stronger imagination.'

I tried to suppress my smile. 'So what do you want me to do?'

He sighed. 'Listen, Michael . . .'

'*Citizen* Michael.'

A wry smile. 'Listen, I know you find *The Social Contract* boring . . .'

I looked at him, alarmed. 'I didn't say that.'

'I saw your face during the readings. And Joy . . . Citizen Joy told me you borrowed it, and then gave it back.' I started to speak; he put up his hand. 'It's all right. I'm glad you tried, at least. And I understand: it *is* difficult. Alex and Isobel are the same as you. So what I want you to do, if you can, is try to take the best parts, the important parts, and make it more exciting. I don't mind how. You can organise little plays if you want, like we did for the Bastille. I just want to communicate the book's message in a more interesting way. So . . .' He pulled the book from his pocket and handed it to me with a hopeful smile.

'Thanks,' I said, wearily.

'Just try. And if you need help, you can always ask Citizen Joy. It was her idea.'

Over a late lunch, Alex and Louis told us their plans for the first night raid. 'You remember that house we passed on the way here?' said Louis.

With an effort, I cast my mind back to the distant day of our escape. 'Oh, with the *CHIEN MÉCHANT* sign?'

Louis nodded. 'That's right.'

'Well?'

'We're going to burgle it.' Alex grinned.

'It's not a burglary,' said Louis. 'It's a revolutionary act. We're going to take what we need for the Republic and leave our Declaration of Independence.'

'Our what?'

'You can write it this afternoon, Citizen Michael.'

Louis woke me in the middle of the night. I said goodbye to Joy and Isobel, who were staying to 'guard the shelter'. They were not happy about this, but we had only four bicycles, and we didn't know how dangerous the raid might be. Isobel gripped my hand and whispered, 'Don't get caught.' Joy said, 'May Jean Jacques watch over you, Citizen Michael.' They kissed me at the same time, a pair of lips on either cheek.

I crawled through the archway, and felt water on my face. I looked up. The sky was black. Tiny raindrops floated in the air. There was a warm wind. In the path outside the shelter, Louis and Alex sat astride bicycles. Mine was leaning against a tree. Louis told me to hurry up.

It was a long, hard ride. When we reached the road, we stopped to catch our breath. All I could hear was the wind in the trees. For a moment sheet lightning lit up everything around us: the forest, the cornfields, the lone house on the hill. 'Let's go,' said Louis.

We hid the bicycles and climbed the tall wire fence. At the top we jumped down and landed on the lawn. Despite the sign outside, no nasty dog lurked in the grounds. We walked towards the black bulk of the house. The trees around the property shivered violently.

And then, the whole garden was illuminated.

'Movement alarm,' muttered Alex.

'Good of them to light our way,' said Louis.

The driveway was carless and all the shutters were closed. We reached the front doorway and gazed up at the walls. They were white and seemed immense.

'What now?'

Louis looked around the garden. There was a stone outbuilding at one end. 'Come on.' He started to run towards it.

I watched four black shadows chase his feet across the bright lawn. They shrank, grew, mutated with each stride. I was running, too. Somewhere behind me I could hear Alex panting.

By the window of the outbuilding Louis took off his T-shirt. He wrapped it around his fist and smashed the glass. Alex and I lifted his feet and he crawled headfirst into the darkness. There was a sound of something tumbling inside, and then the door opened. I walked in. Smell of petrol, buzz of neon.

Everything shone metallically: scythes, shears, strimmers, forks, spades, hoes, rakes, pickaxes, wood axes, wood saws, a chainsaw, all hung in neat vertical lines on the white walls. It looked like an exhibition. At one end of the building squatted a gigantic sit-on lawnmower.

Louis took a wood axe from the wall and pushed it towards me. The handle was smooth, the head heavy. 'What am I supposed to do with this?' I asked.

He smiled at me. 'Use your imagination, Citizen Michael.'

The shutters were a delicate shade of yellow. I thought of buttercups, baby chicks. I swung the axe. A huge crack opened in the middle of one shutter door. I stood still and listened. There was no sound but the distant voices of Louis and Alex, the whisper of rain, and my own breathing. Beyond that, the silence seemed huge, unnatural.

From the corner of my eye I saw Louis running towards me. He was carrying some kind of grey pole. I took another swing: the crack opened. My hair was soaked with sweat and rain. I pushed it back from my eyes. The nerves in my forehead felt excited; there was a cold, tickling sensation where my hand had touched the skin.

'Aim dead centre,' said Louis.

I arched my back, bent my knees, swung again. A dark split opened between the shutters. Louis slipped the grey pole into the gap and pulled hard. There was a wrenching sound and then a clean, hard pop. The right shutter hung limply, like a broken wing. I could see my reflection in the window. I could taste rain in my mouth.

Louis pulled himself up to the sill. A soft crash and he

jumped into darkness. I followed him and paused in the window frame. Something hung over me for a moment – a shadow, an idea, a vague memory. A light came on, revealing a long, red-walled room.

I entered.

14

A Secret History

It was late evening and the other four were asleep in the shelter. I couldn't sleep – as usual at this time, my head was buzzing – so I got dressed and went for a walk.

The sky was pale and clear, and there was a full moon. The forest looked like another world. I stepped through the ghost-light with a pen and notebook in one hand and an empty bottle in the other. I filled the bottle in the river and walked to Elbow Pool.

I drank some water, then opened my notebook and read through the day's work. 'The History of the Republic of Trees', it said. And then, nothing.

We had completed our first week as a republic, and Louis had asked me to write the Official History. He wanted to leave copies in all the local village schools. 'Show of strength,' he'd said, and I'd nodded, knowing what he meant.

For some reason, though, I was having trouble starting it. What was wrong with my memory? It wasn't that I *couldn't* remember, rather that I didn't believe in my memories. They seemed false, suspicious. Still, I had a job to do. Frowning hard, I began to write.

THE HISTORY OF
THE REPUBLIC OF TREES

Day zero: The Lawgiver talks to Jean Jacques Rousseau and the Republic of Trees is born.

Day one: The Prince names his ministers. Raid on mansion near Riennes: we take food, wine, plastic sheeting, tools, guns and bullets; leave our Declaration of Independence.

Day two: Implementation of revolutionary calendar. The Minister of War and the Prince begin construction of the Great Deterrent. Raid on Luzar farmhouse: we take five chickens; leave our flag.

Day three: Raid on holiday camp near Lies: we take a guitar, a bicycle, food, paints and paper, Diet Coke; leave the words to our national anthem.

Day four: Raid on duck farm in Turennes-Sourban: we take four ducks; kill a guard-dog; leave two illustrated commandments from our bible.

Day five: Work completed on the Great Deterrent. First Glorious Celebration of the Republic.

Day six: Raid on *boulangerie* in Mont de Marrast: we take bread; leave illustrated commandment. Second Glorious Celebration of the Republic.

Day seven: Work begins on the Official History of the Republic.

I read it through and sighed unhappily. These were only notes, of course – I could flesh them out later – but still . . . I did not believe a word. There was nothing there but ideas and actions, ceremony and progress. And yet it could not really have been like that, could it?

I decided to read through my notebook, from the beginning. It was mostly ideas for propaganda initiatives, but there were fragments of diary, too.

Day one

I've finished the new calendar. All the old deities are out, and so are Roman Emperors. As for numbered months which refer to the wrong numbers . . . why has no one ever sorted out this mess before?

The others gave me names of pet dogs, rock singers, household objects and star signs, but, as Minister of Propaganda, I decided we needed a more unified system. Believing in equality, I stripped all twelve months back to thirty days and declared the remaining five days a national holiday to be held just before and after new year – which was now, of course, Day One.

By happy coincidence – or was it Providence? – the first of these five days was the day of Joy's arrival. The holiday I thus called the Time of Joy. Her eyes filled with tears when I announced this. Isobel came up to me afterwards and said, 'That was nice of you.' The truth is, though, that had Joy been called Muriel or Annabel or any other name, there is no way I would have named the holiday after her.

I was surprised when Louis told me that Danton's poet friend Fabre D'Eglantine had come up with the same five-day holiday back in 1792, though he called it the *sans-culottides*. Louis also told me that each week had been decimalised, so there were ten days instead of just seven, and that each day had been given the name of a different food or agricultural tool, but that seemed overcomplicated.

I also decided not to change the names of the seasons, as – hard though I tried – I could not think of any words in the English language more beautiful and strangely descriptive than winter, spring and summer. I went for fall rather than autumn, though, because it sounds sadder and simpler. I also like the way it mirrors the verb spring, its opposite in the calendar year, descending while the other rises.

On the following pages were my sketched designs of the flag – a simple tree (brown trunk, green leaves) against a blue sky, with five gold stars in an arc above to represent the five of us – and my notes for the Declaration of Independence: '*Our elders and betters are sadists and liars. We want to live in nature. Goodbye cruel world.'* After that, there were several versions of the national anthem, and then some more diary entries.

Day two
When we got back to the shelter I could hear a strange buzzing noise through the doorway. Inside, a suede-headed Alex was shortening the last few hairs on Louis's head with the stolen electric shaver. Hairdust hung in the air.

What are you doing?' Isobel asked.

'It's more comfortable in this heat,' said Louis.

'Do you want one, Citizen Michael?'

It was funny: I had just been thinking of ways to make us look unified; to stand out from the mass of France as citizens of a new republic. I was imagining uniforms, special hats, badges. 'I think I will.'

'Michael,' whined Isobel. 'I like you with floppy hair.'

'I think it'd suit you, Citizen Michael,' said Joy.

Isobel glared at her. 'Thanks a lot, Citizen Joy.'

'Sorry,' she said. 'I just think it would.'

Alex held the mirror as Louis shaved my head. The whiteness of my scalp came as a shock next to the brown of my face.

'Feel it,' said Alex when Louis had finished. 'It's dead smooth.'

I ran my hand along the top: it tickled. I looked up at Isobel. 'What do you think?'

She said sadly, 'You look like a soldier.'

'He is a soldier,' said Alex.

Day three
Joy's fingers brushed the strings and those stirring opening chords echoed in the garden. Isobel stood next to her, holding the paper on which I'd written the words. Behind them, the frame of the guillotine seemed more surreal

than menacing. The blade had not been fitted yet, so it looked like a huge empty mirror, or a trompe-l'oeil painting of blue sky and green trees. Isobel pouted sweetly as she sang.

> We left it all behind
> We shed the dying skin
> We came to a place of love
> From a world of greed and sin . . .

I watched Joy play the guitar. She has no musical talent, but she's the kind of girl who practises and practises. Her face was set and tense.

> Give us freedom, give us freedom
> Equality in the trees is best.
> Oh we will not return
> To your jails of . . . oh no, not again!

There was a clang of guitar strings, and the music stopped. Alex laughed.

Isobel: 'You were early again, Joy.'

Joy: 'No I wasn't, Citizen Isobel.'

Isobel: 'Of course you were. I've told you before –'

Joy (quietly): 'I wasn't early.'

Isobel: 'Look, it's not a big deal. We can do it again, but this time –'

Joy (more quietly): 'I wasn't early.'

Isobel: 'For God's sake, stop repeating yourself. It's not the point. Let's just –'

Joy (almost inaudible): 'I wasn't early.'

Isobel (to us, rolling her eyes): 'Shall we just agree to disagree, then?'

She put a conciliatory hand on Joy's shoulder. Joy stared at the hand.

Joy: 'I was not early.'

Isobel: 'Jesus, why do you have to be so stubborn?'

Louis: 'Why don't you just play it again, Citizens?'

Joy (to Louis): 'I wasn't early. Was I?'

Louis: 'I don't know. I couldn't tell.'

He was lying, of course. We all knew Isobel had made a mistake – she'd sustained the second note longer than she should have done. But the point was, surely, that it wasn't important.

Day five

The heat was at its peak, and even in the shelter there was no escape. We should just sleep in weather like this. But the revolution has a raging pulse – it pushes us on. Alex and Louis were out on a reconnaissance mission, scoping possible targets for the next raid. Isobel was gathering fruit. Joy and I had to come up with a three-line quotation and illustration to leave at the scene of the crime.

'If the state, or the nation, is nothing other than an artificial person . . .'

Joy's voice sounds leaden when she reads from the bible. In normal conversation she speaks musically, the note rising and plunging as she concentrates all her energy on sounding friendly and attentive. But Rousseau's words lie heavy on her tongue, each equally important so the emphasis never changes.

' . . . and if the most important of its cares is its preservation . . .'

'I wish I'd been there to help him write this book,' I said, rubbing my eyes. 'I could have made it a lot snappier.'

Joy laughed. She thought I was joking. 'Not everyone can have your gift for concision, Citizen Michael,' she said, when she realised I was serious. 'And Jean Jacques has written more pleasurable books than *The Social Contract*, I agree, but it's a profound work, none the less.'

'If you say so,' I mumbled, looking out at the dark shape of the guillotine. The boys had just finished it. High up, the sharpened steel sheet glinted like a smaller sun.

'Listen to this bit: I'm sure you can get a pithy one-liner out of this . . .'

I looked at Joy: her lips were pursed. Was she signalling her disapproval of my talent? But no, irony isn't her thing, really.

'Is there any Coke left?' I said. 'I'm really thirsty.'

Joy said it was chilling in the river for the party. I walked down there and drank some. When I got back to the shelter, she looked at me eagerly. 'Quenched your thirst?'

Deep breath; forced smile. 'Yeah, I feel much better, thanks. Let's make Jean Jacques sing . . .'

'That's the spirit! So, where was I? Oh yeah . . . If the state, or the nation, is nothing other than an artificial person . . .'

Day six

She moved her lips closer to mine. When I breathed out I could feel electricity in my chest. Finally we kissed. I put my hand on her breast. She pushed it off. I pulled away, almost laughing with disbelief.

'What's the matter?'

'I don't know. I feel a bit nervous,' said Isobel. 'Can't we just take it slowly for a bit?'

This was the first time we had been alone together since the revolution began. Six days. It was a long time; but still, it hadn't occurred to me that we would have to start all over again.

I kissed her neck. 'Nervous about what?'

I felt like a champagne bottle that has been shaken and left in the sun: the pressure was building and I needed release.

'You've changed, Michael,' said Isobel.

'We've had a revolution!' Again I had to stop myself laughing. 'We've all changed, Isobel. Life has changed – for the better.'

133

She nodded. 'I suppose so.'

I exhaled through my nose and tried to keep the impatience out of my voice. 'Isobel, I *really* love you . . .'

When I finally got her shorts off, she was dry. She seemed embarrassed about it.

Day seven

Overheard, at the Second Glorious Celebration of the Republic:

Louis: 'But I thought you two were best friends . . .'

Joy: 'She's not taking this seriously.'

Louis (long sigh): 'That's just her personality.'

Joy: 'She only cares about herself.'

Louis: 'Oh, I don't know . . . she's doing a good job with the food.'

Joy: 'She's frivolous. Vain.'

Louis: 'You can't stop her being who she is.'

Joy: 'She keeps a diary.'

Louis (laughing): 'That's not against the law, is it?'

Joy (angrily): 'Why do you always take her side?'

Louis: 'I'm not taking her side.' Pause. 'And I appreciate what you're doing, Citizen Joy, I really do. Thank you for . . .' (inaudible, due to Alex's snorting laughter from another part of the garden) '. . . I just think maybe you could loosen up a bit, compromise . . .'

Joy: 'Revolutions are not about compromise.'

When I'd finished reading, I tore out the offending pages and burned them. Then I reread the Official History I had written. I fleshed it out with adjectives and abstract nouns and read it again. It sounded grand.

It was a lie, of course, but all history is a lie. Robespierre knew that. History is fiction, he said. Or at least, that's what history says that he said.

The important thing about history is that there is only one

version. All competing versions must be erased, deleted, rewritten. There is no space in history for regrets or alternatives. History is a line – it is a single path. If the path forks, then only one of the forking paths can be history. The other path is nothing. It leads nowhere.

The secret history would have to remain secret.

I showed the History of the Republic of Trees to Joy. She read through it quickly and said, 'It's perfect. You're a genius, Citizen Michael.'

'But is it the truth?'

'The truth?' She looked at me blankly. 'It's better than the truth.'

I nodded, knowing what she meant.

15

The Heat

It was hot. Too hot to go outside. Squinting into the brightness, I watched the ducks splash stoically in the glimmer of
water that we called their pond. Two chickens rested in the
shadow cast by the guillotine. They did not sense its danger,
only the slight protection it offered them at that moment.

Alex was sitting at the boundary of shade; the other three
were still asleep. 'Feel that,' he said, indicating one of the
large rocks with which the back wall of the shelter had been
constructed. Facing south, it was exposed to full sun.

'No thanks.'

'You could fry an egg on that.'

'Why don't you try? I fancy a cooked breakfast.'

He smiled thinly. We weren't allowed fires any more.

We sat and watched the heat haze and listened to the others'
breathing.

'Do you want to go to sleep now?' I asked

'Don't think I could. Too hot.'

'You haven't seen anything this morning, have you?'

'Nothing.' He sighed. 'They must have seen us. They must
know we're here. I mean, they can't have missed *that*, can
they?' He pointed to the guillotine with his eyes.

'Things look different from the sky,' I said. 'Anyway . . . I'm
going to the river.'

'Be careful, Citizen Michael. And take a gun.'

I walked through the forest, instinctively bending low, staying close to the ground. The helicopters had made a big
impression on me. Two of them had flown over the garden,
one in the morning and one in the afternoon, but I was sure I
had heard others, far off, buzzing the tops of the trees. It was

the noise, more than anything, that frightened – the horrible chopping sound the blades made against the air. It was so bombastic, I felt; so typical of the adults who ran the corrupt world outside our green borders.

When I reached the river, I held the plastic bottles underwater one by one. I imagined they were kittens I was drowning. I lined up the bottles on the bank and pressed my cold fingers to my face. I took off my trainers and dangled my feet in the water. I sighed and thought how strange it was, this sudden hunted feeling, after so long and so total a silence.

The helicopters had come in response to our sixth raid of the republican era; a raid during which, oddly enough, we did not steal anything at all. Joy had been concerned by the idea that our assaults on the capitalist mainstream might be misinterpreted as mere acts of theft. What was needed, she said, was a grand gesture, a purely political act.

So the five of us cycled to Luzar, entered the *mairie*, and spent two hours quietly going through all the official papers we could find. We wrote, 'CORRUPTION', 'LIES', 'TYRANNY', 'OPPRESSION' and various other revolutionary buzzwords in their blank spaces. We used black ink pens as the forms demanded, and wrote neatly in capital letters. Then we diligently gathered the papers back in their files and stacked them on the shelves where they belonged. Meanwhile, Alex painted the brown front door bright green, and – on my instructions – wrote on it, in red: 'CLOSED DUE TO RADICAL RETHINK OF VALUES'.

Sunlight blinked on the surface of the river and I laughed, then stripped off my T-shirt and shorts and slid into the water.

It was a heavy, throbbing heat, and the plastic sheeting on the shelter roof only intensified it. We sat and talked and slowly sweated. Two at a time, we took a gun and walked to the river. One bathed, while the other kept watch. Louis went with Alex, and Joy went with Isobel. I asked Isobel to come with me, but she said she was tired and needed to sleep, so

Louis came instead. We sat at the water's edge and I sighed. 'The heat is oppressive,' I said.

'We should pass a law against it,' said Louis, and we laughed.

Louis seemed to keep laughing long after I had finished; the ghost of a laugh. When he coughed up a ball of phlegm and spat it into the river, I realised it wasn't laughter but the wheezing of his chest.

'Are you all right?'

'Yeah, I'll be OK.'

'Is it your asthma?'

He nodded. 'The heat makes it worse, and my inhaler's run out.'

'You haven't got another one?'

'I'll just have to get used to it.'

I wanted to talk with him, the way we used to talk in our bunk-beds, but I couldn't think of anything else to say. I looked at him; ripples of light reflected off the water danced on his face. 'What are you thinking about?'

There was a pause, then he said: 'I was listening.'

'To what?'

'Exactly.'

I laughed. 'You're talking in riddles.'

He scrutinised me. 'Do you believe in the outside world?'

'Believe in it?' I frowned. 'You mean do I believe it exists?'

'No, I mean *do you believe in it*?'

I looked into his eyes and tried to think. I saw the grey emptiness that the past had become, the vividness of the leaves and the light all around us. 'No,' I said, 'I don't.'

A smile slowly formed on Louis's face. 'Me neither.'

It was evening when Isobel touched my hand. I felt a mild electric shock in my fingertips. 'Do you still want to go for that walk?' she asked.

She may have looked tired then; I didn't notice. When I looked in her eyes all I saw was my own face reflected: the elated smile; eager slits for eyes.

Isobel walked ahead of me. Her white dress, stained yellow under the arms and around the neck, was imprinted with a dark sweatmark the length of her back. I watched her move for several beats, the slow swing of her hips, the rifle dangling from its leather strap.

I caught up with her; touched her hand. She pulled it away.

'I've had enough,' she said quietly.

'What do you mean?'

She said nothing, but stopped walking. I stood in front of her and put my fingers under her chin. The fold of her neck was damp and hot. 'Chin up,' I said. She didn't laugh. I pushed the hair away from her face. She was flushed maroon and radiated heat. A few tangled hairs stuck to her damp skin; I moved those, too. Her eyes were glassy. I kissed her hot lips. There was the barest flicker of reciprocity; a reflex perhaps.

I inserted my tongue and she pulled away as if shocked.

'Wha-at?' I pleaded.

'No more.' It sounded as if she were talking to herself. She wobbled slightly, as though she were about to fall.

'Just a bit further,' I said. 'Come on . . .'

With my hand in the small of her back, I half guided, half pushed her towards Elbow Pool. She sighed when she saw where we were going.

'Lie down,' I ordered, and she sank to the grass in the shade of the oak. She lay on her back, breathing through parted lips, her eyes half closed. It's funny how closely despair can resemble desire.

I put my gun on the ground next to hers. I kissed her shoulder. It was warm and yielding, salty to the taste. 'No . . .' she murmured. I kissed her neck. 'No . . .' I kissed the top of her breast. She said nothing, only sighed.

The silence of the people permits the assumption that the people consents.

A little later, we were both naked and slippery with sweat. There was something inside me, desperate to get out. 'Isobel, I want you so much . . .' I whispered.

139

She was like a warm corpse.

After a while I got angry. 'What's the matter with you?' I shouted. 'You're not even trying!'

I looked at her face. She was sneering.

Enraged, I started to scream at her. I parted her legs and knelt in the hot space between, my hands pressing down on her wrists. I felt the balance of power tip towards me, and then away again. She did not resist. She looked bored.

'You don't love me any more, do you?' I said.

There was no answer. Time seemed to have stopped. I looked up at the bright green leaves, down at the pile of stones on the beach, across to the surface of Elbow Pool, where sunlight glinted, down again at Isobel's suntanned body, her face turned away. I have been here before, I thought. It was exactly like this –

My mind went blank.

'Citizen Michael!'

It was Louis's voice, calling me, warily, from far off. I dressed quickly. So did Isobel. We did not look at each other. Neither of us spoke.

The longer I brooded on this episode, the more embarrassed and ashamed I became. And that shame made me angry. I lay in the sweltering dusk, staring at the beads of precipitation on the plastic sheeting above me, clenching and unclenching my fists.

But it was too hot to maintain any kind of energetic emotion, and the anger soon faded. I felt sad: I had loved her so much. I felt betrayed: how could she treat me like this? I felt resigned: I knew it would end this way. I felt bittersweet: we did have some wonderful times. I felt optimistic: perhaps we could rekindle it after all? I felt horny: her naked body, her naked body! I felt confused: oh, why does it have to be so hot?

I must have fallen asleep because the next thing I knew I was sitting in a small grey room, at a table. At the other side of the table sat Louis. His hair was longer and he wore a sweatshirt. I began to explain that it was important for him to restart the revolution. 'Revolutions need momentum,' I said. 'Without the barrelling speed of events, the sense of a mass of which you are but one part, you can suspend your belief and let selfish thoughts creep in. I am alone, you may think. We are all alone. None of this really exists. It is all an illusion.' Louis looked at me like I was crazy. His face was grey.

Soon after that, I woke up.

I thought about asking Isobel to interpret the dream for me, but she was pretending to be asleep; and besides, its meaning was clear when you thought about it. It was a vision of a possible future. It was a warning.

I told Louis about my dream and he nodded. 'I understand.' A few moments later, he clapped his hands and we came to attention. He had been thinking, he said. Listen: what do you hear? Nothing, we said. Exactly, he said. There are no helicopters. There never were any helicopters. What we heard was the sound of our fear. Do you understand? Yes, we said. If you believe something does not exist, he said, then it does not exist. It is time to stop believing in the outside world. It is time to stop hearing the helicopters. Yes, we said. The important thing is the revolution, he said. That must continue. I felt myself growing light and hard again as he spoke, like water freezing. With relief I listened to the urgency in his voice. Times, directions, targets. My task was to write an Oath of Belief. 'Something to bind us all more closely to the Republic,' said Louis hurriedly, and I nodded, knowing what he meant.

'Citizen Isobel,' he said, 'I want you to arrange a feast for when we –'

'I want to go home.'

I looked at her. She was sitting on the air mattress, her diary open on her lap. She looked tired but resolved.

'Sorry?' said Louis.

'I want to go home. I've had enough.'

She stared back at him, ignoring the astonished silence that grew around her words. I wondered how long she had been practising those words in her head: forming the syllables, soundlessly, with her tongue and teeth.

Louis looked shocked. His mouth moved, but he did not speak.

And then, from the other side of the shelter, a small voice arose.

'Citizen Isobel, don't you understand what Citizen Louis has been saying?' It was Joy. Her voice was calm, measured, reasonable.

Isobel closed her eyes and shook her head. 'What's happened to us?'

'It's called a revolution,' said Joy, gently. 'Let me explain it to you. The world outside the forest no longer exists. It is dead. Your parents are dead. They always were, in fact, as I think you know. You live in the Republic of Trees now. We have laws. You must obey them. This is your home. You can never leave. You must never leave. You will never leave. Now do you understand?'

There was a long pause between each sentence. In those pauses we could hear Isobel sniff and weep. When Joy had finished, there was no sound at all but Isobel's muffled sobs and our steady breathing.

After a few moments, Louis went over and put his arms round Isobel's shoulders. She buried her face in his neck. He stroked her back. 'Probably just tired,' he muttered. 'The heat can do funny things to your mind . . .'

Louis took Isobel's hand and the two of them walked into the garden. I could hear their voices, but not what they were saying. Without a word, Joy moved her sleeping-bag between mine and Louis's. Isobel's air mattress was pushed back against the wall.

I was drunk that night: the drunkest I had yet been. We all were, except Joy, who never drank, and Isobel, who fell asleep on the air mattress in Louis's arms. Louis walked out to where we were lighting a fire and sighed, 'I wonder what brought *that* on.'

I avoided his eyes.

'Maybe you were right,' said Joy. 'The heat can affect people. I mean, she can't have been serious. If she really wanted to go home, that would be . . . Well, she would have been breaking the law.'

I felt the law stretch across the space above us all, protectively. What would happen if someone broke it? All the horror of the cold universe might pour down on our heads. I looked up at the moon and the stars, like holes cut out of the black sky. What lay behind the blackness? What manner of light?

'Pass the bottle, Alex . . .'

'The wine's finished,' he said. 'I'll go and find that bottle of *eau de vie*.'

'Yeah, good idea.'

Louis called me over and spoke in a low voice. 'Listen, I've been thinking. Perhaps Citizen Isobel's problem is that she doesn't really know what to believe in. There's that bit in *The Social Contract*, you know, where Rousseau says some people have trouble believing in the "artificial person" of the state because it doesn't seem real to them.'

I nodded. I knew the part he meant.

'And he says, I think, that the non-believer might seek to enjoy the rights of a citizen without performing a citizen's duties . . . something like that.'

'The growth of this kind of injustice,' said a toneless female voice behind us, 'would bring about the ruin of the body politic.' It was Joy.

'Yes,' said Louis. 'That's it. So I think what we need is something – I don't know what – but something *solid* to believe in. Something you can see.'

'Like an icon?'

'Could be,' said Louis. 'An image? A ritual? I don't know. Maybe you could work on it with Citizen Joy. Have a think.'

Inspiration came quickly. I squinted at the trees, black against royal blue, and saw luminous eyes shining from each of them: thus was born the Great Eye of the Republic. The eyes watched me benignly, wisely from the trees, and I thought: it's a sign . . . I am seeing the Truth.

Alex made a gasping sound and passed me the bulky plastic bottle of *eau de vie*. 'Don't smell it,' he warned. It was home-made. He had found it in the barn of the duck farm, on a shelf next to bottles of lawnmower petrol and white spirits. I drank some, coughed, and drank some more.

Alex grinned at me. 'Gives you a thirst, deceit, doesn't it?'

My heart banged. 'What?'

'This heat. It makes you thirsty.'

'Oh . . . yeah,' I said, and took another swallow.

When I woke, I found Joy watching me. 'How are you feeling?' she asked.

'OK,' I lied.

There was a sort of convulsive sucking noise at the back of my skull and green spots before my eyes. I couldn't feel my left foot. My heart was speeding.

The hangover was bad, but far worse were the voices. They seemed to come from various parts of my head – my right temple, my left cheek, the centre of my forehead – and from deep inside my chest. They were hysterical, panic-stricken, paranoid, in pain, enraged, all of them screaming at the same time, trying to warn me of something, pleading desperately for me to remember something, or to do something, or to stop doing something . . . I couldn't tell what. I tried to ignore them.

'I brought you some water,' said Joy, passing me the bottle. 'I thought you might need it.'

'Thanks.'

It was ice-cold – fresh from the river, I guessed. I drank a few mouthfuls, then felt sick. I closed my eyes and rubbed my face. It felt strange, as if I had borrowed someone else's.

Joy was smiling oddly. 'How's your memory?'

I remembered the incident with the duck. We had guillotined it. Alex strapped it to the plank and Louis untied the rope. The duck's head bounced on the grass, its bill open in surprise. How we laughed! After that, my memories were vague and dark. 'I don't know. Why?'

'Just wondering.' She touched my forearm. 'I'm going to walk down to the river this morning. Why don't you come? I think we need to talk.'

I nodded and lay back, surprised at the panic and despair that overcame me when Joy spoke those words.

'So,' said Joy, as we reached the river bank, 'what do you think will happen with you and Citizen Isobel?'

I made a sort of neutral, puzzled expression with my face; an I-don't-really-want-to-talk-about-it expression.

Joy did not take the hint. 'It's just that when you two went out for a walk yesterday, you both seemed fine, but when you came back it was . . . kind of tense. And then Isobel said all that stuff last night . . .'

She waited for me to respond. I ignored her and sat on the grass by the river.

'I mean, it's none of my business if you guys had a fight, of course, but if your relationship starts to have a bad effect on the morale of the Republic . . .'

I sighed and leaned forward to wash my hands in the river. 'Look, she didn't say anything to me about wanting to leave. I think she was just feeling down. It was hot.'

Joy sat next to me. 'You know, I really like Citizen Isobel . . .'

I laughed. This was one of Joy's favourite phrases. I used to think it presumptuous of her even to say so, like an earthworm praising a butterfly for its beauty. It was so obvious – how could you *not* like Isobel? – that it would have been better left unsaid. Now, things were different.

'Why are you laughing?'

'*But* . . .' I said. 'You really like her, *but* . . . Isn't that what's coming next?'

'No, honestly, I think she's got some wonderful qualities. She's beautiful, of course. Charming, intelligent . . .'

Vain. Frivolous.

'You know, when I first saw you guys together, I thought: they look like the perfect couple. Like you were up there' – she reached up with her hands – 'and I was down here, looking up.'

I snorted at this ridiculous image, and yet it felt true: that was how I had thought of us, too.

'And then I got to know you both,' she continued, 'and I thought you were both wonderful people. And a good couple too, except . . .'

'Except what?'

I watched the river bubble and froth as it moved gently past. The bubbles were caught for a second in sunlight and you could see the colours of the rainbow in their delicate skins.

'I just got the impression that you were totally in love with her, and maybe she was . . . taking advantage?'

'You don't know what you're talking about,' I said angrily.

'Maybe not,' said Joy. After a silence, she added: 'So . . . you really don't remember *anything* about last night?'

I sighed. 'I remember chopping off the duck's head.'

'Right, but that was pretty early on. What about later?'

I closed my eyes, saw the memories flash. 'We ate the duck. We sat around the fire and talked.'

'Who?'

'All four of us. And then . . . you and me.'

'Do you remember what we talked about?'

I concentrated. I could see Joy's face, earnestly nodding in the firelight, her fingers on my wrists. I had a feeling I was crying: I could feel water on my cheeks and the voices squealing in my head. The next memory I had was imageless, but I could feel warm flesh and breath near my face, on my chest, on my stomach . . .

I shook my head. 'I don't remember.'

'You were upset,' she said, as though inviting me to guess.

'What about?'

'About Citizen Isobel. You said you . . .' She stopped, her face solemn. 'Actually, I don't think it's fair to tell you if you don't remember. Perhaps you didn't mean it?'

'Didn't mean what?'

'Then again, *in vinas veritas* and all that . . .'

I looked at her blankly.

'It's Latin,' she explained. 'It means you tend to tell the truth when you're drunk.'

I was growing tired of this game. 'What did I say?' I demanded, putting my hands to my face. I felt nauseous, so I took a deep breath. An odd smell: acrid, heady, familiar and yet unfamiliar. It seemed to come from my hands.

'You said you had always found me attractive . . .' Joy's voice wobbled as she said this. I sniffed again, and thought about that bittersweet scent. 'And you put your hand . . .' She looked up at me, her mouth frozen around the next phrase. 'What's the matter, Citizen Michael?'

When I had finished throwing up, I leaned back against a tree trunk. Joy was holding my hand. 'I'm sorry,' I said.

'It's OK, I don't expect anything, of course. I know I can't compete with her . . .' Her voice warbled on and I felt bad. But good, too, in a way. 'As long as you know that I love you and that I'll always be there for you – as a friend or whatever you want. I mean, if they were to get back together . . . You seemed so pessimistic about it all last night when I told you . . . I'm sorry about that, by the way, the shock. I thought you knew already, it wasn't . . .'

I sat forward. 'Told me what?'

There was silence.

'You don't remember that, either?'

'What?'

'About Citizen Isobel and . . .'

'What?'

'Citizen Louis.'

I touched my throat, still sore from the vomit. 'What do you mean?'

'I'm really sorry, I thought you knew . . . They both told me about it, so I just presumed they'd told you, too.' Joy looked at me, her face full of tenderness and concern. 'You remember now?'

I shook my head, watched the ground. An ant balanced precariously atop a long blade of grass.

'They used to be boyfriend and girlfriend. I don't know when exactly, but it was still happening here, I think – in the forest. Citizen Michael, I'm so sorry. I think it was wrong of them not to tell you. It kills me to see you like this. Love can be so cruel.'

Hands to my face, I watched the ant waver, almost fall, then crawl down the bending stem.

16

The Demons

I found the two of them sprawled together in a far corner of the garden. They were wearing the all-white uniforms I had designed – one-piece, short-sleeved, made of light cotton. I looked down and realised that I too was wearing the uniform. It was strange; I had no memory of getting changed. I blinked away these thoughts; they were useless now. I moved towards the lovers.

My brother had his arm round Isobel's shoulders and her head was leaning on his chest. I could see the curls of her hair, touching his neck and the underside of his chin. Her eyes were closed. He was talking to her in a low voice. His eyes followed my progress through the garden. 'It's all right,' he said to me. 'Citizen Isobel is feeling better. Aren't you?'

She opened her eyes and sat up. She managed a thin smile. 'I'm sorry about yesterday.'

I gave her a dead eye.

She froze. 'What is it?'

'Citizen Louis, I want to talk to you.'

'Sure.' He smiled. To guess from the look on his face, you would have thought this was some sort of happy ending. His arm remained dangling over Isobel's shoulder, his fingertips lightly touching the bare skin of her upper arm. I pulled him violently away from her.

Isobel gasped and Louis's eyes grew large, first with surprise and then with anger. 'What are you doing?'

I pulled him further away from her and hissed, 'Why didn't you tell me?'

'Tell you what?'

But he had guessed; I could see the guilt in his eyes.

'About you and . . .'

She was out of earshot.

He looked round at her; the expression on her face was frightened and uncomprehending. 'Listen, everything's fine,' said Louis. 'I just need to talk to Citizen Michael about something, OK?'

She nodded and bit her lip. She looked at me. I turned away.

Louis and I walked into the forest; not towards the blackberry bushes, but the other way – north – to the border with the field of cows. He led and I followed. Neither of us spoke.

Though not yet noon, it was hot and still. We looked out from the last line of trees. The cows had gone. At the far side of the field, the ground sloped into thick forest and rolled high up another hill. The trees looked beautiful and mysterious from that angle, green and black and agleam.

'When did it start?' I asked.

'A long time ago. Two years. She was *my* first love, too, you know.' He gave me a rueful smile.

I had not been ready for this reply. 'Two years?'

Feeling shocked, I sat down. Louis sat next to me. I stared at the ground where our stumpy shadows crossed the border below the barbed-wire fence. The twisted metal thorns cast a sort of necklace across both our black throats.

'The first time we went to their house,' he said. 'You remember we played hide-and-seek?'

'Of course I remember. You abandoned me in a rose bush.'

'Oh yes, I'd forgotten about that. Anyway, Alex was counting, and you went off to hide, and Isobel took me to her bedroom.'

'We weren't allowed to hide in the house.'

Louis laughed. 'That's exactly what I said to her – "We're breaking the rules." But she said, "We're not playing any more." And she kissed me.' He paused, as if reliving the moment. 'Then, in the pool, she kept rubbing her body against mine.' He looked suddenly embarrassed. 'Well, that was how it started.'

We were silent for a while. To me, the memory of that day was like a child's painting, its colours bright and flat. Blue sky, white mountains, yellow lemonade, green lawn, Isobel's red swimsuit. It disturbed me that Louis could have seen depths in those colours to which I was blind. I decided this was a valuable lesson. Surfaces are lies. We cannot believe our eyes. And the truth is – the Truth is – behind, beneath, beyond.

'I still don't understand why you didn't tell me.'

'You were only a kid. What would you have thought if I'd told you that? Besides, I was worried that if I told somebody – anybody – it might not be true any more.'

'But for *two years* . . .'

'Yeah, but for most of that time we weren't even speaking to each other. You know what she's like.'

'You mean she kissed other boys?'

He laughed coldly. 'You could say that.'

'So why not end it?'

'I did – earlier this year, before we escaped. I'd had enough. I wanted her to promise she wouldn't go with anyone else, and she said she couldn't give me that.'

'Oh, I thought she meant . . .'

'Sex?'

I nodded.

'No, it wasn't that. I mean, I wanted to, but she said she was a virgin and . . .'

'*Said* she was?'

Louis shrugged. 'There are rumours. I don't know if they're true. I've never asked Isobel about them. I heard she's had sex with several guys. Older. Not schoolboys.'

Whore. The word made me think of the image it had con-jured in my mind when I was younger: a birthday present beautifully gift-wrapped in white, with a gold ribbon and bow, one corner of glossy paper torn away to reveal a hint of hideous living flesh – scarlet, bulbous, quivering – like a still-beating heart.

Louis saw the look on my face, and hurried the story on. 'Anyway, I wasn't going to invite her to the forest. But she found out what we were doing, and she came to me. She was so excited about it.'

'And in the forest?'

'What do you mean?'

'Joy said you were still doing it here.'

He sighed. 'Only once. The day I finished the map.'

I closed my eyes. The evening after our first time in Elbow Pool.

'She said she'd found a place where blackberries grow. She asked me to go with her.'

'So why did it stop?'

'She was upset with me about something.' He glanced at me, to test whether I knew what he was talking about.

'You and Alex?'

A blush and a grimace. 'Yeah.'

'Go on.'

'She was jealous. We had a row. She said two could play at that game. As soon as you came back from the hunt, she took you to the blackberries instead of me.'

So she had hurt him, too. I felt pleased, for a moment. And then I realised what it meant. I was a pawn. I was her revenge. It wasn't even flattering – it was not as if she'd had much choice.

'You could have warned me.'

Louis laughed. 'You should have seen the look on your face when you came back.'

I closed my eyes and remembered that first kiss. The after-image of the field burned yellow inside my eyelids.

'Let's go to the river,' said Louis. 'I'm parched.'

'You go. I want to sit here for a while.'

'Are you still angry?'

'Not with you, no.'

He stood. A hand on my shoulder. 'Don't hate her, Michael.'

I clenched and unclenched my fists, then let my eyes drift soothingly over the distant treetops. 'Why shouldn't I hate her?'

There was no reply. Louis had gone. I heard his footsteps rustle lightly behind me, then melt into silence. Finally there was no sound at all but the ceaseless moan of flies and the demons screaming in my head.

The ground seemed to roll, sea-like, under my prone body. I imagined it was the world I could feel, spinning through space. Occasionally I felt an unpleasant jolt of black memory, like a door being suddenly opened and then closed.

I don't know how much later it was when I sat up again, but I was sitting by the river with Alex. He was fishing. I felt drowsy and nauseous, but it was shady by the water and a cool breeze shivered through the trees. I looked up at their golden boughs. Something about the simple beauty of those silhouetted branches made me feel sad; there was a purity to the trees which put my human failings to shame. As they moved in the wind, I imagined they were shaking their heads at me, disappointed.

'Have you caught anything yet?' I asked.

'Patience,' sighed Alex. 'Are you feeling any better?'

I didn't respond so he looked at me. 'Fucking hell, you're white as a ghost.'

'I'm OK.'

'You should give it a rest tonight.'

I smiled. 'I feel like a drink now, actually.'

'I'm serious. You were well out of it last night.'

Something in Alex's tone alerted me. He normally thought it was funny to get drunk.

'What did I do?'

His eyes widened with horror. 'Don't you remember anything?'

'You mean getting off with Joy?' I said it nonchalantly, though I couldn't stop myself blushing.

Alex turned away. 'That was the night before . . .'

My heart thudded. The night before? Alex said something else, but I didn't hear him.

'What did I do?'

'Oh! I thought I had a bite then . . .'

'*Alex* . . .'

He gave me a look, filled with pity. 'You shouted. A lot. And you cried. A lot.'

'And?'

'That's it, as far as I know.'

'What was I shouting?'

'I don't know. You were in the shelter; I was outside with Louis. You should ask Joy – she was in there with you.'

I found Joy in the shelter with a tin of paint and a glistening brush, trying out different designs for the Great Eye. There were green paper eyes staring up from all over the floor. Joy grinned when she saw me.

'Hey . . . so what do you think?'

'They look good.'

She was wearing the white uniform. It suited her, I thought.

'Which one do you like best? They're all subtly different, if you look. The numbers of lines in the glory around the eye, whether the pupil is coloured in or left blank, that sort of thing . . . What's the matter, don't you like them?'

'Alex told me I was shouting last night. He said you'd be able to tell me what it was about.'

Joy looked crestfallen. 'Are you sure you want to know?'

I nodded firmly and she placed the paint tin on the ground. 'You were upset. With her. You made a few personal remarks.'

154

'Like what?'

She took a breath. 'You called her a whore. You swore a lot. You told her she'd broken your heart. "People die of broken hearts," you said.'

I put my hands to my face. 'How did she react?'

'She looked at you like you were a piece of shit. She just ignored you, Citizen Michael. And listen, if you want my opinion, you had every right to say what you said.'

'What happened then?'

Joy sighed. 'You followed her around a bit more, yelling. You started crying. Sobbing. You were really upset. Citizen Michael, we all understand. I just felt so helpless.'

'And in the end? What happened in the end?'

'You came to me. We had a long talk and I . . . did my best to comfort you. I'm really sorry for your pain.'

Joy's eyes were wide and intense. I nodded, feeling sick again. 'Where is she now?'

'She went for a walk, I think. Your brother's in the garden.'

'Right.' I moved towards the back of the shelter.

'Citizen Michael?'

'What?'

'I'll leave you alone so you can talk. But I won't go far. If you need me, just call.'

I sat in the mouth of the shelter and looked out. Louis walked towards me, topless and tanned. How could I ever have believed that she preferred me to him? Him with his broad shoulders and ridged stomach and balled pectorals and quivering biceps; and me with my protruding ribs and curved spine. Next to my brother, I felt like some failed experiment.

Louis was grinning. In his hands, cupped together, were half a dozen ripe tomatoes; so red, in the sunlight, they looked like jewels. He put them close to my nose. 'Smell them,' he commanded. They smelled like the earth they had come from. 'Not like the ones from the supermarket, are they?'

I shook my head and forced a smile.

He sat down next to me. 'Are you still upset?'

'I'll be OK.'

'Did you catch anything?'

'No. Citizen Alex is fishing.'

'Fishing!' Louis looked euphoric. 'Good idea. We can fry the tomatoes in the same pan, make a sauce . . .'

'You seem happy,' I ventured.

'The world hasn't actually ended, you know, even if it feels like it has.' He put a hand on my shoulder. 'It gets easier. I know it's a cliché, but time *does* heal.'

I bit the inside of my cheek. 'And now – are you . . . ?'

He shrugged. 'I'm not sure. We haven't really talked about it.'

'So you might . . .'

'Listen' – his eyes close to mine – 'I honestly don't know. I love her and I think she loves me. But we've got the same problems we had before.'

'And me?'

'She loves you too.'

I snorted. I felt like I had a large stone in my throat which stopped me swallowing.

'And so do I,' continued Louis. 'We all do. Remember, we're all in this together. The most important thing is the Republic.'

'Yes,' I said. 'That's the most important thing.'

'And Citizen Michael? Leave her alone for a bit, will you? I don't think screaming at her is really going to help.'

I blinked slowly, as though absorbing this reprimand. 'I'm going to have a rest,' I said.

As soon as Louis had gone, I found the bottle of *eau de vie* – it was hidden in his rucksack. I unscrewed the blue cap and sniffed. It smelled of oblivion, of nothingness. Holding my breath, I poured some down my throat. It scorched; I gasped. I drank again. Then I replaced the bottle where I had found it.

My nausea faded and the sky took on a warmer hue. Evening was coming, food and talk and fire. I wandered outside, sat on the grass, and let the sun bless my face in its fading rays.

I woke to the scent of frying fish and tomato sauce. The sun was setting and the air had cooled. I felt a little stiff but otherwise magnificent, and I told everyone this as I moved through the garden, feeling their concerned glances flicker over me. There were no voices in my head now, only a serene excitement about the future.

'Honestly,' I said as we sat around the fire, 'I feel absolutely fine now. Better than fine. I just needed a rest, I think. Mmm, this sauce is delicious . . .'

On my way out to urinate in the woods, I stooped to take the bottle from Louis's rucksack, and carried it with me outside. I gulped several mouthfuls and hid it in a tangle of nettles and weeds. Soon after that, everything turned black.

Slowly and painfully, I got up. I could hear the low, disgusting murmur of the flies through the wall. The noise increased as I walked out into the harsh light of the garden, squinting at the vulgar colours.

The air was windless and smelled rotten. There was no one around. Everything was as it had been the previous evening – the tomatoes, the guillotine, the fire hole, the chickens, the last duck – except for a strange pink shape like a gigantic smashed rose in the middle of the grass.

I rubbed my eyes and peered through the brightness. It was Isobel's air mattress, deflated and scrunched violently into a heap. There were, I noticed, lines of what looked like dried blood half concealed in its folds. I stared at it for a moment and then at my fingers, which were stained crimson. With my heart beating unnaturally fast, I picked up the mattress and laid it flat on the grass.

It had been slashed several times with a knife, in erratic diagonals. But more disturbing still was the message scrawled in dark red letters across the ripped canvas. The five letters had been painted wildly, as though the author were deranged, but the word they formed was clearly legible.

It said . . . **WHORE**

THREE

17

The Trial

Under a crimson sunset, Isobel was watering the strawberries. I had given them up for dead, but now they looked healthy and ripe. And it was not only the strawberries. The melons and cucumbers and courgettes had grown enormously, and the tomato plants were as tall as small trees.

I had only just got out of bed and I guessed I was not truly awake yet. I felt too floaty, too serene. I was aware of something different in the garden, or in the atmosphere around us, but I couldn't tell what it was.

Something fell, slowly, from a tree above. It looked like black snow. Only when it landed and dissolved on my outstretched fingers did I realise it was a flake of burned canvas. I looked up and saw other flakes hanging from the surrounding branches, like frail and dusty fruit. Behind me the cold, blackened remains of the air mattress glinted from the fire hole. Last breaths of smoke escaped weakly.

Isobel was wearing her uniform, but it looked darker. At first I thought it was just the effect of the setting sun, but as I moved closer I realised the material had been dyed red. Of course, I thought, remembering. She is the accused.

She bent from the waist as she poured tiny measures of water on to the dry soil, surrounding each plant with a circle of life. I watched her buttocks, spread enticingly, through the thin cotton of her uniform and felt a sleepy desire.

'Where are the others?' I asked.

Isobel shrugged. I saw the purple bruises on her arms, the repaired rip in the thigh of her uniform. Her hands were shaking and I felt bad. I wanted to say something reassuring, but could not think of anything.

There was a long silence, and then I was aware of a shadow moving beside me on the grass.

'Hello, Citizen Michael.'

I turned.

Joy stood behind me, smiling solicitously. 'How do you feel?'

'Fine.' I felt myself blush. Had she been here the whole time? Had she been spying on us? 'Where were *you* hiding?'

'I wasn't hiding,' she said. 'You just didn't see me.'

We looked at each other for a few moments.

Finally, Joy laughed. 'Citizen Michael, are you still asleep?'

'No . . . why?'

'Haven't you noticed anything?'

'What?'

'Look!'

I followed her eyes. Suddenly I saw what I had only sensed earlier. The trees were in the same places as before, they had not grown or changed shape . . . but now they looked back at me with eyes at once inhuman and familiar.

'I've been busy this afternoon,' explained Joy. 'I've painted a hundred eyes.'

I stared in disbelief. How had I not seen them before? Everywhere I looked there were eyes, gazing from the border of the garden and beyond. They were exactly as I had imagined them: bright green, with rays of light pouring out.

Isobel murmured, 'It's spooky.'

I shook my head. 'I find it comforting. Like every tree is your guardian angel.'

'That's what I think too,' said Joy. 'No one should mind being watched. Unless they've got something to hide.'

I scanned the multitude of all-seeing eyes and tried to think how it made me feel. It's like new flowers, I thought; the sudden flowering of belief.

The Truth . . . revealed.

Isobel held out the empty bottle. 'I need more water for the plants.'

162

'Citizen Michael can get it for you,' replied Joy.

'Sure.' I took the bottle and turned to leave.

Joy touched my arm and whispered, 'Don't take too long. I need to talk to you before it begins.'

'The trial?'

'Yes,' she said. 'We need to prepare your defence.'

Down at the river, I held the bottle underwater and listened to the hiss and gurgle of the current. My defence. As soon as Joy said those words, I knew I must have suffered another memory lapse. I tried to calculate from the details of the scene in the garden how much time I had lost. The eyes on the trees. The burned remains of the air mattress. The change of colour in Isobel's uniform. All of this might have been accomplished in an hour or two . . . but did that explain the ripening of the strawberries? I gave up: guessing was hopeless. It might have been an hour or it might have been a week. Such measurements, I knew, had no meaning here.

Feeling thirsty, I drank the contents of the bottle and filled it again. I looked at my fingernails: they were bitten to the quick. I felt my hair: freshly shaved. But when had that happened? I could not remember. It occurred to me that I was still suffering from the effects of my concussion, and that this was not normal. The trouble was, who could I talk to about it? I did not want the others to think I was cracking up. I did not want them to talk about me the way they talked about Isobel. The best thing to do, I decided, was keep quiet and listen carefully to what people said. That way I could work out what I had missed, and act accordingly. In all probability it wasn't as important as Joy made it sound. Her tone of voice was naturally solemn anyway.

When I came back from the river it was turning dark and the scene in the garden had changed. Isobel's green tent bulged from the grass, and all around it a strange light shone: a ring of brightness in the trees. I stared and realised that the eyes on the trunks were shining, phosphorescent in the gloom.

'There you are,' said Joy, emerging from the tent and zipping it shut behind her. 'Come on, we need to talk.'

'Where's Citizen Isobel?'

'Inside,' replied Joy, indicating the tent. 'These are the new arrangements.'

I put the bottle down and followed Joy out of the shelter. We went north. She held a torch, though it wasn't yet dark enough for us to need it. We reached the border of the meadow and sat down. I stared at the empty grassland, the forest that rose in darkness at the other side. How different the trees looked, now the sun had set. They seemed almost threatening.

'I came here with Citizen Louis,' I said, then remembered that I had no idea how long ago that was. 'The other day.'

Joy's mouth compressed sadly. 'How do you feel about all this?'

'I don't really know how to feel,' I said carefully.

'I understand. It must be very difficult. I know how close you were.'

Were? Was she talking about me and Louis? Or perhaps me and Isobel? I nodded, indistinctly, and waited for her to continue.

Joy was speaking slowly, gently, as though to a child. 'I don't think you should take it personally. Obviously I cannot agree with his decision, but . . .' She turned to me abruptly and held my hands between hers. 'Citizen Michael, please don't worry. We have a strong case, and I know the Judge.'

'The Judge?'

'Yes. And it's the Judge we have to persuade, not anyone else. Now, you have to tell me truthfully. Are you guilty?'

I tried to keep the panic out of my voice. 'Guilty of what?'

Joy smiled at me inscrutably. 'Well, quite. I feel the same. Technically, it may be a crime, but morally . . .' She squeezed my hands. 'Besides, *her* crime is a far greater one. The Judge will see that, I'm sure. I promise you, Citizen Michael, we'll turn that uniform white again as soon as we possibly can.'

I looked down at my sleeves, and my torso. The cotton was dark. I picked up the torch from the ground and switched it on. A small white circle on my chest faded into yellow, and orange, and, on the outer limits of the glory, bright red.

I was the accused.

The shelter was illuminated by a single candle: dark red, heavy as a rock. We had stolen it from the mansion, on that first raid. Louis, Alex and Joy sat around it, their faces sombre. I sat in the space they had left for me. The flame threw sinister, flickering, blood-tinted shadows on to the walls behind us.

I looked around the shelter. There were still damp clothes hanging from the tree trunk, old socks draped over axe handles and packets of rice, but without Isobel's possessions – her lotions and bracelets and sprawling worn knickers – it seemed like another place. A barer, purer place.

Something else was missing, too, though it took me longer to work out what it was. When I did, I got an empty feeling in my chest. Her scent had gone.

Just then, I noticed a new light in the garden, coming from the tent. Isobel must have switched on a torch to read: I saw her silhouetted through the thin canvas, her profile distorted by the angle of the light. Her limbs looked thin and her head huge, like a skeleton surmounted by a beach ball. We all looked at her, but none of us said anything.

The ground was hard, so I folded my sleeping-bag twice and sat on it like a cushion. Then I sighed, raised my face, and waited for the process to begin.

Still no one spoke. They seemed to be waiting. Joy sat to my left; Alex to my right. He was staring into space, sucking on the end of a biro. Louis sat directly opposite me. He stared at the ground. Between Alex and Louis there was a large empty space. I thought about the positions in which we were sitting, and then I understood: it was star-shaped. But because Isobel was inside the tent, there were only four points to the star.

I looked at Joy: she was flipping through a notebook. When at last she glanced up, I caught her eye and gave her a questioning look. She leaned close to my face and whispered, 'Not long now.'

I put my mouth to her ear. 'What are we waiting for?'

She looked at me curiously, then replied, 'The Judge.'

I opened my mouth to ask another question, but she put a finger to her lips.

I yawned and rubbed my face and wondered again what all this was about. I could only presume that the 'crime' of which I was accused was the mutilation of the air mattress. At first, reaching this conclusion, I had felt relieved. It seemed so minor, so unimportant. I even had a vague memory of Joy helping me to burn it afterwards; of her laughing as the hot grey flakes rose and flew across the garden. And yet, the longer I waited for the trial to begin, the greater my crime seemed to loom. I looked around the shelter and saw the others' unsmiling faces. I looked at the space reserved for the Judge, and remembered again the shock I had felt when I saw that scrawled word, written in red, and the blood-like stains on my hands. What had I done? What had driven me to it? I felt my chest fill with a large, uncomfortable shape. I swallowed drily. I knew now what the shape was. Guilt.

Thirsty, I turned round and groped in the darkness for the water bottle I had left on Joy's sleeping-bag. When I turned back, I noticed that the other three were all looking into the empty corner – towards the star's missing point. I unscrewed the cap as I watched them, lifted the bottle to my lips. And then my eyes found what they were staring at. I screwed the cap back on the bottle and dropped it to the ground.

'Arise, Citizens, for the Judge!'

Joy's voice was stern, metallic. She, Louis and Alex all stood, and hesitantly I did the same. The shelter span around me. Suddenly the air seemed too close, too thin. I closed my eyes and the shape of the candle flame burned on, silver-green, in the darkness. Slowly it faded, and a second image, the same colour, took its place.

The all-seeing eye.

When I opened my eyes, I was sitting down. Despite being cushioned by the sleeping-bag, my legs and buttocks were numb, as though I had been in the same position for a long time. Everyone in the shelter exhaled and the candle flickered. Louis told Alex he could stop writing; Alex shook his wrist and grimaced, then winked at me.

I looked across at where the Judge had been. The space was empty. Joy touched my hand and whispered, 'You were very brave. I'm proud of you.'

I shook my head. 'What happened?'

'What do you mean?' She was frowning, concerned.

I said, 'Nothing, I . . .'

And then my memory began to return, in flashes. I closed my eyes and saw the figure – a human figure, or so it seemed – dressed all in white, with a white mask over his face. There had been no holes in the mask – as though the Judge needed neither mouth nor eyes. Instead, painted on the white in luminous green was the Great Eye.

I remembered staring at the Judge as Louis, and then Joy, spoke, hearing their words but not really understanding them. I remembered the candle being blown out, and the absolute darkness, relieved – faintly at first, and then dazzlingly – by the shining eye. And then I knew who the Judge was.

Lord Rousseau.

'The Judge was very impressed with you, Citizen Michael. You've been found innocent. Look . . .' She was gesturing to my uniform. I looked down, and saw, in the candlelight, that it was no longer red. 'You're free. It's over.'

But what had I said? Of what had I been accused? If I had

167

been found innocent, then it couldn't have been the air mattress, could it? I wanted to ask Joy, but didn't dare. Already her expression was troubled.

'Citizen Michael, are you OK? Do you understand what I'm saying?'

'Yes,' I said. 'Thank you. I think I need to go and lie down.'

'Of course,' she said, 'you must be exhausted. Do you wish to be present for the interrogation of the traitor?'

'The traitor – you mean Citizen Isobel?'

'Not any more. Your innocence proves her guilt. She is the traitor now. Do you wish to . . .'

'No . . . no, I'd like to sleep, if that's all right.'

'Of course. You can sleep in the tent. Citizen Alex, would you fetch the traitor, please?'

I turned to look at Louis before I left the shelter, but he was staring at the flame of the candle as it guttered. A moth flew close to the light and I saw its shadow loom monstrously over Louis's shoulder. I walked out to the tent. Coming the other way, Isobel passed me in silence. It was dark; it was possible she hadn't seen me. Alex followed behind her and I whispered his name.

'Yes, Citizen Michael?'

'Could I look at the transcript of my interrogation? There's something I'd like to check.'

'Of course you can,' he said, and passed me the notebook. 'I've got another book in the shelter. Give me that back when you've finished, won't you?'

'Yes, I will. Thanks.'

Inside the tent, the air smelled of vanilla – of her – and of something else. There was another smell in the tent. A bad smell. It seemed to come from the ground. I sniffed a few times, trying to locate it, and then gave up. It was only a smell: I would get used to it.

I switched on the torch, made myself comfortable on Isobel's sleeping-bag, and began to read Alex's notes.

INQUISITION OF CITIZEN M
BY CITIZEN J
MINUTES BY CITIZEN A
IN THE PRESENCE OF THE JUDGE

INQUISITOR: Citizen Michael, do you swear on *The Social Contract*, in the name of our Lord and Judge Jean Jacques Rousseau, and under the holy gaze of the Great Eye that everything you say will be the Truth?

CITIZEN M: I do.

INQUISITOR: Will you please tell the court exactly what occurred earlier today with regard to Citizen Isobel.

CITIZEN M: Well, we'd fallen out, as you know. But we made up this morning. She apologised for her behaviour, and I forgave her.

INQUISITOR: How were you feeling at this point?

CITIZEN M: Happy. Relieved. I thought things were back to normal between us.

INQUISITOR: How would you define normal?

CITIZEN M: We were in love. Or . . . I thought we were, anyway. I was in love with her.

INQUISITOR: So you were perhaps less on your guard than you should have been, considering her recent behaviour?

CITIZEN M: Yes, that's fair. I was stupid. I'm sorry.

INQUISITOR: Don't apologise, Citizen Michael. Everybody has weaknesses. Where did you go to on your walk?

CITIZEN M: Elbow Pool.

INQUISITOR: Please tell us what happened there.

CITIZEN M: We talked for a bit, and then . . . we got undressed. We started playing.

INQUISITOR: What kind of playing?

CITIZEN M: She touched me, we kissed. After a while we got into the water. We played a bit more.

INQUISITOR: Did she bring you to ejaculation?

CITIZEN M: No.

INQUISITOR: Did you penetrate her?

CITIZEN M: No! No . . . we were just playing.

INQUISITOR: And then what happened?

CITIZEN M: She asked me if I loved her. I said, 'You know I do.' She smiled and said, 'Close your eyes and wait here. Don't move a muscle until I come back, or you'll ruin the surprise.' And . . . she said she loved me.

INQUISITOR: Did you believe her?

CITIZEN M: Yes, I believed her.

INQUISITOR: Would you like a handkerchief, Citizen Michael? That's OK, take your time. So, you closed your eyes and waited?

CITIZEN M: Yes.

INQUISITOR: For how long?

CITIZEN M: I don't know. You know what it's like here, with time.

INQUISITOR: Uh-huh. And what made you open your eyes?

CITIZEN M: Well, suddenly it seemed like I'd been waiting there a long time. I listened, and I couldn't hear anything. I felt . . . not exactly afraid, but –

INQUISITOR: Suspicious?

CITIZEN M: Not until I realised my clothes had gone.

INQUISITOR: What did you do then?

CITIZEN M: I searched for them. Luckily, I found the shorts quite quickly . . .

INQUISITOR: And that was when you raised the alarm?

CITIZEN M: I went back to the shelter, yes, and . . . well, you know the rest.

INQUISITOR: You told us what had happened, and Citizen Louis ordered us each to go in a different direction to search for Isobel. You volunteered to go east. Why was that?

CITIZEN M: Because we were on the east side of the Republic when she vanished. I thought that was the most likely place for her to go, and I'm probably the fastest of us, now Citizen Louis is suffering with his asthma.

INQUISITOR: Sure. Was that the only reason?

CITIZEN M: Well . . . I felt it was my fault that she had escaped, I suppose, so I wanted to put it right myself.

INQUISITOR: A noble sentiment. Why don't you tell us the rest of the story, Citizen Michael? What happened after you left the shelter?

CITIZEN M: I ran back to Elbow Pool and looked for markings on the paths near there, but I couldn't see anything distinct, so I crossed the river and looked on the other side. There was some soft mud on the bank there and I noticed a fresh footprint in it.

INQUISITOR: Belonging to Citizen Isobel?

CITIZEN M: Yes. So I stood with my foot in the footprint and looked up – to see the view she would have seen.

INQUISITOR: What did you see?

CITIZEN M: Well, a lot of things, but what caught my eye was the entrance to the Underwater Forest, and I remembered when we first went through there that Isobel had loved it. It was just a hunch, but I thought I'd better follow it because if I searched the area methodically she'd have time to escape.

INQUISITOR: So you went into the Underwater Forest . . .

CITIZEN M: And up the slope. I knew I was on the right track because I could see soil scrapings where the ground had been disturbed. There was a broken tree root too, and the break looked new. I kept going to the top, but I didn't know where to go after that because it's a crossroads. There's a wide path going across in both directions, and a couple of smaller paths going down into the forest.

INQUISITOR: So what did you do?

CITIZEN M: I climbed a tree. I thought I'd be able to see better from up there. In fact, I couldn't really – because the lower leaves obscured my view – but when I got halfway up I heard something. A girl's voice. I could tell it was coming from my left, so I climbed back down the tree and took the wide path that way. I ran as fast as I could, and stopped a couple of times to check if I could still hear the voice.

INQUISITOR: Could you?

CITIZEN M: Not the first time, but the second time I did. I guessed she must be near the edge of the forest if she was calling for help.

INQUISITOR: Wait a minute, Citizen Michael. Did you say she was calling for help?

CITIZEN M: Yes. She shouted, '*Au secours!*' I heard it clearly the second time.

INQUISITOR: And are you sure it was Citizen Isobel?

CITIZEN M: It was Citizen Isobel, yes. Anyway, I ran then, because I knew the Republic would be in danger if she raised the alarm. But I reached the edge of the forest, where the road goes to the house we raided, you know? And . . . she wasn't there. I couldn't see her.

INQUISITOR: She'd left the forest?

CITIZEN M: Yes. She didn't get far, though. I found her a little way down that road, in the other direction . . . There's a village down there and she was close to it. But she wasn't running. She was kneeling on the ground and crying.

INQUISITOR: Was she still shouting for help?

CITIZEN M: Not until she saw me.

INQUISITOR: And then she called for help?

CITIZEN M: Not really. She just screamed. And ran into a cornfield that bordered the road. Luckily the corn still isn't fully grown, so I could see her head move as she ran.

INQUISITOR: So you were able to apprehend her?

CITIZEN M: Yes, I rugby-tackled her, and put my hand over her mouth to stop her screaming.

INQUISITOR: Now, think carefully, Citizen Michael. Did you see any villagers? Could anyone have seen you or heard the cries of Citizen Isobel?

CITIZEN M: No, that's the weird thing. This was a village – only a small one, but still . . . maybe thirty houses? And there was no one.

INQUISITOR: There's something I don't understand. Why did

Citizen Isobel stop short of the village? Why didn't she bang on doors?

CITIZEN M: But that's what I mean. I think she did. The more I think about it, the way she was kneeling when I found her, where she was, how far ahead of me she'd been . . . I think what must have happened was that she entered the village and knocked on people's doors . . . and no one answered.

INQUISITOR: No one at all? In a village of thirty houses?

CITIZEN M: That's right. It was like a ghost village. No one in the fields. No cars on the road. And when I managed to stop Isobel screaming, there was just . . . silence. I mean, I could hear birds and the wind and so on, but that was all.

INQUISITOR: Fascinating. And you managed to bring Citizen Isobel back without any further incident?

CITIZEN M: I wouldn't say that. She fought like crazy to start with. Bit my hand. Scratched my face.

INQUISITOR: Were you forced to use violence?

CITIZEN M: I pulled her arms behind her back, but it was hard to keep my hand over her mouth like that and make her move at the same time. She kept kicking.

INQUISITOR: That explains her bruises, then. Do you remember how the rip in her uniform occurred?

CITIZEN M: No, I don't remember. It might have happened when we were fighting, I suppose. Or when I tackled her. But it could have happened before that, when she was running. There are so many thorns. I don't know, sorry. I wasn't aware of it at the time.

INQUISITOR: Fine. And she came quietly after that?

CITIZEN M: She tried to escape once more, when we were on the road, but as soon as I got her into the forest, her body went all floppy. I relaxed then. I knew everything was going to be all right.

INQUISITOR: Just one more question. Are you convinced in your own mind that Citizen Isobel was attempting to escape the Republic permanently?

CITIZEN M: I'm afraid she was . . . yes.

INQUISITOR: Thank you, Citizen Michael. You have been a great help. And thank you on behalf of the Republic of Trees for successfully finding and returning Citizen Isobel.

That was where it ended. I put the notebook on the ground and switched off the torch. I lay back on the sleeping-bag, exhausted, and thought about my testimony. Was it the truth?

It was odd: when I read it, it had been as though I were experiencing it for the first time. Yet now, having been through it, I felt like it was part of me. It was a memory – as real, as substantial, as any of my other memories.

Was it the truth?

It had to be. The Judge had found me innocent, after all, and he saw everything. I believed in him and he believed in me. Therefore, I believed in my testimony.

Even if it wasn't the truth, it was something more important than that. It was history. It was . . . the Truth.

When I closed my eyes, I saw the Great Eye beaming down at me.

And then I fell asleep.

When I unzipped the tent, the sun was shining silver through the trees. The dew was cold on the grass. I looked at the entrance to the shelter – I could see figures moving.

I walked towards them. Louis and Alex came out into the garden, talking quietly, faces down. I said, 'Morning,' and Louis glanced up at me. 'Oh, we were just coming to wake you. It's time for the verdict.'

'The verdict? But I thought she was –'

'The Judge left the decision to us. Some things came up in Citizen Isobel's interrogation that cast doubt on your statements.'

'What things?'

174

'It doesn't matter. You don't need to hear them. I don't suppose you're going to change *your* verdict, are you?'

I stared at my brother. He looked away. 'Come on. It's too late for this now.'

He turned and I followed him into the shelter.

We each had to write our verdict on a piece of paper. There were only two possible answers. Abstention was forbidden. My pen hovered over the paper as I weighed my decision.

It was quiet in the shelter, like an examination room: all of us were looking into our minds and wondering what the future would be like after we had finished. The air felt close. I saw a lizard dart across a stone, heard a scrape of pen on paper. I looked up; Joy was smiling complacently. She was sure she knew the right answer.

From the corner of my eye I could see the shadow of the guillotine on the grass. It looked enormous in the daylight. At night its dark verticals were camouflaged by the forest, but now I looked and had to rub my eyes to check it was really there.

It was.

After a moment I became aware of the others watching me. I looked back at them. They were all sitting, waiting, their papers folded in the space between us.

'Take your time, Citizen Michael.' Joy smiled.

I nodded, sighed, tried to concentrate.

I looked at the piece of paper. It was small, a rectangle that fitted inside my palm. It had been torn from an exercise book using a ruler so two sides were perfectly straight but the others were rough with hundreds of tiny, loose fibres. There were four horizontal lines in aquamarine and a single vertical in bright red – the margin. Near the bottom right-hand corner there was a dark little flaw in the paper's weave, like a freckle.

I felt a sudden, overwhelming desire to escape. I could see the trees swaying gently, green and gold, beyond the garden, and I wanted more than anything to sneak out unnoticed and climb into those hidden, unreachable places.

Six eyes bored into me. I swallowed, drily. Oh, to swim and drink in the cool river water . . .

I wrote my verdict and folded my paper. I placed it next to the others.

18

Operation Butterfly

'Good morning, Citizen Michael. And how is your faith?' Joy smiled as she spoke. She had made coffee as usual and was waiting for me in the garden. It was another beautiful morning. The sunlight gleamed from the eyes on the trees and I felt good.

'A hundred per cent,' I said. 'And yours?'

'Yes, mine too. I was just thinking about your ideas. About how we might implement them.'

'Which ideas?' I asked.

'The ones from yesterday. About sleep deprivation and so on.'

'Oh yes?'

I had no idea what she was talking about, but I had learned by now the pointlessness of worrying about my memory lapses. Clearly there was a pattern of forgetting, but equally clearly it was not having an adverse effect upon my work. And Joy, I was sure, did not suspect.

'It's interesting, your idea of the two selves, dwelling in the same mind. The nightself and the dayself. The sleepself and the wakeself. The change of the guard. I think you may be on to something there.'

'Thanks,' I said.

'Perhaps, if we can change *both* her minds, then . . .' Her voice drifted into a familiar reverie.

'Mmm. So how were you thinking of implementing it?'

'That's the trouble. I can forbid her to sleep, but I can't stay in the tent with her all the time.'

'No.'

'And I understand your desire not to become . . . physically involved.'

'Yes.'

'So we need to find some way to make her feel she is being watched, even when she is on her own.'

'Like the Judge,' I said, thinking aloud.

'Yes. Although, of course, while she does not believe, she will not be able to see him. It's a vicious circle. Some kind of representational image, perhaps?'

I nodded. 'I'll have a think.'

'Thanks.' Joy took one last sip of coffee, then passed me the cup. 'Well, I'd better get to work. Wish me luck.'

'Good luck.'

She bent her face down towards mine, and we kissed. On the lips. Hers were soft and warm. I felt a pleasant flutter in my chest.

'May the Great Eye watch over you, Citizen Michael.'

'Like a sun that never sets, Citizen Joy.'

When she had gone, I finished the coffee, ate some cereal, and tidied away the breakfast things. Then I went down to the river, to perform the morning's ablutions. And to think. It was always on those river walks, mind drifting as I moved through treeshadows, that I found the inspiration I needed.

And this morning, halfway there, it happened again. A green eye watched me from a nearby tree, and suddenly I stopped walking, stopped seeing. For a moment I even stopped breathing. My hands were in the air. 'Yes,' I said aloud. 'That's it! That's what we'll do. And we can call it the House of Eyes.'

It had been a relief to get back to work. After all those private torments, and the grimness of the trial, the business of the Ministry seemed blessed with a reassuring impersonality. Here I was able to stop obsessing over the still-warm entrails of my first, dead love and to focus on details of a cooler, more manageable kind.

It may seem odd that I was able to confront my new task so objectively, but propaganda is a black-and-white art; there is no room for ambiguity or doubt. Your task is to persuade, to convince, to convert; to put across, to win over, to bring round; and yes, if you prefer, to indoctrinate, to brainwash, to compel.

Or, in the beautiful phrase I eventually settled on as the ideal description of our challenge, *to make believe*.

But in order to make someone else believe, it is necessary for you yourself to believe. To take on trust, to know for certain, to have faith, to swallow whole, to eliminate all doubt. To transform yourself from a poor, fallible human being into a vessel of divine will.

It had taken me most of a morning, up on the high branches, communing with the Great Eye, letting the hot, dry sun bleach out my weaknesses and fears, to reach the required level of inner strength.

Nature helped. I thought of the trees' disappointment in me the day of my hangover; the purity of their beauty. I watched the buzzards sail, wings still, in the flawless blue above. I gazed at the imperious mountain tops, electrifyingly clear on the horizon.

'Great Eye,' I prayed, 'give me the purity of the trees, the serenity of the birds, the immovability of the mountains, and I will, I promise, bring you a fifth believer.'

The wind stirred in reply and I knew it was to be.

And oh, the glorious lightness of not feeling! The miraculous calm that descends when you cut out the cancer of enfeebling, illusory, romantic love and replace it with the deeper, the purer, the infinitely greater love of god and republic! Righteous and holy, I climbed through the trees with nothing in my head but the challenge of elevating the traitor to this same perfect plane of unquestioning faith.

Quickly we developed a routine, Joy and I. We ate lunch apart from the others, in our office at the front of the shelter.

179

This enabled us to discuss strategy in private and to avoid wasting time in idle chit-chat. We were working to a strict deadline. Isobel had to be made to believe before the seventh sunset or she would suffer the punishment for non-belief.

She was guilty of that, beyond doubt. Louis may have claimed that the facts behind her escape attempt remained unproven, but, as Joy pointed out, this was basically irrelevant. Isobel was guilty of what Rousseau called 'the greatest crime'.

I had nodded in recognition as Joy quoted the passage to him. 'If anyone, after having publicly acknowledged the Republic's dogmas, behaves as if he did not believe in them, then let him be put to death, for he has committed the greatest crime, that of lying before the law.'

Louis hadn't known what to say then. All he'd managed in response was another liquid cough and a plea for us to pardon her. It was Joy who suggested the idea of the chrysalis, though I came up with the name – Operation Butterfly. It was an inspiring thought. Isobel the traitor, the spiritual caterpillar, had entered the cocoon. I did not know what state she would be in when she emerged, but I prayed her soul would be transformed, that her belief would grow wings and take flight.

After lunch, Joy returned to the tent. As to what went on in there, I knew only what Joy told me. I didn't wish to know more. What goes on inside a chrysalis is mysterious, and rightly so. I heard no screaming; nor did I see the skin of the tent bulge with movement. There was never any suggestion of physical violence. Sometimes I heard murmured voices – Joy's mostly – and, had I moved closer, I would have been able to discern words.

But I was not curious. The idea of the real girl inside the theoretical shell of the traitor disturbed me, so I stopped believing in her.

Belief, I understood, was the only reality. If you did not believe something existed, it did not exist.

I thought, therefore she wasn't.

*

While Joy was in the tent, I consulted the Dictionary. It was not an ordinary dictionary – of words and their meanings – but a special one, of dead people's thoughts and ideas. Louis had brought it from home, though it was actually a library book. It had a yellow sticker on the inside cover saying, 'FOR REFERENCE ONLY: DO NOT REMOVE FROM PREMISES'.

The Dictionary now became my favourite book. I read it greedily, hoovering up wisdom like dust. I sucked in history, science, art, literature, philosophy, politics, poetry, life, love and death in great, random, century-spanning gulps. I ignored the attributions: for me, each quotation was a simple signal of Truth. Or rather, it was the raw material of persuasion. After all, the Truth was clear to me. What I needed was proof – and that was what I sought as I drew my finger down the dense lines of the index, in a fever of anticipation. Something in here, I told myself, will make her believe. Something here will save her life.

However, it would not be fair for me to exaggerate my role in Operation Butterfly. In truth, I was not much more than a researcher, a honer of words. At Joy's request, I scanned the Dictionary for quotations about belief, or virtue, or duty, and picked out the ones I liked. Then I translated them into English and customised them to suit the Republic's purposes.

After each session, Joy returned and we discussed the traitor's response to the latest round of talks, and what our next move should be. Sometimes she rushed back to the tent for another session. At other times she judged that the traitor would benefit more from a period of reflection, and instead the two of us sat and read the Dictionary together, or talked about how life would be when our makebelieve work was finished.

If the session threatened to be a long one, I would take a stroll outside the shelter – walking down to the river to fill the water bottles, or picking redcurrants and raspberries from a new patch of brambles I had found. Or I would go climbing.

Always in these moments I lived in the present, on the surface, like a bird. It was a pleasant way to exist.

When I came back from my wanderings, I was more relaxed. Sometimes *too* relaxed. One time I sat in the garden with my eyes closed and let the sun warm my skin. Without meaning to, I fell asleep – and had the worst dream I'd yet suffered. Like all the rest, it was grey, and took place in a small room. But this time the door opened, and there was Isobel. She sat across the table from me and stared. I remembered the look in the boar's eyes just before we killed it. I tried to move, but I couldn't. When Isobel opened her mouth to speak, I awoke, with a scream.

For some time afterwards the grey image clung to my eyes. I had to rub my eyelids furiously, and pinch my arm several times, in order to erase the dream. Even later, back at work, I felt the dream had infected me somehow. I caught glimpses of it in the corners of my eyes. I had to pray to the Great Eye to make it disappear.

During this time, I felt there was something I couldn't quite remember, some important memory that hissed, like a river, just out of sight. I could not see or name the memory, but I sensed its largeness and some connection to the grey dreams.

But then I snapped out of it. This was no time for dreams and memories. It was a time for discipline and focus. All the time I was awake, I made sure I concentrated on the solid bright surfaces around me.

The mudbrick shelter, the sun-painted leaves, the dry grass below, the pale sky above. The black typed letters in the Dictionary. The electric-green eyes on the trees.

When darkness came I would stare ever harder at those eyes. I would lose myself in their shining until they were all I could see.

Joy emerged from the tent, smiling grimly. Her skin looked pale and greasy and there were tired lines around her eyes.

'Good makebelieve?' I asked, looking up from the Dictionary.

'I think we're beginning to get somewhere. It's difficult, though. There are so many levels of deceit to dig through.' She sighed. 'Oh well. We must stay positive, Citizen Michael. We have to do our best.'

I nodded and put down the Dictionary. I could see stars from all the reading I'd done. 'I've got some more Truths for you.'

Joy looked pleased. 'That's great. Can you show me?'

'Let's go out in the sun.'

The two of us sat with our backs to the shelter wall. To my right, I could hear the flies buzz over the animal carcasses. In front of me I could see the green tent, its skin smooth and motionless, and its long shadow stretching sideways on the grass. A chicken scratched near the entrance.

I gave Joy the paper with the Truths written on it and she read them out in her inflexionless voice. '*Whatever one believes to be True either is True or becomes True in one's mind.* Wow, that is so profound! Who wrote that? No, don't tell me – you're right, it doesn't matter. What's the next one? *A belief is like a guillotine, just as heavy, just as light.* That's beautiful, Citizen Michael, though I'm not sure the traitor will appreciate the simile. Still, it's good to remind her of the alternative, I suppose.'

Joy rubbed her temples and sighed.

'Read the rest,' I said.

She smiled and sat up again. 'Of course.' She read from the sheet of paper: '*Extremism in the defence of liberty is no vice! Moderation in the pursuit of justice is no virtue!* Ha – that's one for me to remember, I guess. It is quite upsetting at times, you know, seeing her like that . . .'

She looked at me, her eyes large. I nodded sympathetically and turned her round so I could massage her shoulders. She sighed. 'That is *so* good. Can you feel all the tension in my muscles?'

'Just relax,' I said, and motioned to the sheet of paper that shook slightly in her hands. 'Read the next one.'

'Wow, this is a long one! *We have only to believe. And the more threatening and irreducible reality appears, the more firmly and desperately we must believe. Then, little by little, we shall see the universal horror unbend, and then smile upon us, and then take us in its more than human arms.* Oh, that is so . . .'

There was a silence while she looked at me. I could see a hint of tears in her blue eyes, and their myopic intensity made me feel uncomfortable. To break the spell, I told her about the report. 'It's finished,' I said. 'Would you like to see it?'

OPERATION BUTTERFLY – DAY ONE

In makebelieve numberone, Traitor = ultranegative. No eyetouch with Persuader. Traitor mouthdemanded only that she pleasedesired Citizen L, and she pleasedesired 'freedom'. Persuader mouthsignalled that, numberone, Citizen L = uneyetouchable. Numbertwo, freshair = pleasereward for Truth. And numberthree, freedom minus belief = lawforbidden. Persuader mouthsignalled that freedom and belief = only halfequals of sameword – BELIEFREEDOM – which (for quicksake) = belief. Traitor eyecried and mouthdamaged Persuader. Makebelieve numberone = terminated.

In makebelieve numbertwo, Traitor eyetouched only ground and mouthcircled 'Go away, go away'. Persuader obeyed.

Persuader mindmade to open longer feartime between makebelieves numbertwo and numberthree.

At start of makebelieve numberthree, Traitor lipsmiled at Persuader. Traitor's mouthresponses mindarrowed pastdays of Republic zeropoint, with special moutharrow on pastfriendship between Traitor and Persuader. Persuader mouthdemanded Traitor why she mouthcircled pastdays. Traitor mouthresponded, eyeswet, 'Please can you talk to me normally, Joy? Please can we just be friends again?' Persuader mouthsignalled to Traitor that friendship minus citizenship = lawforbidden. Persuader mouthsignalled that friend and citizen = only halfequals of sameword – CITIZENFRIEND – which (for quicksake) = citizen. Traitor made onlynoise.

In makebelieve numberfour, Persuader mouthdemanded, 'Do you believe?' Traitor mouthresponded 'Yes.' Persuader mouthsignalled that Traitor = perpetuliar. Traitor mouthpleaded, 'I'm not lying!' Makebelieve = terminated.

Makebelieves numbersfivesixseveneight-nineten all terminated for same makewhy. To punishelp Traitor, Persuader mindmade to makeless Traitor's energyflow in, numberone, mouthfood, and numbertwo, mindsleep.

Makebelieve numbereleven = breakthrough numberone. After longtime onlynoise, Traitor mouthconfessed, 'I've been lying. I don't believe.' Persuader mouthsignalled that she would helpunish Traitor for nonbelief.

It was evening and the sky was the colour of a lovebite: yellow and pink directly above us, a livid purple over the trees. The air was fragrant with the steam of stewing rabbit and wild thyme. Alex licked the wooden spoon and mumbled something positive. He grinned at me. I smiled back, then looked at Louis.

He was still frowning over the piece of paper in his hands, though I knew he had finished reading it. 'What kind of language *is* this? It's certainly not English.'

'It's the language of the revolution,' I explained. 'As Minister of Propaganda, I believe the Republic needs to develop its own language. That will take time, so for now the language is in the process of being revolutionised.'

Louis raised his eyebrows ironically. I felt he was slighting my work.

'What's the matter?' I said. 'Don't you *understand*? Don't you *get it*?'

Louis looked at me with horror and hatred for a moment, then turned his attention to Joy. 'How could you have known she was lying, Citizen Joy?'

'She has a history of lying. As you know.'

'But what if she was telling the truth?'

Joy sighed. 'She has already admitted that she was lying, Citizen Louis. And besides, if she was telling the truth initially, then that would mean she was lying in the second instance.'

'But what if next time she tells the truth and you still think –'

'Listen. Sorry to interrupt, but it seems to me the real problem here is the traitor's intrinsically corrupt, untrustworthy nature. Her "personality", if you prefer. I have no doubt that she will lie to us again, and again after that. In my opinion we need to keep stripping away these layers of insincerity until we reach the true blankness underneath. The dreamself. The nonperson. Then, and only then, can we begin to "rehabilitate" her.'

A scowl crossed Louis's face. 'But how can you possibly do all that in five days, Citizen Joy?'

'Perhaps we can't, Citizen Louis. We can only do our best.'

Louis took a breath. 'Citizen Joy, I'm worried that your personal dislike for the traitor is affecting your judgement.'

'That's not true at all,' said Joy, looking genuinely surprised and offended. 'Unlike your judgement of her, mine is
purely objective.'

'You don't like her, though, do you?'

'Personally, I neither like nor dislike her. As a traitor, I naturally abhor her. As a potential citizen, I'm doing my best to
help her.'

'She's very pretty, don't you think?'

'Evidently you think so, Citizen Louis. I presume prettiness
partly explains the peculiar hold she has over you.'

It was like watching a game of tennis: Louis chipping over
disguised lobs into the corners, Joy belting them remorselessly back to the centre of the baseline.

'You were close friends not so long ago.'

'Before her treachery, yes.'

'And yet you seemed oddly eager to kill her.'

'My desire was for justice, that's all. But you opted to pardon
her. Therefore, I accept that she has been pardoned and it is
now my job to help rehabilitate her.'

Louis, losing his patience, leaned forward and spoke
louder. 'Look, Citizen Joy, it's obvious you're jealous of her.
I'm just warning you now that if you –'

We waited while Louis's coughing fit was precipitated into a
ball of yellow phlegm which he spat on the grass behind him.
He wiped his mouth and muttered, 'Excuse me.' He tried to
speak again, but his voice was drowned out by ghost-voices
wailing from his lungs. It sounded like a distant folk orchestra,
all accordions and harmonicas and paper-and-combs.

'Citizen Louis, are you sure you're OK?' asked Joy. 'That
cough sounds quite nasty to me. You might have caught
some sort of infection. Perhaps you ought to rest for a while?'

Louis glared at her, but was still unable to speak. Finally he
nodded, and Alex led him across to the shelter.

When Alex came back, the three of us divided the rabbit
stew and ate it in silence. It tasted good. I drank some cold
water and leaned back on my elbows.

'Nice rabbit,' I said.

'Thanks,' said Alex.

There was another long silence. Finally Joy said, 'I think perhaps we ought to put up the other tent this evening. If Citizen Louis is infected, we'll need to protect ourselves. What he has might be contagious.'

19

The House of Eyes

In the dream I was in bed and I could not move. I was staring up at the thin walls and I was trying to sit up. But I couldn't. Everything was grey.

I opened my eyes and stared through the clinging greyness. It was like a dawn mist, obscuring the interlacing branches, the spots of daylight, the vague shapes of the others' empty sleeping-bags. I knew where I could be, where I wished to be, but not yet where I was.

Forget the dream, a voice urged. See through the dream. *Believe*.

I repeated my favourite Truth to myself.

> We have only to believe.
> Then, little by little,
> We shall see the universal horror unbend,
> And then smile upon us,
> And then take us in its more than human arms.

It started off silent, my mantra, but by the time I reached the end I was speaking loudly, confidently. The mist dissolved and the objects in the shelter shone clearly once again. I saw the eye we had painted on the ceiling and sighed with relief. Was it death that I had seen in the dream? Was it the land of the dead? For a moment there I had thought perhaps . . .

For a moment there I had stopped believing. That was what had happened. It occurred to me then that believing was the soul's breathing. The body breathed, the soul believed. If you stopped doing either of these things, the world ended. I thought of Isobel, alone in the tent. We must save her soul, I told myself. We must make her believe.

I walked to the edge of the garden. Joy was not visible, and

I guessed she must already be inside the tent. Working. Makebelieving. There were two tents now, facing each other, a body's length apart. In one lay Louis, struggling to breathe. In the other lay Isobel, struggling to believe.

It was Day Three of Operation Butterfly. So we had lost another night. Isobel had slept – again we had failed to dethrone her dreamself. Still it commanded its dark dreamempire, in a hemisphere beyond our reach. Lawless. Accountable to no one. Another night gone. That left only four. Then would come the seventh day. The seventh sunset.

Joy had left me some coffee. I drank it quickly – it was cold – and started work. I picked up Joy's notes on the previous day's makebelieves and looked through them. They were sparse, plain, a little brutal-seeming in places. An outsider reading them might have imagined that we were merely torturing Isobel, which was certainly not the Truth.

That was where I came in. It was my job to rewrite Joy's reports, and simultaneously to create a new language. A new language for a new republic. Treesian. Arbrish. Freespeak. Revolangue. Well . . . the name could wait. The important thing was to take each word of the old language and demand that it justify its existence. Already I had a list of more than a hundred words waiting to be executed. Unpatriotic words. Superfluous words. Overused words. Misleading words. Ugly words.

Louis mocked my mission. 'Guillotines may break my bones,' he said, 'but naming cannot hurt me.' But Louis was wrong. Naming *could* hurt.

I took Joy's notes and went for a walk through the forest, in search of inspiration. As I moved past trees, bracken, stones, rabbit holes, I examined the words that named these objects, these sights. How appropriate were they? Could the objects even exist without their names? I thought of my favourite English words – river, tree, sun – and wondered whether it was truly the sounds of the words I found beautiful, or the picture, the feeling that the word conjured? The *meaning* of the word.

But what is meaning? Can it exist without the word? What if the words define what we see? What if saying (thinking, believing) river, tree, sun, makes us *see* river, tree, sun, even if what is *there* is – let us say – bed, wall, striplight. Or, let us say rather, Truth, Love, God.

Yes, yes, I thought (excited now), what if the *words* are the thin coverings? Translucent dustsheets protecting the true meanings that lie beneath the surface. What if it is the *words* that reflect the light, and thus obscure the Truth? After all, we live in a universe of illusions: the sky is not blue, the earth is not flat, the moon does not change shape. There must be something beyond all this. If only I could kill all the words – burn them, annihilate them – might I see through these coverings, these tricks of the light, to the spiritual world that surely glowed beneath?

I stood on the sand, looking out at the sunlight glinting on the surface of Elbow Pool and wondered what I was truly looking at. What was truly *there*. I knew what I could see, or thought I did, but . . . what if I saw only words? Expectations. What if I saw only what I had been taught to see? How, then, to see the Truth?

And, at once, I knew the answer.

Believe.

I wrote down as much of this as I could remember – it came in a flash – and then settled down to work on the report.

OPERATION BUTTERFLY – DAY TWO

In makebelieve numbertwelve, Traitor mouthcircled Citizen M's Truths eightyseventimes, but then became mindmessed. Persuader mouthsignalled that Traitor's energyflow = zero until she yesmanaged to mouthcircle Truths onehundredtimes. Traitor eyecried and mouthdamaged Persuader. 'You're trying to kill me,' she mouthlied.

Makebelieve numbertwelve = terminated.

Persuader mouthdemanded, 'Do you believe?' Traitor mouthlied 'Yes.' Makebelieve numberthirteen = terminated.

At start of makebelieve numberfourteen, Traitor mouthpleaded, 'Sorry.' Traitor yesmanaged to mouthcircle Truths onehundredtimes. Persuader mademore Traitor's mouthfood. Traitor mouthswallowed foodenergy and mouthsignalled that she pleasedesired more. Persuader mouthsignalled that desire minus fear = lawforbidden. Persuader mouthsignalled that desire and fear = only halfequals of sameword – FEARDESIRE – which (for quicksake) = fear. Persuader mouthdemanded, 'Do you believe?' Traitor mouthlied 'Yes.' Makebelieve numberfourteen = terminated.

In makebelieve numberfifteen, Traitor = mouthless. To helppunish her, Persuader mouthassured Traitor that if she yesmanaged to mouthcircle new paper of Truths, her pleasereward = freshair. Traitor mouthwhispered, 'Thank you.'

Makebelieve numbersixteen = breakthrough numbertwo. Traitor yesmanaged mouthcircling of Truths. Persuader mouthdemanded, 'Do you believe?' Traitor mouthresponded, 'No, I don't believe.' Persuader mouthanked Traitor for her mouthonesty and mouthsignalled she would return soonlater for freshaireward.

I read through the report, then looked up at the river, trees, sun, hoping to surprise them; to catch them out of wordisguise. But still they glinted back at me, exactly as before. You tricks of the light, I thought. I'll see through you yet.

Back in the garden, Alex was plucking a dead hen. Its severed head lay forgotten, a single black eye staring up at him from the grass.

'You didn't catch anything, then?'

He looked at me aggressively, the headless bird doing the splits between his hands. 'No, I didn't. It's not easy on your own, you know.'

'Sorry,' I said, taken aback by his anger.

Muttering something, Alex pulled a handful of feathers from the corpse and let them fall to the grass.

'What's the matter with Citizen Alex?' I asked Joy, as I handed her the report.

'Frustrated,' she replied, reading through it quickly. When she had finished, she said, 'That's excellent, Citizen Michael. As ever.'

'Thank you,' I said. 'Maybe I should go hunting with him this afternoon?'

She looked at me blankly. 'Why?'

'You said he was frustrated.'

'Oh, I didn't mean he was frustrated about the hunting. Anyway, you've got a job to do this afternoon.' She was smiling as if at a private joke.

'Have I?'

'The House of Eyes?'

The large object in my chest moved slightly, brushing against my heart and lungs. 'Oh,' I said. 'Yes, of course.'

The light was green, that was the first thing; it stained my hands and gave the air a weird, otherworldly glow, like the nightlights the Americans used on television to help them drop bombs.

It smelled of her, that was the second thing; the air felt humid and heavy with her accumulated breaths, and the vanilla perfume was here in double concentration, almost pungent, so that it dried the back of my throat and made me cough.

There was another smell, too; the bad smell that seemed to come from down below. It gave me a strange feeling, that smell. Luckily, when I took the lid off the tin, the bad smell was masked by the sweet, toxic scent of the paint.

I knelt on her sleeping-bag and watched the slow, smooth movements of my hand. The sleeping-bag felt warm and soft beneath my bare shins. The softness and warmth triggered a memory.

Regret, I told myself, is only halfequal of sameword, FORGETREGRET. Which (for quicksake) = forget.

I think therefore she isn't.

I think therefore she isn't.

I think therefore she isn't.

When I'd finished my mantra, I breathed deep and pushed the clutter of her things away from the wall. The silky inner lining was lax, so I had to put one hand on it to keep it tight while I painted. The paint ran in a few places, giving the image a melting, horror-movie look.

Green on pale grey: it looked undramatic now, but at night, in darkness . . . those eyes would shine; they would burn into her. They would see through all her lies and her acting, to the emptiness inside. The rotten core.

High on hate, eager to hurt, I pressed too hard. The bristles parted, the brush slipped and a dribble of paint ran down the lining, towards her open rucksack. I put my finger under the small bulb to halt it and looked down at the pile of her things that I had saved.

I could feel my heart contract and spurt, contract and spurt. I dried my green fingertip on the edge of my T-shirt and began to rifle through her possessions. A heavy, clinking toiletry purse. A stolen hand-mirror. The tube of sun-cream – nearly empty, encrusted with a sticky brown residue around the nozzle. Those blue satin shorts. As I lifted them up I became aware of the bad smell again. I sniffed the shorts: they smelled of her vagina and dried suncream. But still the bad smell came, thickening and strengthening. I put my hand to my mouth. Where was it coming from?

I picked gingerly through the rest of her possessions, but none of them could possibly be responsible for that foul, rotten, retch-making stink. I put them all back in her bag and moved it to the side. The smell grew worse. Much worse. And then I saw it. On the groundsheet where the bag had been was an incision, in the shape of a three-quarter circle. I lifted the edge and nearly passed out.

Frantically I unzipped the tent and breathed fresh air. I felt the sun on my face and calmed down. But I had to find out. What was underneath that flap?

I held my breath and crawled back to the door in the ground. I lifted it and stared. It was a hole. A hideous, warm wind rose from it. At first I imagined it was a toilet, made by Alex or Joy, but when I switched on the torch and pointed it down, the light faded to nothing in the blackness.

Again I put my head outside the tent and inhaled. The air inside was almost unbreathable now. It stank worse than shit; like something ancient, primordial, evil.

I held my breath and crawled back. Again I shone the torch down. Could it be a tunnel? Was Isobel planning to escape? But that did not explain the smell; and besides, how could she have dug such a thing? Where would all the earth have gone?

Warily I put my hand down the hole, expecting at any moment that my fingers would touch something soft, disgusting, possibly alive. But there was nothing; only a faint sense of blown heat, as though somewhere in that monstrous pit burned a fire as black as night. As I leaned further down, I almost fell – and a surge of vertigo went through me. How deep *was* this hole?

One more breath of fresh air and back I went again. This time I shone the torch into the hole and then, with a shiver of apprehension, I dropped it.

Down it fell. The light shrinking, blinking, vanishing.

No sound.

The hole must be bottomless.

Astonished, I put my ear to the hole. At first all I could hear was the throb of blood – the sound of my own feardesire. But then I detected it: a tiny noise, far off in the distance, as though someone were shouting to me from the other side of the world.

I listened closer. It *was* a voice. A human voice. A girl's voice. What was it saying? And then I heard.

I drew back in shock. The voice had said my name.

20

The Truthflowers

When I woke, we were inside the same sleeping-bag. We lay like naked spoons, glued together by sweat. I could smell the vanilla perfume on her neck, feel her hair tickling my nose. I couldn't remember how we had ended up like this, but it didn't seem to matter much. Oh Isobel, I thought, I love you so much . . .

It was still quite dark: all I could see was the back of her head silhouetted, and beyond it some floating yellow circles of light on the mudbrick wall. I blinked away the grey remains of my dream and put my hand on her hipbone. I stroked its soft curve, sensing the warmth that pulsed from the other side, and loosed a long sigh of relief and bliss. Everything was all right. It had been nothing but a dream . . . The trial and the House of Eyes and . . . they were not real. We were still together, the two of us. Closer than ever.

I stirred between her legs and she said, 'Mmm.' She sounded as though she were still asleep, but soon I felt the swell of her hips and reached my hand around to touch her breasts. That was my first surprise: they were larger than I remembered. She muttered something, and then she yawned, and stretched – I felt the muscles in her back tighten against my stomach and chest. I thought, her back feels wider, stronger. Then she spoke.

And I felt myself sinking.

'Good morning, Citizen Michael.'

'You,' I said.

She turned round, slowly. I could see her eyeballs straining white in the darkness, could feel her breath on my face, could hear, but not see, her smile. 'Thank you for last night,' she said. 'You were very loving.'

I did not say anything. There was warm water in my mouth. I closed my eyes and tried to remember what had happened. Another blank. How could we have ended up together like this? Had I been drinking? But my mouth was not dry. My head did not hurt. I wanted to escape, to get free of this unbearable heat and closeness, but Joy was rubbing her body against mine. 'Oh,' she moaned, 'I wish we could stay like this for ever, don't you? Just the two of us. And this feeling.'

I said nothing.

When Joy had finished and had turned away, searching for tissues, I slid quickly out of the sleeping-bag. I felt cold and silly, standing there naked, groping in the darkness for my underwear. Finally, after muttering a few curses, I became aware that Joy was watching me. She said sleepily, 'What are you looking for?'

'My boxer shorts. Do you know where they are?'

'Uh-uh. You kinda tore your clothes off last night. And mine. You seemed in a hurry.'

She sounded amused. I bit my lip and continued searching. In the end, I gave up and put on my uniform.

'Where's Citizen Alex?' I asked.

'Citizen Alex? Well . . . here, I guess.'

Horrified, I turned round and looked. His sleeping-bag lay near the opposite wall, deformed by a familiar large bulge. I shivered with disgust and hissed, 'But –' and then couldn't think what to say.

'But what, Citizen Michael?'

'Who was guarding the House of Eyes?'

'Oh.' Joy yawned. 'We don't have to worry about that any more, do we? She's hardly likely to escape in her current condition.'

I frowned for a moment, unsure what this meant, then shivered again and went outside.

*

At the edge of the garden, I rubbed my eyes. I was still tired and thought I must be seeing things. I looked again. Gradually, through the blue haze of dawn, I began to see clearly. The garden was alive with words.

The first surface I deciphered was the north wall of the blue tent, the House of Air. **'YOU MUST BELIEVE'**, it said in those slashed red letters. I could see similar scrawled messages, in different colours and sizes, all over the garden, but could focus on only one surface at a time, so the background was a dazzling blur. And in the corners of my vision the symbols seemed to move. It felt like the garden had been invaded; like these new words and images were not merely painted surfaces, but something alive, hanging and writhing in the air – ghosts, magic flowers, manifestations . . .

As I struggled to articulate this new feeling, I took a few steps into the garden. The further I progressed, the greater my amazement grew, for now I sensed these lifeforms swarming and dancing behind me, all around me. I turned and they froze, and I read the huge, bright green letters on the wall of the shelter.

'THE TRUTH . . . REVEALED!'

I stared at these words in astonishment. It was as if the wall had read my mind. The words told me what it was I had been striving to express. 'Yes,' I said aloud. That was it. The wordisguise had gone. I was seeing the spiritworld that lay beneath material surfaces. I was seeing the Truth.

I walked deeper into the garden, eyes moving from surface to surface, too fast to read anything but too slow to absorb the dizzying whole. I stumbled on something and looked down, and realised I was standing at the centre of a Great Eye carved into the grass. Its pupil, its iris, its outline and glory stared back at me. My perspective seemed to telescope backwards and forwards as I looked at this, so that the black lines appeared first to be lines of soil above the surface, and then to be nothingness, hollowness, viewed through narrow slits in the ground. I almost swooned then: the feeling was vertiginous, as though I were staring down into the bottomless pit I had seen beneath the groundsheet of the tent. Instantly I looked up, expecting the sky to be filled with jet-trail slogans or the sun to blaze down in the shape of an eye.

But the usual high, blue firmament rose over the forest, and slowly I began to calm down. I put my fingers into one of the slits and touched earth immediately. This was man-made, I realised; it was the work of trowels, not miracles. Still, I couldn't shake off the feeling of ecstatic certainty that had filled me when I read those words on the shelter wall at the very moment I was thinking them. The feeling that I had, finally, arrived. At the place to which all paths led.

THE TRUTH . . . REVEALED!

Smiling now, I started to wander around the garden, reading the slogans one by one. I soon realised that they were mine; that someone – Joy, I guessed – had painted the phrases I'd chosen. As if they were divinely ordained. As if they were gospel.

On the other wall of the shelter: '**WHATEVER ONE BELIEVES TO BE TRUE EITHER IS TRUE OR BECOMES TRUE IN ONE'S MIND**'.

On the western face of the House of Eyes: '**LIBERTY EQUALITY FRATERNITY OR DEATH**'.

In small letters across the suspended blade: '**A BELIEF IS LIKE A GUILLOTINE, JUST AS HEAVY, JUST AS LIGHT**'.

In a vertical line of single letters down the slender trunk of a young birch: '**STRENGTH THROUGH JOY**'.

And then I looked at the letters again, and for the first time I felt uneasy. Though less violent and wild-seeming than before, they were recognisably in the same hand that had painted '**WHORE**' on Isobel's burst air mattress. And that hand had been . . . mine.

Or had it?

Dark suspicions bubbled in the back of my mind. I began to wonder about Joy, imagining a secret malice hidden behind her show of love. But if she *had* written that word on the air mattress, and these words, all over the garden, what was she trying to achieve by the deceit? I thought about this for a few moments, but all I could come up with was the idea that she was trying to make me believe I was losing my mind. And why would she want to do that?

There was one other possibility, of course, but I liked the idea of that even less.

I was still reading the slogans when Joy emerged from the shelter. Her uniform was half unbuttoned and her hair unbrushed. Her skin glowed pink. When she reached me, she put a hand on my forearm and smiled shyly. 'Sorry, I couldn't get up earlier. You wore me out last night. In the nicest possible way, of course.' She put her head on my chest, her arms round my back, and whispered, 'I love you, Citizen Michael.'

In a dry, hurried voice, I said, 'The garden looks amazing.'

She glanced around. 'It certainly does. You did a wonderful job.'

This was the answer I had been dreading. 'Did I?'

'Of course! It's so overpowering. When the traitor sees this, she'll just *have* to start believing . . .'

'No. What I mean is, are you sure it was me who did it?'

Joy took a step back and gave me a puzzled look. She was half smiling, as though unsure whether I was joking. 'Who else could have done it? It's a work of genius. You know, yesterday afternoon, when I came out of the House of Eyes and saw that slogan on the shelter wall, "THE TRUTH . . . REVEALED", I was just . . . *wow*! You'd never told me that one before. It just seemed to sum up the whole thing to me.' She looked at me and blushed. 'Sorry, I'm babbling, aren't I?'

Joy became uncomfortable because she thought I was staring at her, but I was looking through her now, thinking about what she had said: 'yesterday afternoon'.

'What's the matter?' she asked. 'Did I say the wrong thing?'

'No, I'm just a bit confused. That day when I painted the House of Eyes . . .'

'Another stroke of genius!'

'Yes, but . . . when *was* that?'

Joy shrugged. 'The other day.'

'Not yesterday?'

'Well, no. Yesterday was . . .' She blushed again. 'What is it? What's wrong?'

'Nothing's wrong,' I said, and put a hand on her shoulder. She hugged me tightly, buried her face in my chest.

'Nothing's wrong. I was just . . . losing track of time.'

To my relief, we separated then. Joy went down to the river to get washed. She asked me if I wanted to come, but I said I ought to check on my brother. She squeezed my hand and said, 'What an angel you are.'

The air in the blue tent was warmer than the air outside; it was also staler, more breathed. I hung open the tent flaps and crawled inside. I could see the dark letters through the walls of the tent, could read the slogans backwards. I wondered if Louis had noticed them, if he understood what was happening in the world beyond his sickbed.

He was asleep and looked calm. When I got closer, though, I could hear his chest wheezing. It was a strangely complex sound, the kind of noise a computer might make before it dies; a song of electrical decay.

Louis's head was surrounded by a halo of crumpled tissues. I said his name quietly. He opened his eyes and looked at me. For a moment he seemed not to recognise me. Then he said, 'You.' He didn't sound especially pleased to see me.

'How are you feeling?'

'Exhausted.'

'Your chest sounds better.'

He coughed. 'I was freezing last night. All my muscles went into spasm because I was shivering so much.'

'Do you want me to bring you a blanket?'

'Forget it. Just pass me the water.'

I found the bottle on the groundsheet beside me. 'It's

empty,' I said. 'Do you want me to go to the river and fill it?'

He nodded, lay down and immediately closed his eyes.

'You're welcome,' I said.

His lips seemed to curl into a sneer then, but he was probably asleep. I must have been imagining it.

The sun was blazing over the treetops when I came out of the tent, and again I found myself disoriented by the chaos of painted colours. It was all I could do not to fall over. I put a hand on the tent in front to steady myself. When the dizzy spell had passed, I realised I was pressing down on the western wall of the House of Eyes and staring at the word **DEATH**. Momentarily unnerved, I removed my hand and stepped back, and it was then that I heard her.

I knew it had to be Isobel, though it didn't sound like her at all. It sounded at first like a small child moaning in its sleep. But the longer and more closely I listened, the stronger became my sense that there was something more frightened or anguished underneath the moan – as though the child were having a nightmare and in the dream it was screaming, but what came out of its mouth was only a muffled hint of what it felt.

I frowned: there was a memory, or a thought, somewhere in the depths of my mind. For a second there it had surfaced, I had glimpsed it, but now it was gone.

The sound continued. I walked away.

There were just three of us for lunch – me, Alex and Joy. It was not the most memorable of meals: we ate rice, which Joy managed to overcook so that it ended up as a kind of grey sludge. The conversation was dull too, at first, without Louis and Isobel. It occurred to me then that the three of us were really rather uncharismatic; the kind of people whom no one ever wants to sit next to at school dinner, so they end up together, on the last table, hating one another for the thick silence in which they eat.

However, revolution is a great ice-breaker. It turned out that this was not merely lunch but the second session of the Revolutionary Tribunal. By keeping quiet and listening, I discovered that, in the absence through illness of the Prince, we had agreed to perform his duties together. All decisions would be joint decisions. The Tribunal's first session had apparently been dominated by my suggestions for what I had called the Truthflowers. Joy congratulated me on the conception and execution of this initiative, and I nodded. Then Joy read from the agenda, while Alex took minutes.

'The first item concerns Operation Butterfly. I'm afraid there have been no further breakthroughs. My only suggestion is that we move the traitor out of the House of Eyes later today and leave her to mindcircle the Truthflowers, until the time comes for her belieftrial, which is' – Joy consulted her notes – 'tomorrow morning.'

Tomorrow morning. How many days had I lost, then? Two, three, four? My mind could not process the calculations.

'Any questions?' Joy was asking. 'Yes, Citizen Michael . . .'

'Could I see yesterday's report, please?'

'You want to look at it again?'

'I just want to check a few details.'

'Of course.' Joy smiled. 'I'll give you a copy after the Tribunal. Now, the second item regards the WasPrince and yesterday's wordisgrace. To sneak into the House of Eyes, against Tribunalaw, and to make those hurtnames about the Minister of Propaganda and the Truthflowers . . . Well, we all agreed it was a disturbing development. Thankfully, the medicine we gave him seems to be working. Citizen Michael, you visited the WasPrince this morning, didn't you? How did you find him?'

'Fine. A bit thirsty, but . . . um, could you just remind me, Citizen Joy, exactly what he said about me yesterday?'

Joy gave me a surprised look.

'I've just forgotten the precise wording,' I explained.

'Certainly, Citizen Michael.' She consulted her notes. 'He mouthlied you were a "short-dicked evil little monster". He then mouthcircled the false accusations made by the traitor against you. But I don't see any need to go over *those* again.'

'No,' I said. 'Of course not.'

'My suggestion is that we move the WasPrince to the House of Eyes this evening, and that one of us begins make-believe sessions with him tonight. I am afraid that if we leave it too late, we may find the rate of beliefdecay irreversible. Citizen Michael, would you be OK to act Persuader?'

I stared at her, unable to speak. All I could do was shake my head, feebly.

'You feel too emotionated? I quite understand. In that case, I will conduct the sessions myself. We must hope that your brother's hatelove for me does not have an adverse effect on his progress. It would be a tragedy to lose two of our citizens in such a short time.'

The rest of the Tribunal passed smoothly. We agreed to dig a grave for the animal corpses in order to eradicate the fly problem. We endorsed Alex's suggestion that he spend the afternoons hunting in order not to diminish our food supplies unnecessarily. My proposed renaming of the WasPrince as 'the patient' was accepted unanimously. There was an uncomfortable moment when I accidentally used Isobel's name, and a look passed between Joy and Alex, but I explained that I was feeling tired after my efforts in the garden and they both smiled understandingly.

After the session was over, Joy gave me the report. She went to check on the patient, while Alex set off for the hunt. I found a comfortable spot in the corner of the garden where I could sit and read.

The single sheet was covered by my handwriting. I had used a black biro. Because of the closely spaced words and the pressure I had exerted, the other, blank side of the page appeared to be in Braille. I touched this pattern of bumps nervously with my fingertips as I read.

In makebelieve numbertwentythree, Traitor skindamaged Persuader.

In makebelieve numbertwentyfour, Traitor = punishelped.

In makebelieve numbertwentyfive, Persuader mouthdemanded, 'Do you believe?' Traitor = mouthless. Persuader mouthsignalled that mouthlessness = nobelief. Traitor = mouthless. Makebelieve numbertwentyfive = terminated.

In makebelieves numbertwentysixseveneightnine, Traitor = mouthless.

In makebelieve numberthirty, Traitor mouthscreamed onlynoise. Makebelieve numberthirty = terminated.

Onlynoise forever. Makebelieves = absoterminated.

That was where it ended. The sun was still shining on the piece of paper, glinting at certain angles from the clotted black ink with a pretty iridescence. I looked at the guillotine, which stood close by. There was a crust of dried blood on the semicircular wooden trap at the bottom, where the necks went. For a few moments, I thought I might be sick, but by staring at the shaded parts of the trees across the garden, I was able to push down the feeling.

The stillness of the trees lulled me into a feeling of peacefulness. The world, I saw, had not ended; nature was enduring, unconcerned. Thinking that I must, somehow, have misunderstood, I skim-read the report again. Then I put the sheet of paper on the grass, as though it might somehow be infected with the evil it described.

I was sitting up. From that distance, at that angle, the words were unreadable. I told myself that those little black squiggles meant nothing, that they were only words, scratched lines, no more significant than the sum of ink and pulped wood from which they were formed. But then I caught sight of the tent, the words splashed blood-like on its taut green skin:

'**YOU SHORT-DICKED EVIL LITTLE MONSTER!**'

I blinked and the message changed back, but against my will I began to imagine what lay inside the tent. No longer Isobel, no longer the girl I had loved, but ... *what?*

I think therefore she isn't.

I think therefore she isn't.

I think therefore she isn't.

21

The Gift

It was late afternoon when I remembered Louis's empty water bottle. I didn't feel like talking to him, having learned what he had said about me, but I had promised him water, so I took a walk down to the river. I needed a wash anyway – I could smell Joy's dried fluids on my skin – and I needed soothing. In Elbow Pool I could float and forget. I thought it would be nice to forget for a while.

I unrolled my towel and spread it over the grass and the sand, then I took off my uniform and walked into the pool. I plunged my head underwater and came up feeling refreshed. Nothing else in life, I thought, makes you feel quite so alive, quite so *in the moment*, as this: resurfacing, the water cold and mercuried on your skin, your eyes seeing rainbows, your lungs sucking hard, your heart pumping fast. Plunge and breathe. Contract and spurt.

For a while I floated, staring up at the blue sky and the gently tossing treetops, thinking nothing. Then I saw swallows, darting across the space between the trees. Oh to be a bird, so dreamless and pastless and free . . . Jean Jacques was right: if we could only regain our innocence, our animal souls, we need never be unhappy again.

And then I did something that I hadn't done for what felt like a long time. I began to daydream.

I thought of the oak whose branch I had leapt from that first time. The way it bloomed from its thick, dark stump of trunk into a mushroom cloud of green leaves. I thought myself inside it, following those secret inner paths. I climbed all the way to the top, from where I looked out at that great, waving sea of green, receding all the way to the horizon.

There was a bird near the top of this tree – this tree of my mind. He was a swallow, and I wished myself inside his head. The forest seemed even huger from there, each branch a kind of tree in itself; the whole place plunging down beneath my delicate clawed toes, deeper than I could see, as though I were floating on the surface of an ocean and all those humans below were but weird plankton, rooted miserably to the sea's bottom, grumbling in a complex language that no other creature had ever felt the need to learn.

So I was tiny and the forest vast. And yet, as I took off with a flicker of wings, it shrank. As I rose into the blue, the sunlight on my feathers, as I swooped and spiralled, dived and soared, the green mass below me lost its sweltering gravity, its sucking power, and became merely a patch of green in the mosaic of colours, the mosaic of possibilities, below me.

Life was mine; the forest was mine. I dived into it, as I had always dreamed of doing. I swam through it. And when I was tired of that, I rocketed free from it. To be forever elsewhere, that was my idea of liberty.

Now there was no Republic, there were no boundaries. Now there was no law, no gravity or memory. And oh, to be rid of those heavy weights! To leave them buried in the bed of the river and float away . . .

I was feeling pleasurably clean when I got back to the shelter. I was thinking about the evening ahead and getting excited. I was imagining the warm carcass that Alex would bring back. I was anticipating the smell of roasting flesh and the warm spot the wine would make in my chest. I was remembering the parts of Joy's body I had touched that morning and wondering what had repelled me so; she was a girl, after all, and the sun was warm and soon the past would be buried. I was feeling good.

That was when I decided to celebrate. In the empty shelter, I changed out of uniform into my best pair of jeans and my only unstained T-shirt. In the blue tent, I left Louis's water bottle near his pillow and found some aftershave in his rucksack. I splashed it on my neck and chin and wrists, then I sniffed. I smelled like going out. I opened a recently stolen bottle of wine, poured myself a cup, and sat in the garden, watching the Truthflowers shine and quiver in the last rays of sunlight.

Joy appeared some time later. She was dressed in Isobel's gingham dress, and she had done something to her hair and face. Her eyes seemed simultaneously darker and brighter, and her lips thicker and more sensual. As she leaned over me I caught a scent of vanilla.

'You look beautiful,' I said, my words slurring.

She smiled shyly. 'It's just the lipstick that makes you say that. I don't know what made me wear it.'

'I didn't know you had any.'

'Oh, I haven't. I took it. From her.'

'Didn't she mind?'

'Well, she didn't say anything. I took a few things, actually.'

Her voice was low, warm, full of secrets.

I touched her hair. It was, I saw now, pinned off her neck by Isobel's pink and blue butterfly grips. Joy sighed and her lips touched mine. The soft adhesion of lipstick, the jets of warm air, the taste of synthetic cherry. It all seemed so abstract, so sweetly impersonal. She might be anyone, I thought, as I watched a blue butterfly catch the sun in its nest of dark hair.

A second touch of lips and then her tongue in my mouth. The sound of our breathing. 'Mmm . . .'

Joy sighed and moved her face away. 'I like your tongue,' she said. 'Do you like mine?'

It was such a bizarre question, I had to laugh. Or maybe it wasn't so bizarre really; just direct, to the point. It was her tongue, after all, with which I had been playing; it was not a communion of souls.

'Yes.'

'More than hers?'

I shrugged. 'Hers is nice, too.'

'Was, you mean.'

Yes, I thought, it's over. No more kisses with Isobel. I am not like Louis, doomed to eternal longing. At that moment, I felt nothing for Isobel beyond a certain curiosity and concern. I hoped she would pass the belieftrial, rejoin the Republic. I hoped it would be sunny tomorrow too, and that Alex would catch something to eat. If not, then . . . well, life went on.

'Yes. Was.'

'Good.' Joy smiled, and kissed me again. 'Oh, I almost forgot!'

'Forgot what?'

'I've got a surprise for you. Hang on a minute!'

She ran to the shelter, then returned more slowly, her hands behind her back. 'Close your eyes and hold out your hands.'

When I opened them, my hands contained a gift: a small, rectangular box wrapped in old, slightly yellowed newspaper. In the middle of the box, written in Joy's squarish handwriting, was my name, followed by a single X, which I took to be a kiss. The dot of the 'i' had been drawn as a smiley face.

'What is it?' I asked.

'Guess.'

It felt ludicrously light. I shook the box: something inside it made a strange, dull flapping sound. For some reason, I imagined a caught butterfly. Dead by now, of course.

'I can't.'

'Read the back,' said Joy.

I turned over the package. It said, 'S.W.A.L.K.'

'What does that mean?'

'Sealed with a loving kiss.'

I was touched. 'Thank you, Citizen Joy.'

'You're welcome. Aren't you going to open it?'

I didn't speak. I couldn't speak.

'What's the matter?' asked Joy.

I was looking over her shoulder, at the corner of the garden near the guillotine.

'Oh, you've just noticed?'

There was an enormous, pale blue worm asleep on the grass.

The worm spoiled my evening. Every time I began to relax, to enjoy the scented smoke or the way my limbs floated slowly through the air when I tried to walk or lift food to my mouth, I would see it, like a mote in my eye, and the laughter would sound hollow in my ears.

'Can she breathe?' I asked. 'Shouldn't we let her out?'

'I've already untied her,' explained Joy. 'She can come out whenever she likes. She's staying inside because she wants to.'

We were standing quite close. Even though we talked in low voices, it was likely that Isobel could hear us. The thought made me grip the neck of the wine bottle more tightly.

'I suppose we'll have to crack the chrysalis ourselves if she doesn't do it soon,' continued Joy. 'Otherwise she won't have time to take in the Truthflowers. I know it's a long shot, but you put so much time and effort into them, I think we ought at least to give them a chance. If she still doesn't believe after *that* . . . well, she'll only have herself to blame.'

I stared. The chrysalis – of course. That was what the sleeping-bag looked like; not a worm, but a cocoon. But what stage had the metamorphosis reached, inside? What would emerge – a winged imago, or the same ugly, crawling larva? Or could it be worse than that: some grotesque inbetween, some unfinished pupa, never meant to see the light?

The chrysalis moved, a sleepy wriggle, and instinctively I took a step back.

Joy looked at me curiously. 'You have nothing to feel guilty about, Citizen Michael. Whatever comes out of there tonight, you've done the best you can. We all have.'

'I wasn't feeling guilty,' I said. 'What made you think I was?'

Joy shrugged. 'Come on, I can hear Citizen Alex. And he's whistling, so he must have caught something.'

Alex had shot a wood pigeon. He was very pleased about this and told us about the kill in great detail. Then he went down to the river to wash himself while Joy started a fire and I plucked and emptied the carcass. It took me a long time because my hands were shaking. I kept turning around and checking that the chrysalis had not opened. For some reason, I imagined the creature that came from it might be dangerous.

To give my mouth something to do, I drank wine from the bottle. If I concentrated on the dark shape in front of my eyes, the feel of the glass circle between my lips, the trickling sensation in my throat, I could almost forget about the blue thing in the corner of the garden.

Soon I was so drunk I laughed at anything. Alex opened another bottle of wine and I laughed. Joy put her head on my shoulder and I laughed. I tried to stand up and I couldn't and I laughed. Yet, as soon as I walked through the shelter and out into the forest, I felt hellishly sober. I watched my piss steam from the nettles, hoping it would make me laugh, but all I managed was a weak smile.

When I got back to the garden, Joy and Alex were standing over the chrysalis, talking.

'It's time,' said Joy, when she saw me.

'But it's not even dark,' I protested.

'Why should it be dark?'

I didn't know what to say. I just thought it should be dark.

I watched as she knelt down and pulled at the zip. It slid smoothly, like a scalpel opening flesh. A bad smell rose from the gap.

To distract myself, I opened my gift. It was a long, pink, severed tongue.

22

Fall

I lay in the tent, in darkness. I was the patient now. Joy had said so. I was unwell, she said. I was unwell and she would make me better.

If only I could sleep and forget. I longed for the sleep I had known in childhood: the deep bath of nothingness, the black sea of innocence. But sleep would bring the dream, I knew, and I did not want the dream. The dream was too death-like. It seemed too real.

To try to clear my head, I unzipped the tent and walked into the garden. All was quiet. The Truthflowers shone dimly but they did not illuminate anything else. I tripped over a taut rope and caught myself on sloping canvas. All I could see was darkness and the shape of my hand and **FRATERNITY OR DEATH**, my own words glaring accusingly. The House of Eyes. Louis was in there, alone. I was the patient now, and he was the . . .

I paused, frowning. What word had I found to describe his condition? Oh yes, that was it: the suspect.

I walked on through the maze of bright words and soon sensed the guillotine's dark bulk looming over me. As I got close, I heard a moan. The sound came from the darkness near my feet. I turned and retraced my steps. There was no escape that way.

I was thirsty and I knew Louis had water, so I edged my way round to the front of the House of Eyes and pulled the zip. I put my head through the opening. The air smelled of damp and illness and something much, much worse.

I held my breath and listened. For a moment it sounded like the moan I had heard in the dark, but it wasn't. It was just Louis, trying to breathe. The sound of a thousand lost souls screaming in eternal torment. It was just Louis's asthma.

I searched with my hands, but couldn't find the water bottle. It was completely dark. I felt all over the groundsheet, all around Louis's body. Then I pushed him out of the way and felt below where he had been lying. And there it was. The incision.

I lifted the flap. The bad smell. The warm wind. I edged closer and put my hand into the hole. The vast nothing. The bottle must have fallen down there, I thought. Perhaps we must all fall down there in the end.

I leaned down into the blackness, arms first, head, shoulders, torso, and then I was falling

falling

falling

A long time passed – or so it seemed. I could hear ticking. Tick, tick, tick. Everything was grey.

I found myself in a place that looked like a park – large, flat gardens with wooden benches and plane trees and tarmac paths. The grass was covered with crisp plane leaves and the smooth shapes of their shed bark, like pieces from a jigsaw puzzle. The trunks of the plane trees were the colour of milk. Their branches, pruned carefully to reach out sideways but not upwards, formed a kind of knotty firmament. The thin light came through in puzzle-shaped stabs that stained the ground with bright crescents and oblongs and horseshoes.

I could see other people, walking around slowly, or sitting on benches, or feeding pieces of bread to sparrows. No one shouted or laughed, except the sparrows.

It was a big park; there was plenty of room to run around, and yet no one did. I could have climbed the plane trees, but I had no desire or energy for anything of the kind.

I walked to the nearest bench and sat down. It was very comfortable. I leaned back into its curve and looked at the branches of a plane tree. I stayed like that for some time. Later I watched a leaf fall, in slow, diagonal waves, to the ground.

Some time after that, I heard a bell. I stood up slowly and walked towards a long building in the middle of the park. Other people were moving towards it, too. I looked in their eyes and saw nothing but my own reflection. Were these the dead? I wondered. Where were we going?

And then I began to feel frightened.

We went through the door, one after another. Inside, the building looked like a school or a hotel – lots of long corridors with closed doors. I could hear ticking.

Tick, tick, tick.

Was I dead, too?

Tick, tick, tick.

I closed my eyes.

The darkness parted and light came in. The space in the darkness was a tall, thin triangle, but the shape of the light was different. It was tunnel-like and golden. It shone from the triangle and made a bright oval on my chest. It warmed my heart.

After a while, I found I could lift my head and look down at this sunbeam; could look into its champagne depths, where particles of dust whirled. It was as if they were snowflakes that never landed, as if the sunbeam erased gravity, stopped time, and let them hang there for ever, now falling and now rising, now shimmering and somersaulting, in their infinity of shapes and shades. I knew it was not life, but I was grateful for the illusion. The dust was dead – the dead parts of ourselves – and here it was given beauty, a kind of afterlife, by the burning of a distant fire in cold, black space. And I thought: there is death in life; there is life in death.

A voice in the darkness said, 'How are you feeling?'

Born again, I thought. That's how I'm feeling. But I could not say it. My tongue lay thick and dry in my mouth. When I finally made it move, all it could say was, 'Water.'

Sharp plastic touched my lips and then water came. It came so fast I felt like I was swimming in it. I could feel it pour down my throat. I could feel streams of it roll over my face and on to my shoulders.

'Take it easy,' said the voice.

I gasped, breathing. Plunge and breathe. Contract and spurt. Oh, to be dreamless and pastless . . . For a moment, there I was, but I could feel it returning now. Re-forming.

'Where have I been?'

'I don't know, Citizen Michael, but I'm glad you're back. I thought we'd lost you.'

Joy's face slowly materialised above mine. Her eyes and mouth were in shade but the edges of her hair shone like an eclipse.

'Lost me?'

'You were out cold. Oh, I'm so relieved . . .'

I listened. I could hear Joy's tear-stained breaths, and beyond them muffled birdsong, and below that the pulse in my ears. But that was all. I could not hear ticking.

'Out of time,' I muttered.

Joy shook her head, and dust flew from her hair into the sunbeam. The motes became frantic. 'No. Not at all,' she said. 'You're not out of time. You're *in* time. We waited for you. Now you're back, we can go ahead. Do you understand?'

'No,' I said, and she laughed.

'Take your time, Citizen Michael. There's no rush. Take all the time you want.'

But there was no time, I knew that. No time like the present. Was this the present? Or was this some other, more obscure tense? The perfect conditional. The unreal past.

What if . . . If only . . .

'Was I gone a long time?'

'It felt like for ever,' said Joy. 'You must be hungry!'

I thought about this. 'Yes, I suppose I must be.'

'I'll make you some breakfast. What would you like? An omelette? Boiled eggs?'

'Anything,' I said.

'Sure.'

'Joy . . . do you know what happened?'

'You had a bang on the head. We think you must have fallen.' She stroked my cheek. 'Oh, I'm so glad you're OK. Welcome back to the land of the living, Citizen Michael.'

I was hungrier than I'd realised. Watching Joy's plump fist thrashing the fork around the plastic bowl, turning the white and gold to pale yellow, I felt my stomach tighten and rumble. Alex was out hunting; I sat with my back to the shelter wall; Joy knelt in front of me, smiling and talking, her words coming in short, tight breaths as she stared at the flawless destruction in the bowl.

I half listened as Joy told me about the latest crop of tomatoes, about Alex's plan to steal a cow, about her ideas for new Truthflowers. Finally she stopped talking, stopped whisking, and looked down at what she'd done. 'Well, I'd better put the pan on the fire,' she said.

'You haven't told me about . . .'

'The traitor?'

'And the suspect.'

'Oh yes, the suspect.' Her voice was dark, shielding.

'What's the matter? What's happened?'

She sighed. 'The suspect is not well. He's not . . . *responding*?' The last word was inflected upwards, like a question, and Joy's eyebrows rose in unison.

My gut burbled tactlessly. 'Not at all?'

'No. Not at all. Shall I show you the reports?'

I shook my head. 'Later. But you don't think . . . ?'

'It's too early to say. We shouldn't give up hope, yet. Who knows, when the traitor has gone, perhaps things will look differently to him.'

'Yes,' I said. 'Perhaps.'

I could feel her eyes on my face. I ordered it not to betray me. I remembered the tears I had shed when the chrysalis had

opened, and I remembered too Joy's disapproval, her *concern*.
I had been unwell. I was better now. There was no need for
her to be concerned any more.

'And the traitor?' I asked, in a casual, neutral voice.

Joy was over by the fire now, pouring the yellow liquid into
the hot pan. She prodded the mixture with a wooden spoon.
She looked up at me curiously. 'Like I said, we waited for you.'

'So' – I felt a grin edge nervously across my face – 'when is it?'

'Whenever you're ready, Citizen Michael. We can arrange
the day around you. Eat breakfast. Go for a walk. Get washed
if you like. And when you're ready, we'll do it. There's no
rush. She doesn't have any other plans, as far as I know.'

'No.'

Joy tipped the pan sideways, letting the juice flow to the
edge. I cleared my throat. 'With the suspect, has there been
any . . . ?'

'Any what?'

'Damage?'

Joy stared at the pan. 'You can't make an omelette without –'

'No.'

'*Eh voila!*' Joy triumphantly slid the smoky yellow mass on
to a plate and delivered it to my lap with a knife, a fork, and
a kiss on the forehead. 'Will I make a good wife?'

I signalled to her that I couldn't answer; my mouth was full.

I took Joy's advice and went for a walk. She offered to come,
but I said I'd prefer to be alone for a while, and she understood. 'Just think,' she whispered as I left. 'Soon all this will
be over and we'll be able to start again. We'll be free.' I nodded
at her and smiled and said, 'Yes.' I had already decided by
then. My mind flashed ahead to the beauty of the final solution. Yes. Soon. I kissed her on the mouth and said, 'I love
you.' She blushed and said, 'I love you too,' but I didn't care
about that. The decision had been made.

It was a beautiful morning. I followed the path east at first,
but when it forked I chose randomly and continued to choose

randomly as I went along. I was looking at the trees not as landmarks or symbols but as trees. They were my friends and this was my home. I stroked their gnarly old barks as I walked, pulling off flakes of dry paint where I could, and whispering to them, 'Yes, we'll be free soon.' I looked up to those great gold-lit boughs and saw them nod gracefully, and I knew.

Out beyond the realm of the eyes, I started to climb. I could feel the trees' energy pulsing in my fingertips as I clung to them. Their branches cradled me, gave me spring and lever-age. It took me a little time to rediscover my rhythm, but as soon as I had it I felt my buzzing consciousness slip away. It seemed to melt, almost, as I swung and leapt and pulled, so my head was filled not with ideas and words but with a kind of dark water. The dark water swashed around, stirring up images, daydreams, memories. Yet I saw all of these as they truly were: not solid and daunting realities, but mere passing ghosts, evanescent reflections on the surface of a bottomless pool.

I climbed to the top of a beech and looked south. The hori-zon was clear and I could see the whole, vast span of the Pyre-nees. Snowless, in the summer light, the mountains looked flat, almost like film-studio cut-outs, yet there was a living gleam to their brown flanks that made me think of cows or horses. They seemed to breathe and pulse, even as they loomed there, dwarfing us all. Ideas and words, republics and gods, all withered in their shadows.

I looked above me at the scarless blue and saw a dark shape gliding: a buzzard. It rode the air in circles, calmly watching the green and brown below.

I thought of the ridiculous eyes I had painted, all those ridiculous words, and I laughed. The trees, the mountains and the buzzard all laughed, too. 'Soon we'll be free,' I whis-pered, and the wind caught my words. I heard them hiss and disappear across the treetops. The secret was out.

Through the small eyeholes of the mask I could see the suspended blade, but not the traitor, whose neck was securely fastened into the hole. I looked at the other three in their identical white uniforms and Great Eye masks – Alex, to my right, leaning against the wood, his hand on the rope; Joy, to my left, her blue eyes flickering intensely at me; the Judge, facing me, behind the guillotine, still and impassive.

Apart from the muffled thud of my pulse in my ears, the silence was absolute. No birds sang. No leaves whispered. My face was hot and damp with my own breaths. I steeled myself and looked down at the traitor's head.

It was a shock.

I closed my eyes, but her after-image remained.

Her eyes staring into mine. Those soft, grey eyes, familiar and yet unfamiliar. There was no irony in those eyes any more. No twinkle. They stared at me, filled only with horror.

Embarrassed, I looked away.

A moment passed. I inhaled and she inhaled.

I had often thought of death when I was young, and always I had imagined it the same way. I was in the school classroom at St Argen, kept behind during *recréation* to finish an exercise, and the other children were outside in the sunshine. I sat at the desk and watched them move against the green trees, the blue sky, the black tarmac, everything shining in the light of the sun. In the classroom it was dull: a grey pallor clung to every surface, and the yellow electric bulb only made it seem darker, less lifelike. On my desk lay the exercise I had to complete: mathematics, a foreign language, impossible to understand. On the wall ticked the round, white clock, its black hands immobile at half-past two. It ticked, but even the thin, red second hand did not move; merely vibrated in the same place. Tick, tick, tick. Not a second passed, ever. It would be like this for infinity, I thought: two-thirty in the afternoon, the exercise unfinished; the children outside, and me in the grey classroom. Sidelined. Forgotten. Non-existent.

I was outside the school window, watching Isobel stare at the impossible exercise, her face taking on the dead, grey hue of that ill-lit room. I could feel the sunlight on the back of my neck, could hear the inviting calls of my playmates to join their game. A choice: the playground or the classroom.

The land of the living or the land of the dead.

I looked at Isobel, strapped to the plank, her eyes screaming, and then I looked away. There was nothing I could do. Better her than me.

I inhaled and she inhaled. I held my breath; she held hers, too. A pause. I exhaled, and she never did. That was death: the overlong pause.

And I breathed again, thirsty for air.

Her head lay on the grass now, but I did not look at it. I knew that a whole universe had been extinguished, and yet it meant nothing to me. It did not affect me at all. Call it a failure of imagination.

I looked up. The Judge had disappeared. Joy and Alex had removed their masks and were laughing, nervously. I took off my mask and turned, for no particular reason, towards the House of Eyes.

Louis stood watching me. His arms were tied behind his back and his mouth was gagged. His eyes screamed accusingly.

For a brief moment, I was unnerved – I thought he might come at me – but then I saw Alex moving towards him threateningly. Reassured, I turned to Joy and whispered in her ear. Three words. I felt the soft flesh of her lobe on my lower lip, and sensed the shocked thrill in her face, her quickened breath, when I spoke those words. Then I kissed her on the cheek – it was flushed – and walked away.

I lifted myself on to the next branch and paused for breath. I saw a deer nibbling ferns below me. A bee swam drowsily past my face on its way to a thrilling date with some nectar-dripping flower. I felt young and exhilarated and alive. Soon I would be free. I sniffed: there was a freshness in the air. Almost like spring, I thought. Or like fall.

For a precious moment I straddled the branch and let my eyes be dazzled by the cornflower sky, the virescent leaves, the long, life-giving splashes of gold sunlight that illuminated rotting tree trunks and bleached bracken. This was all good, I thought. This was all that mattered.

I started to climb again, feeling happy, feeling better and better as I thought of the three little words I had whispered to Joy. So simple and yet so potent, those words, they would liberate my soul, would cleanse the forest of its dark spirits, would set us on the path to the true promised land.

As I ran through these thoughts, I stood on the very edge of an oak branch, balancing, lightly bouncing, testing it for strength and spring. Only three words – 'kill him now' – and only two bodies, for the time being. But I had made the decision, and I felt lightened by it. It would not be easy, the course I had in mind. It would require nerve and valour and cunning. But I could do it, I was certain. It would be a leap of faith, that was it. A leap of –

'Hey, Citizen Michael!' Alex's voice, somewhere behind and below me. 'Look what I've got!'

Gracefully, I pivoted on the branch. There was Alex, finger-tall on the ground, his arms out and raised, like Christ's. And from each hand dangled a familiar face. Two down, two to go, I thought, and laughed.

In the euphoria of the moment, I lost my balance. The forest swam below my feet. I felt blazingly, precariously alive.

ACKNOWLEDGMENTS

My thanks to: Richard Manley, Eric Maycock, Carol McDaid, Matthew Taylor, Keith Taylor and Pat Taylor, all of whom read this book in its pre-revolutionary form; to David Godwin, for belief; to Lucy Owen, for propaganda; to Lee Brackstone, for sharpening the blade; and most of all to Odile, Oscar, Milo and Paul-Emile, for making the real world worth the return.